ELEANOR

ALSO BY RHODA LERMAN

Call Me Ishtar
The Girl That He Marries

Eleanor

A Novel

by

RHODA LERMAN

HOLT, RINEHART AND WINSTON · NEW YORK

Published by Holt, Rinehart and Winston, 383 Madison Avenue,
New York, New York 10017.
Published simultaneously in Canada by Holt, Rinehart
and Winston of Canada, Limited.

Library of Congress Cataloging in Publication Data
Lerman, Rhoda.
Eleanor.
1.   Roosevelt, Eleanor Roosevelt, 1884–1962—Fiction.   I.   Title.
PZ4.L613El   [PS3562.E68]   813'.5'4   78-15140
ISBN 0-03-021066-6

Designer: Amy Hill
Printed in the United States of America

TO CURTIS ROOSEVELT,
WHOSE GRACE AND WISDOM LED ME, PAINFULLY,
TO KNOW HIS GRANDMOTHER

EXCURSION ONE
The Canteen, Summer 1918

IN WHICH I LEAVE FOR
THE CANTEEN

The rewards of war, to be sure, are quite different from the rewards of marriage and that is perhaps why, in the summer of 1918, after thirteen years of marriage to Franklin, war so tempted me. I was thirty-three that summer and awakened by war, much as the city had been awakened. Sleepy, obliging, genteel Washington swelled, suddenly voluptuous with summer heat, teeming with strange men, sodden with new vapors, diseases, desires, her streets and alleys widening to welcome war because war, we had found, the city and I, was passion and passion was a partner with whom I in my daydreams against the black stage of my life with Franklin had danced long and lonely.

On July 9, 1918, Franklin left on the U.S.S. *Dyer*, secretly, with only the splash of the oars and the clink of chain as he was rowed out to the darkened troopship, and because he was gone, whatever it was that had tempted me now drew me and

I was free to answer. It was a dangerous time for me, a time between the daydream and the real, a time when the walls between them bent and buckled and I couldn't tell if I were holding them up or pushing them down. I cried often.

Franklin was Assistant Secretary of the Navy then, under Josephus Daniels. We rented a home in Washington, shared a house with Franklin's mother in New York, owned a summer cottage next to hers in Campobello and belonged, ultimately, with her in Hyde Park in the big house. I was thirty-three, Franklin was thirty-six. We had five children: Anna, twelve, James, ten, Elliott, almost eight, Franklin, four and Wee Babs John, two. I was too thin, too tall and too tense. I had shingles, nightmares, constipation, a world of daydreams to ease the pain of my days, twice as many teeth and three times as much energy as anyone else I knew except my Uncle Ted, and very little courage. There were some things I could not bear.

And so it was perhaps just as well, the way I felt, that Franklin had gone off. It was to have been our second honeymoon. Instead, that summer, that fall, I spent in the canteens.

In Washington, I served the men who were going to war. From tea to dawn, from dawn to tea, until two or three in the morning, day after day that summer and fall, under the steaming tin shed of the canteen at Union Station in Washington, I served the men. A Navy League Auxiliary tea might keep me away or a lunch at the New Willard, less often at the Powhatan, or a Liberty Loan speech by Mr. McAdoo or a lecture by a British flier who had been a German prisoner. Sometimes I would visit the wounded and insane at St. Elizabeth's Naval Hospital. But more often than not I was at the siding of the railroad station. When the troop trains moved in, my heart beat wildly to the shaking of the foundations and when they moved out, as inexorably they did, with their sad freight, my heart emptied until the next train, the next whirlpool of men waiting, hundreds of them, with tears and songs and greetings and the emptiness that I, among others, would fill for a few hours in the lives of these men who were leaving for war. We were all very serious and I, everyone thought, more so than the others.

But in the New York canteens, I danced with the men who had come home from the war with ribbons and medals and gold fourragères. Franklin wrote: "Don't get so tired in New York. Please." Mama wrote to Franklin: "Eleanor was in Hyde Park. She came up from New York and she is thin with exhaustion. Whatever is she doing there?" And I wrote: "I have spent hours today working at the canteen in New York but feel that I have in some way contributed to the war effort."

I danced with the doughboys. With long and tall and short and fat and Boomers and Scooters and Billies and Willies and Horaces and Morrises. I didn't care with whom I danced. I had no tiny pencils wrapped in silk and no engraved programs in which to write names. I danced fox-trots and waltzes and I told the boys, when they inquired, that my husband was in the Navy but I would never tell them which ship. They didn't really care. They just wanted a girl to hold, a smile, sometimes a name. They held me; I smiled. Some went over again. Some went home.

I exchanged names, I knit sweaters and socks and over-the-tops for their puttees and wove in, when I was at the borders of my gray knitting, a long piece of my own auburn hair as a blessing. They held me. Some waited to dance with me and hummed "Mademoiselle from Armentières" as they waited, shuffling on the sidelines, reeking of cheap pomade, fresh wool and free smokes. I closed my eyes and wondered what that woman was like, that Mademoiselle from Armentières, and the men spoke haltingly about my eyes, their wives, their apple trees, a hill full of goldens gone from the rains, letters, their units, their rifles, their fear, going back, going home, war. "Certain possible death," they would say, hushed. Or "possible certain death." Some knew my husband's name and they danced with me all the more, weaving feet and fate and asking me "When does he say it's gonna be over? Will there be a Navy battle? That's what I wanna see, a Navy battle."

I bought them tiny Bibles like my father's to wear in their breast pockets. They brought me little bits of violets and flags for my lapels. The buttons of their tunics brushed the flosses and silks of my chemise. "It won't be over too soon," I promised them. "Oh, Dem Golden Slippers," I would sing. "Golden slippers I know so well." And they'd answer: "Gonna lead me straight to hell," and I would laugh a silvery laugh and shame them. I thought of them as my children— and of course, most of them were much shorter than I—but I liked their arms slipping around my waist, their brass against the lonely lump of lead in my stomach. I wore my After the Shower gown of French gauze sprinkled with glistening steel beads; I wore a coat-of-mail dinner frock with miles and miles of looped ribbons overlapping in black silk cascades. And I pinned their violets in my hair. Franklin wrote from Europe: "Don't get so tired in New York. Please." It was in Washington I tired, not in New York. In New York I blew up red balloons with bicycle pumps and I wore brown velveteen with wide panniers and strung the balloons across the pressed tin ceiling of the storefront recreation hall on Eighteenth and Fifth Avenue and we sat like ladies of the night in our gowns from the House of Callot, sat in the parlor and waited for the dark, for the doughboys to arrive, and then we turned on the Victrola and each of us took turns winding it, a large lovely lily blossoming with my music.

Sometimes we served cider and doughnuts, sometimes lemonade and doughnuts, sometimes coffee and doughnuts.

"I have seen the war," Franklin wrote. "I have found four Hepplewhite chairs with our crest." I have feet of lead and hammertoes and shingles.

My heels were thin and turned, my slippers torn and my

soles ingrained and pitted with the glassy sands we sprinkled on the wooden dance floors.

Some men came again and asked for me, I understand. Some left little notes. They called me Lady. I wrote little notes to their wives and found small donations for their families and then took the train back to Washington and hummed the songs of the dance hall as we passed through Jersey and Philadelphia and Baltimore and then slowly, in front of my linen closet on the second floor outside the bedroom, my throat would close as I put myself and the linens away.

"But you have ten servants, Babs," Franklin had said once when he caught me at the linens. "What are you afraid of? A rumpled sheet? Relax. You can't control *everything*." By "everything" he had not meant the linens; he had meant himself.

Over the damask cloths and the percale sheets and the seersucker spreads Franklin preferred, I would hum "Mademoiselle from Armentières, parlez-vous," over and over until my smile and my voice cracked and the wicker baskets were emptied and waiting for the next week's load. Finally I couldn't sing or smile. I stood before the linens and tied ribbons around the stacks of towels and the melancholy I felt poured out on the sidewalk, on picnics with the children, at balls and dinners, on Sunday excursions in the Stutz, and there was no musette bag, no valise, no kit bag, nothing to pack up my troubles in, nothing to contain my shame except the shingles raging on my spine and around my throat in an ever shifting map of my soul. "Can't we just have fun, Babs?" That was Franklin's plea when he was home. I would sit winding balls of gray wool from hanks of gray wool off the arms of a chair or a child who squirmed in the process and I would knit. Then I would run my fingers along the silken fringes of a painted silk lampshade, Fontainebleau scenes in fabric paint, around and around the light, along the fat gold tassels of silk on the drapes, bulbs of cords and upholstery fringe and braided butler pulls, until my fingers were numb with the nub of the silk and then I would kick off a shoe, slip off my hose, and pick purposefully at the dry patches of skin on my heel and lift the skin off in little squares and strips. There was something inside me that my own fingers, tearing and ripping, sought to free.

But I was free that summer, freer than I'd ever been. The children were in Hyde Park with Mama, Franklin gone, no one to care for, no one to wait for, no schedule. It was the first summer since my marriage that I was neither nauseated, pregnant as a cow nor nursing a large and hungry Roosevelt. My friend Isabella said I looked like a nineteen-year-old. "Slim and lovely," she wrote from Colorado where she lived with her husband, Bob, whom I think once loved me. "Hardly a matron." We were both very much matrons in the proscribed, circumscribed, circumspect conscriptions with all the rules and roles of the upper class. But that summer, even the air smelled different to me: metallic, acrid, tart. Something burning. Metal parts wearing thin.

At daybreak, dimly, one July morning not long after Franklin had left, I heard the cry of the troop train approaching Union Station. There was nothing to keep me from it. Although the moon was still in the sky, although it was not yet dawn, I rose and left my house, left the sleeping servants, hurried along N Street to the garage and rapped softly on the door for our chauffeur. Huckins, chamois-gloved and pomaded when he at last emerged in his uniform, delivered the Stutz to the curb, helped me into the driver's seat and took his place smartly on the running board.

"Ready, Huckins?"

"Yes, madam. Ready, Mrs. Roosevelt."

And with a complaint from the tires on the cobblestones, we were off.

I, a matron, with my hair brushed high, too much rose water behind my knees, too much color rubbed into my cheeks, the scarlet cross on my chest, my Red Cross cape flying behind me, the wind rushing at my teeth—Franklin had neglected to replace the windshield—ribbons of steam curling toward me from the railroad tracks, and rose petals, beaten by the night's rain, strewn on the curb, I thundered toward Union Station as if it were the Front. Past the solid red-brick houses with their box-hedged yards and their three-stepped stoops, their striped awnings and screened piazzas, past the cast-iron fences and cast-iron lightposts and wasteboxes at each corner of each clean sidewalk, past each precise front yard, each backyard just large enough for a war garden, a swing, an arbor. Past, past, past.

Huckins, poor soul, I'm certain regretted ever having agreed to teach me the technicalities of the Stutz. He, like Franklin and Mama, thought I should have an electric car and drive round the city streets in an upholstered living room with a tiller to steer by and flowers in a vase, no faster than thirty miles per hour and no farther than twenty-six miles from home. I wanted to drive the Stutz.

As we drove toward the canteen, Huckins' drooping mustache blew upward into a Cheshire-cat smile, while he clung to the doorpost and mouthed over the engine: "Madam, the cart. Madam, the curb. Madam, the pig. Madam, I beg you." And I smiled and ignored him in much the manner Franklin smiles and ignores me when he doesn't wish to listen and I drove on at high speed startling an occasional darky hymning his slow self across the street, stampeding an early morning dairy horse and his clip-clop milk wagon over the cobblestones, ice wagons, peddlers, pushcarts, tubs of oysters, racks of rabbits and manure everywhere and Huckins' gold-crown eight-dollar Painless Dentist set of teeth shut and rattled as the Stutz took the trolley tracks, circled Lafayette Square, the White House, and the shuttered windows of the house from which dear, brilliant, bitter Henry Adams watched the presidents come and go and laughed at them all.

9

IN WHICH MAMA SUGGESTS
A SECOND HONEYMOON

That the summer of the war would be a second honeymoon for Franklin and me had been Mama's idea. Mama had suggested it on a day already too warm for spring in Hyde Park. It was late in May. The first wave of American boys were on their way to Belleau Wood and the sky over Flanders was orange with bursting shells. Over the Hudson, our sky pressed in upon us, heavy, close, stagnant, swarming with maddening gnats, and over the greening Catskills above the river haze, traces of heat lightning cut at the sky. We sat on the back porch of the big house, Springwood, Mama's house, fanning ourselves, Mama sighing occasional full-bosomed suffering sighs, I knitting and waiting for her pronouncements, as I had come to her with an entirely different idea.

The river side of Springwood still sprawled, uneven, gray board and batten, pieces, porches, parts, underhangings, overhangings, as comfortable as it had been when Mama came to it as a bride. But the front side of the house which faced the highway had been redesigned by Franklin, a team of obsequious architects, a great deal of cocoa-colored stucco and Mama's capital. Three years before, when Franklin had unfurled the blueprints for me as if they were holy scrolls and Springwood the New Jerusalem—I shall not continue the analogy to its son—he explained how the two new wings on either side and an extended roofline would balance the old house, how the new façade between the wings would connect them and how the elegantly terraced porch running across the front would give Springwood a rich symmetry. What he meant was that it would be more like the other pretentious homes up and down the river. Unrolling another scroll, Franklin showed me the two master bedrooms on the second floor of the south wing, the narrow sitting room between them, the balcony and, on the first floor, running the entire length of the wing, his library. Nothing had been left out of the library wing. Detail after detail, cherry paneling, miles of shelves, the circular space for the Winged Victory, the wood boxes behind hidden panels near the fireplaces so logs could be brought up from the cellar with a handlift, locked cabinets for the treasures, crevices and recesses for the urns. "And no bathrooms, Franklin?"

"Good Lord!" Then he smiled and his eyebrows jumped that impish half inch. "You don't suppose Mama would give up her snuggery . . . turn that into the bath? It's right off the library."

"I don't suppose."

"No, neither do I."

A year later, when we drove up to the new Springwood for the first time, I said: "And no footlights, Franklin?"

"Babs, you know how much I want you to like it."

I did know and because I knew, I chose the sitting room for my bedroom. "So Mama," I explained, "can have the other master bedroom, the large room."

"As you wish," they'd both said, Franklin and Mama, looking at each other. I was the bad child whom they would discuss later. But I had already punished them by framing their pretentiousness with my monastic cell.

"Splendid," Franklin hissed as soon as we were out of Mama's hearing. "You can finally come between me and my mother."

"Really, Franklin, that's horrid."

"I'm simply being amusing."

"I'm not amused."

"You never are."

And I, in my own way, made quite certain neither Springwood nor the patterns of its life, nor of Mama's life, would become mine. I did not know then that two years later, in the spring of 1918, I would need Mama and all that Springwood meant to save my own life. But there we were two years later on the back porch, looking over the Hudson, rubbing oil of citronella on each other's arms and necks and sitting on wicker rockers newly repaired with twists of pliant green willow, the new knots and lengths still unpainted, the old wicker white and peeling, creaking on the porch slats as Mama and I rocked together. Mama was a big woman, almost old, impeccably wrapped in the wisdom of a life lived without compromise and without question. I had seen her that morning at the train station sitting straight-backed in the rear of her new Cadillac brougham, the seat next to her piled high with baskets of chickens and vegetables on their way to my house on the 10:40 to Washington. Except that I had appeared, unexpected. I had come to her with my dream.

Now we sat and I waited for her judgment. Her face was flat, stubborn and intense, like Franklin's. Flatter. Her mouth still rose-shaped, tight and thorny now in dismay, the dark eyes, cruel and fixed as an owl's, flashing and narrowing in puffy folds, her cheeks heavy purses sagging with my dream.

"I'm sorry, Mama. I didn't intend . . ."

"Hush, child, while I think."

Beyond us, Mama's land sloped and dropped in terraces to the Hudson, a collar of daffodils first, then the pale lacy cloud of blossoms in the apple orchards, then the dark wealth of walnut and pine, and, far below, the marshes and the reed-fringed river. Just beyond the porch, Plog, Mama's manager, was whistling as he polished the Cadillac. The bull was roaring in his stalls in the old gingerbread barns beyond the greenhouses, and farther out, hounds barked, plucking faint chords in the fields.

What I had come to Hyde Park to say to Mama I had already said. "Dearest Mama," I had said with my arms around her neck, her arms around my waist, my chin on her shoulder. "Dearest Mama, it is my dream. I so want to go. Others have gone with their husbands. Ted's wife has gone; a Vanderbilt girl. And someone is *needed* to run the Red Cross installation at Évian. Dearest Mama, I dream of it."

"A Vanderbilt is hardly a model for a Roosevelt, let alone a Delano," was all she had answered. Then, fanning, sighing, rocking, creaking, pleating her long black skirt with thumb and forefinger, back and forth along the sateen, sharpening and flattening the pleat as if it were I, listening to herself, she sat there while I forced myself to knit. Franklin was like that, bred with a bloodstone in him, engraved by the kingdom's finest lapidary, some wonder-filled coded gem of the Delanos ready for emergency. One had only to turn the gem over and, voilà, the answer to anything would present itself, dancing into the light. Not I. I had nothing like that. I've watched them in emergencies. Franklin and Mama don't think. They wait for their answers. Saturnine, taciturn, they sit until the bloodstone turns and takes the light, then sudden mercurial insight, then the pronouncement and then, with that judgmental, monumental smugness around the corners of their mouths and eyebrows arched like keystones, the answer. That day I was the question, the family emergency.

I was the skein of gray wool dancing in my own lap like a small animal as I knit and tugged at myself. I was the large

13

dark clump of gnats along my forearm struggling for freedom, and drowning in the citronella and the wisps of my own fine hairs.

As well as anyone else, better than Franklin would or could, Mama knew me. She knew me when I scuttled away into the spidery corners of my dream world. She knew when my back grew rigid with polite anger. Every day that I wasn't with Mama, I wrote her. And every day, for she was my schoolmistress, I patiently listed my social calls, my invitations, the completeness of our lives, our successes in her society with the children of her friends, Franklin's importance in Washington, my marketing, the children's weights, the new gowns, the rude servants (Butler was insolent), the spring-cleaning, how sweet Franklin Jr. was when he had to be gassed to have the abscesses in both ears lanced, how funny Dicky Bird was because Huckins had cut his nails and nipped a bit of the flesh and Dicky stood on one leg in his cage for three days, how James went to a war movie because Franklin had told him that he could and Anna wished she too could go to the movies as she had never been, how perfectly pleased we all were with the American Geographic Society magazines she had sent, how happy I was to hear that she was putting in new net curtains at our adjoining houses in New York City, 47 and 49, we called them, how I hoped the new bull, Main Sheet of Annandale, would be a great success, how I thought the dairy barn with plumbing would be a grand improvement, and that the old farmhouse would be far more livable for the tenant, Moses Smith, if Mama were to put in a force pump, and how good she must feel knowing that the rye and wheat were already housed. All that. Thank-yous and pleases, calculated requests for things I already had, things I already knew, things I cared nothing about. I trailed it all in lacework letters, the lines crisscrossing each other on the ivory vellum, black-bordered vellum, laced with my female virtues, a spoor of good-wife/good-woman virtues veiled in the gentle compliant complaints, a spoor of dull little family

14

anecdotes which only a wizened huntress like Mama could read and recognize, through the latticed lines, as traces of the madness in my blood.

Mama referred tactfully, in our way, to my inconsistencies and she watched me and calculated me as carefully as she did her milk production—so much feed, so much milk—as carefully as I did her. Like Franklin, she forgot nothing, threw out nothing, wrote down everything. There were journals, ledgers, diaries, household books, piles of letters, piles of calling cards, invitations, trip diaries, small Morocco books and large calfbound books and somewhere, I was certain, some dreadful journal, some Jehovan *Book of Life* lined with illumined peacock papers from Persia and inscribed like fever charts with Eleanor's moods, tempers, depressions, selfishnesses, inefficiencies, inconsistencies—which were my lies—and in special codes the insane geographies and peoples of my dream worlds. That is how carefully I was watched. How to increase the yield of laying hens, simple instructions for zephyr booties and curried pigeon, some symptoms of madness, detecting gas leaks in the sewer pipes, shares of the Delano mining interests, 1891–1909, and what to do about Eleanor. And now I, or she, have added paragraphs, perhaps chapters, perhaps only one final mark in thick ink referring to Évian. I have not yet died but she has weighed my heart from the moment I met her son. Good luck to her if she were weighing my soul. Even Mama couldn't find that. Even Mama. If she could I would be very interested.

Between sighs, for a moment, Mama patted her own knee firmly, decisively, and then mine with the flat of her hand.

"Have you had any more of your moods this spring, Eleanor?" She withdrew her hand and continued to wait, squinting into my future.

"No, Mama," I lied, "I've felt quite well."

My dream world was an odd thing. It was my elsewhere, as real for me as my actual world. It was dangerous only because I wanted to remain in it. I preferred it. I shared it with no one although I had existed in its landscapes since I was eight, when my mother died. Other children I suppose had dream friends and dream adventures, a way of trying one's self on before going into the real world, a way of filling empty places. But I had never let go of that perfect world in which my father was the hero and I the heroine, happy, loved, approved, beautiful and wonderfully, so wonderfully courageous. Shining in silver courage like leaves turned inside out by the wind, gleaming from their undersides. When I was nearly ten and my father died, and his death was told to me with the dreaded long faces of adults in terror of reality, I knew enough to cry in order to please my Grandmother Hall, who had already taken my brother and myself in, to please my mother's sisters, Pussie and Maude. I pleased them with my tears as well as I pleased the visitors who came clucking over us, for Hall, my young brother, and I were now legitimate orphans. "Poor Eleanor" was the leitmotif of my relations' chattering. Everyone always said "Poor Eleanor." They still do, for different reasons. After the next raw December day, after the black umbrellas and the shovelfuls of mud on my father's casket—the same umbrellas and mud of my mother's burial—I slipped back into my dream world with my father, just as I had always been. I let my mother die, my father I kept alive. Nothing can change a dream world. The more painful the real world became, the more I left it. Governesses said I was withdrawn, a little queer, and that I would be quiet for hours on end. They had no idea where I was and how happy I was when I was away.

". . . modern, I suppose . . ." Mama was speaking. I didn't know when she had begun. Her words were drifting out into the haze, gently, as one folds whipped cream into the bavaroise. The ring of bells on riverboats floated up toward us. "I suppose this is modern."

I said nothing.

"No." The words jelled, stiffening swiftly into decision. Her voice changed. "No. I do not approve of your going. I do

16

not approve of Franklin going. War is not a holiday. You are both shirking your responsibilities."

"Oh, Mama! I would never . . ." I protested. "I want to serve my *country*."

She licked her lips as if something bitter had passed over them. "Come now, Eleanor. I am quite done up with the both of you. There are five children. Responsibility is the hallmark of aristocracy. What has came over you?"

"It's a new world, Mama. People don't think in those terms . . . I don't wish to be respectful. I wish to be respected!"

"I'm speaking of tradition, Eleanor. Christian values. That which does not change. Yes. The fixed. Yes." She agreed with herself. "It's all that talk of shirt sleeves. I don't suppose you care to live in a stable as your Aunt Pussie does. I don't suppose you wish that kind of eccentricity, do you? You do know, don't you, that her dear little nine-year-old is made to answer the door? That there are no servants? Is that modern? I say it's madness."

"Madness, Mama?"

This is how it always begins.

"Madness." She let the word hang above us. It is her way to hang her sword, Damoclean, on the thinnest thread and unravel the thread at will. She has only to pull at it to terrorize me. It is her way. After she reminds me that I come from madness, she suggests that I am acting madly and it is, then, merely the tiniest tug at the thread that leads me to obey her . . . if only to save myself from the ends of my family. I know all this but it does not help.

"It is certainly not something a Delano would do. Mark me, Eleanor. That woman is stalking tragedy, Eleanor, and she is not alone in that, not in *your* family."

"Mama, please . . . I beg you . . ."

And would the madness be mine? When I lived with Grandmother Hall at Tivoli up the river, Pussie, in her fits of temper, told me horror stories of my own papa in his last years. Pussie was even more beautiful than my mother. And very cruel. She told me how my mother had Papa declared insane for the inheritance; how he had been barred from our home, from his own babies, found in gutters, in saloons, in the cheap rooms of strange women. She told me all this while her older brother, my mother's brother Vallie, howled from his locked room above us and our lives were streaked, all of us, mine from both sides, with the acid of madness. Mama had opposed our marriage not because Franklin was too young but because of my family, my drunken father, my Uncle Vallie shooting at people across the lawns of Tivoli, my aunts Pussie and Maude playing at their Ouija boards, me, all of us. And now? Would they take my home and my babies from me if I didn't behave in the way of the Gospel according to Mama? Of course I had to control things. Wasn't my malady already beginning?

"I suggest, Eleanor . . ." The fan stopped; the creaking of the rocker stopped. "I suggest, this summer, a second honeymoon for you and Franklin."

"A honeymoon?" I burst into sobs. "I want to go to war!"

In distaste, Mama drew herself up from the rocker. "I shall take your staff and the children and you'll stay in Washington and make certain that boy of mine and you work at your marriage. The both of you. No more bachelor summers for him! And no more heroics for you! You will do your duty as a woman."

"Mama! I will go mad!"

"Come now, none of that. You'll only go mad if you want to."

And I followed her into the darkening house. "Christian virtues, Eleanor. Christian virtues," she intoned before me through the narrow halls, like a great prioress.

"It isn't fair, Mama. Everyone in Washington is laughing at me. It isn't fair what he has done to me. I've done nothing to deserve it. I've been a good wife, Mama . . ."

"Don't be absurd. You make a great mistake to think everything that happens to you is the fault of others."

"This is."

"No. It is not. You are your own worst adversary."

Her walk was that of a squire's wife, a waddle, the walk of a farmwoman just off the horse, with potatoes in both pockets. Dutch, German, not a fault, but a strength in the shadows, a strong thing. "If you work at the preservation of Christian values, I promise you my complete support—particularly in matters that affect my son's marriage. Is that clear, Eleanor? You do understand what I am saying?" She waited without looking back.

"I understand."

She walked on.

"He knows he wouldn't be happy on Miss Mercer's money. What is it you paid her? Fifteen hundred a year? There's nothing to worry about with fifteen hundred a year. I know my boy. Really, Eleanor, fifteen hundred a year!" In the front hall she stopped to stroke the golden bronze shoulder of Franklin's statue gleaming under electric Roman torches. Mama stroked Franklin's shoulder and touched lightly the knuckles of each long graceful finger, carving him still, forming him still. "The torso, it is so beautiful," the sculptor had said. "We only suggest the legs." Mama agreed.

"Why do you think Elliott is the way he is?" Mama asked rhetorically, moving away from the statue. I bit my lip to hold in my anger. I have heard from my servants, from Connachie, the spare Scots nurse, the insinuations of Mama's own acid. "Control yourself, Anna," she would say to my daughter, "don't be like your mother!" "Now, Elliott, that sulking makes everyone around you very unhappy. You must try to be happy and pleasant when your Mummy is sad. All of you," she has said to all of them. "We all must help your Mummy to be herself."

"I know you. You do what you wish, Eleanor, and if you do

not, those around you suffer. Your children are wild and you have obviously not kept Franklin happy."

It was I, my malady, my melancholy, that would pit and pock at the design of the king she'd cast. In the thirteen years with Franklin I have found marriage to be that rare institution in which, in order to survive, one must become a victim. Poor Eleanor. Poor Franklin.

I reached to touch Franklin but at the deadness of the metal my fingers stiffened and retreated. "I am worried. If Mr. Daniels allows him to the Front, Mama, he may be killed."

"Franklin?" She laughed, a fly buzzing in a teacup. "If he goes, I have Mr. Daniels' word that Franklin will not be allowed near the Front." She led me to her snuggery.

"Mama! You didn't!" And motioned me to sit at her feet on a stool.

"Now, now. I was very discreet. I *am* on your side, Eleanor, no matter what you think."

"Mama, it is terrible that you went to Mr. Daniels. It would so embarrass Franklin."

"Be practical. You are both such wide-eyed romantics. I know my boy," Mama said sitting stiffly on a pink horsehair chair. "He doesn't like to fight." She and the chair exhaled.

The snuggery was Mama's sanctuary, a corner of the old house, small and warm with dark wood and bell pulls and chests in every corner for her record books, her ledgers, her girlhood collection of cups and saucers, Kodaks framed in wood and laced with ribbons, a tiny recess. Franklin teased her for its ugliness, drew plans yearly to convert it to a bathroom.

Franklin had two of us really. He had always been able through the years to set each of us upon the other and walk away from both when he'd had what he wanted. And we, locked in combat, would never notice he was gone until it was too late. This time, we thought, we had fooled him.

"I understood as soon as he was selling the *Half Moon*. No reason to sell his father's boat. And I know Franklin loved it.

Well, I said to myself, Franklin is acting like a man straightening out his affairs, a man freeing himself. So I went directly to Mr. Daniels. He may be Secretary of the Navy and he may be Franklin's superior but he is also a very kind gentleman and he understood immediately."

Everyone understands immediately. Mama rang for the butler.

The butler came, nodding, wound the arm of the Victrola, laid the needle on a record, withdrew, and we sat there in the half-light among the heavy silk drapes from her father's China trade, I at Mama's feet, my head on her knees, a pile of records next to us, Mama humming Wagner. I wanted to run across the fields in the twilight, in large loping strides over the hummock of nettles and the spongy mosses but I sat there at her feet, like a dog, desperate for her affection, listening to German tragedies when my own sat like a screech owl on my shoulder and Mama patted my shoulder and stroked my hair and wiped tears from my cheeks with her thumb.

The light faded entirely. The butler came in again and again to wind the Victrola and change the records and finally he closed the Victrola and carried the records back to the library. As we stood, I kissed Mama's cheek. It was no drier than my own. "Dear Mama . . ."

"I'm afraid neither of us can live without Franklin," she apologized. "There may not be happiness, Eleanor. There will be glory."

"I want happiness. I want love."

"I know."

She walked with me to our rooms where we would dress for dinner. At my door, looking older than when the day had begun, she said, "You'll find in the long run that your greatest contribution in this life will be your family. Trust me in that. I am very hopeful for you, child. You are too thin," she added.

I didn't forget Évian. As all things lost, I lived Évian in my dream world. I wrote communiqués citing myself for heroism. I saved lives. I prayed over dying men. I cured. I healed. I

21

loved. Franklin envied me, admired me, loved me. But there was a spot somewhere when I thought of Évian that made it less than complete, like an acid blot on a Kodak—that taste of salt and citronella on Mama's cheek, a taste of her pain. I had thought only of my own.

At the Hyde Park station the next morning, the red and green wooden baggage cart was loaded with Mama's baskets of chickens and vegetables and milk cans, and the stationmaster pulled it along the uneven bricks of the platform with the metal wheels rattling and clunking behind us. Mama led. When the train pulled in from Rhinebeck, the Vanderbilts' stop, the stationmaster scuttled by us, bent over, tapping the iron wheels of the train with a rod, cocking his ear to the ring of the wheel, listening and testing the tone of each wheel for its strength, and Mama in the same manner ran her hands up and down my arms and over my shoulders. "I am on your side, Eleanor. Don't forget that. Nor underestimate it. Fixed things, Eleanor. Fixed things."

I settled into my compartment, into a wicker chair next to a wicker table with a lamp on it. Mama, sitting in the open seat of her Cadillac, grew smaller and smaller as the train poured through the rockcuts and river land away from Hyde Park toward New York. And I made plans for my second honeymoon which had every possibility itself of becoming war.

The sun haloes each block of marsh grass, enriches each clump of poverty grass, deep greens and golds and black glens, water-rotted barges and docks, collapsed granaries and mills from the Revolution, Marble Hill, Spuyten Duyvil, flat cliff faces, the wilderness of my fathers. See the sheep, I tell a child, by habit, for I am alone. See the sheep grazing on the hillside. They look like rocks, don't they? Cinders float from the train past my window and green-blue verticals of light splash and dip into the river. In some car near mine a boy is playing a mouth organ. I know it is a boy from the plaintiveness of the song. "Mademoiselle from Armentières." That song again and forever. I have heard it from the back of hay wagons. I have heard it in the city from the doors of saloons, in Washington, New York, Hyde Park, the points of my endless triangle, wherever I run, the song follows me and reminds me, like a whistling lover eating iron at the grates of my window, of war.

Lying in bed, propped on my elbow, I have watched Franklin in the moonlight. He feigns sleep. His mouth is slack, slightly open, moist. I touch his lips lightly with my forefinger. His eyelashes are long and damp against his cheeks. I put my lips on his cheeks and, as I breathe in, the thin flesh lifts toward my mouth. I release it and move away. Precious beautiful man with the thin breath in your nostrils, your eyelids quiver under my touch. You are so beautiful. "I'm so sleepy, Babs. Let me sleep."

I sigh. He sits up. "Is something bothering you, Babs? Do you want to talk about something?"

"Are you displeased with me, Franklin? Tell me, what is wrong with me?" It is not what I wish to talk about.

"You are ambivalent." He smiles. "Our class is ambivalent."

"We act ambivalent, that is all."

"No, you are ambivalent."

"I am?"

"Yes," he says, "Definitely." He laughs in the moonlight.

"I am not."

"If you are, you wouldn't be able to say that." He laughs.

"That is correct."

He is about to play. "But you do have hesitant sensitivities, tentative senses, sensitive tenses. You do hide what you feel. Ambivalent, bivalved as a clam. Shells and shells and when I open a crack you are very soft and mushy inside. Weepy and whiny and ambivalent. For instance, how do you feel about Mr. Howe?"

"I find Mr. Howe necessary. I am glad you have found him."

"Ambivalent. What do you *feel?* Don't you hate him?"

He is playing with me, with his hands. He is doing a spider doing push-ups on a mirror. His hands flex and spread on each other. "Don't you feel anything about Mr. Howe?"

"Of course I feel." I feel. Shall I tell him what I feel? That I could step on his hands now? Shall I tell him that I feel that he has tricked and cheated me? Shall I tell myself what I feel? And he begins to enjoy his words so much he forgets his feelings. I am excellent at being ambivalent. It drives him wild because he knows I have chosen ambivalence publicly to cover something I will only let him imagine. I am also excellent at being mediocre. I've watched tennis games at Sagamore Hill. There is always one person in the four who must learn to look very capable and very busy because the others never give him a chance at the ball.

I am not ambivalent. I am not a bivalve. I am a snail—my dream world is my safe shell. Inside my shell I am naked as a snail. I love Franklin and I despise him for the pain. I am not ambivalent about my children. I would give my life for them if they were in danger, but I don't adore them in the least. They make me very unhappy. I make them very unhappy. I adore my husband. I don't adore my husband. He makes me very unhappy. I make him very unhappy. I feel terrible guilt that I don't do these things well that other women do so comfortably, so naturally. Is it that I am so unnatural? Or that we are all such liars? Who among us will be the first one to say that her children are bores, that she would not choose one among them as a friend, that her husband treats her as an indentured servant and looks at other women who have not given him children, who do not have ulcers and hemorrhoids and miscarriages and monthlies and dead sons and Griselda moods and headaches and tears? And who will have all those accoutrements as soon as they are chosen. Who is there among us who is happy? As I, Mama adores Franklin, and he eats her heart out.

"You're doing that thing with your tongue again, Babs," Franklin would complain.

"Sorry," I would say and pull my tongue back into my mouth and try to chew on it within my mouth.

"What did I say that so offended you tonight?" I would ask, waking Franklin when I could no longer bear to lie still. "What did I say?"

"Nothing in particular," he would murmur and turn away. "Just try to be a little less serious."

If only it were something in particular. If I stand up straight and stop chewing my nails, will you love me again? If I spend the entire summer in Washington with you, you alone, no children, a few servants, just the two of us, will you love me again?

The train nears New York. Tonight I will spend in the canteen. I love the city. Here my fathers felt, I think, the excitement Franklin feels in Washington. Land, land and more land. Endless Eden-stretches of fish and fowl and rabbits and fruits and freedom, endless rivers, space, mountains, sky, Eden. I feel it still, that excitement . . . the richness of what is ahead. I am muscular, as they were. I am strong. I crave endless space and action and freedom. I remember my father roaring at an ocean. He carried me on his shoulders to the top of a cliff covered with tall yellow daisies and he bent his solid beautiful torso back and roared. My mother scolded him. He was very drunk. "Your mother's emotion; your father's big ocean. Shh!" He turned to her. "I prefer to hear the ocean. We're speaking." I saw very little of him after that. What did Papa want that he couldn't find? I want to be left alone; I want to be loved. Smokestacks belch across a full moon on the East River and trails of vapor embroider the night sky of New York. Here I am powerful and possible. From the train I walk farther and farther back on my heels, my once-braced spine unbraced and straight, my legs very long, vigorous, clicking my heels on the concrete.

My soles are thin and I feel the sidewalk hammering right up through my spine and I walk faster and it hammers faster. My clothes are fine, my carriage graceful, my neck long and thin and elegant and my body powerful. Here I do not look at the pity on other women's faces or the polite impatience in Franklin's eyes. Here I feel powerful and possible. And yet, even as the train took me from Hyde Park, even as I planned my honeymoon I also knew, ambivalent as I must be, that Franklin was planning his mission to Europe.

IN WHICH I DISCUSS SEEDS AND LEAD WITH HENRY ADAMS

I have begun, strangely enough, to treasure the loneliness Franklin left me with. At 2:00 A.M., at 3:00 A.M., at 5:00 A.M., I ride home from the Washington canteen. Beneath a clouded moon ringed with the promise of rain, delaying. Through avenues of gargoyle forsythia bushes and slick vines snaking around wrought-iron fences, under arches of spirit spruces leaning softly against each other, I float from the soft gray woolly mists into the black and sleep a few hours and wake.

Some mornings I sit curled in a wicker swing in the arbor of our garden with the kitchen tabby purring and burrowing in the shade of my skirts. And the sun climbs to noon while I read romances, eat ripe peaches, wipe peach juice from my chin and tears from my cheeks. For the two weeks Franklin has been gone, I've been in love with Mr. Rochester. Jane Eyre's desires become my own and chase each other like white butterflies in the black shadows of my heart. One sunrise I visited a rainbow over the Potomac. I sat under the rainbow with my arms wrapped around my knees down where the rushes hide all of us from the others and watched the blue herons and listened to the katydids until a horseman galloped along the riverbank and the herons broke from the marsh in a soul at the sound, a large swooping soul of birds, shrinking into a single blue dot beyond the rainbow.

If any place is a safe place for me, it is the grave of Henry Adams' wife, Clover, with its Saint-Gaudens statue. Mr. Adams himself visits the grave in Rock Creek Cemetery quite as often as I, but at different times, and if I do see his victoria on the path, I leave. I and that statue called Grief sit together for many hours. Clover Adams took her life, the ladies say, clicking and clacking, but the words are pregnant with a vague promise. Took her life. I too at times have wished to take my own life, to have my own life, to do with it what I wanted, and I wondered so if death were the only way.

"I want to possess my life," I told Mr. Adams once in his parlor. "That's what I mean. There is so much I want to know. I am so curious about *life*, Mr. Adams."

"No, no, no," he admonished me, laughing. "Curious is not enough. It is too distant a word. Oh, no, dear little large lady or is it dear large little lady, curious is not enough. Our homes and our friends . . . we fill our lives with curiosities . . . collections of curiosities . . . our homes and our friends are collections of curiosities about which, after possession, no one is any longer curious. There is no life in curiosity."

"Yes, oh, yes, I understand that. Oh, yes, like the elephants on your mantelpiece."

"The elephants, Eleanor?"

I moved to his mantelpiece and picked up an ivory elephant from the family of ivory elephants lined up from least to greatest. "Everyone we know owns a family of ivory elephants and everyone we know keeps them on the mantelpiece arranged in universal plan from lesser to greater just as it would be for us growing larger, growing greater, all in a row. Never—and I have seen many of those ivory elephants carved from their very own tusks, one after the other—never have I seen them arranged in any design other than a straight line from small to great. Even my parlormaid dusts them from small to great—I have watched her—with her feather duster."

"It's very un-American," Mr. Adams explained to me, "to go in circles. One goes straight to great. Only the child and the old man remake the world after their own hearts—when the parlormaid isn't looking—carefully, courageously, putting the elephants into circles. From now on, I will have those ivories in circles and off the mantelpiece. Promise me you'll do the same, Mrs. Roosevelt."

I ask Mr. Adams odd questions. He gives me even odder answers.

"And what does Grief mean, Mr. Adams?"

Dear Mr. Adams would laugh in that sardonic laugh of his, sitting in his victoria outside my house, passing bunches of violets to my children from inside the quilted velvet curves of the carriage with his secretary, Aileen, beside him. "They come from all over the country and from Europe and offer up philosophies, grand ones, about the meaning of Grief. But any nursery-school jinriksha boy would know. That statue is only a mirror. You bring to it yourself and you are forced to look at yourself."

"What kind of terrible joke is that upon the people who come to mourn, Mr. Adams? Mourn for yourself?"

"Eleanor, dear, you are *too* human." And then he and Aileen would rattle off, down N Street toward Lafayette Square, and I would dwell on his words for hours. I mourned for myself before Clover's statue. I had not yet learned to look for myself, preoccupied as I was with looking for Franklin.

"You are such a secret person, Eleanor, such a secret

person," Mr. Adams told me in his parlor. "What is it you are growing in there? What seeds spring in the cold frame you show us all? When will your summer come? What will your summer be?"

"I don't know. It may never be."

"Your roots go further and further down," he said not listening, his fine New England head buried, bony in his chest, enjoying his own words. "And you stoop. All seed, all promise . . . what grows in you?"

"I don't feel green, Mr. Adams, I feel rather black and old."

"*I'm* old. Black, is it? Then you are not a precious flower? Melancholy? Slow, sad, sour, black. Paralyzed. Yes, you are lead. Metallic seeds, then, planted by the planets in you to become precious metals. Ah." From a shelf of books that began with *Beowulf* and ended with his own, he brought down a new enormous text on medieval mining and tapped the leather cover with a forefinger. "Of the metals. For you. Poor young Herbert Hoover translated Agricola and neither of them, I daresay, had any idea they were writing allegorically. *De Re Metallica.* Allegorical." He tapped the book and then he tapped me on my hand which rested along the carved arm of a chair. "Hidden things, you see. Seeds. Lead. Who said this, Aileen? 'When the deeps are loosened, the great mind breaks forth amid events too private or too sacred for public speech and seem themselves, I know not why, to belong to hidden things.' I've stolen those lines from someone. I know not who. I give them and this to you. You will read it? For me?"

"Yes. Yes. Lead is the greatest challenge. Of course. But you aren't interested at all, are you?" He took the book back and leafed quickly through it. "See here. 'After great forest fires . . . after great forest fires, the silver runs from the blackened forest in three streams. Shining streams. From the lead.' You see, Eleanor, you must endure the holocaust. Lead is very important. You are a lead person. Via longissima . . . the longest way."

"I am lead?"

Twilight fell. Aileen moved nervously to end Mr. Adams' discourse. I could only listen.

"Lead is a great fatherly weight, a ball, a hunk, pulling you down into the lead-drift of the centuries, slow poisoned, down. Even the diamond breaks and still lead persists, endures, travels slowly through the planets, through the mothers of the metals, slowly, beginning with Saturn. Get the lead out of your pants. Saturn, satin, Satan. Resist change. When the psyche of lead is changed, it is a change in history . . . that is what lead means. There is a great task set upon oneself by the lead. It is very grave. That's clever. Sorry. Let it not ever be said Henry Adams was clever. Dear God."

"Shall I change history?"

"Wrap up the tome in brown paper and kitchen string, Aileen. While Mrs. Roosevelt's friends are sneaking off with copies of Marie Stopes, God help us, she can hide Mr. Hoover's work under her apron. I do care about you, Mrs. Roosevelt. I do care."

"I too. I feel . . . oh, but I feel you waste yourself on me."

"Better you than all those others. And you are a wonderful listener. That is what I most love about you . . . myself." Aileen, relieved, and I, confused, laughed. I stood to depart. "You'll change history, little large lady, only if you change yourself. I wouldn't, so I didn't."

Small, angular, son of sea captains and presidents, he reached up to pat my head. "And the wine of life is poisoned by the lead, isn't it? In the drinking cups of the Roman Emperors. Did you know that? You uncle would. The Romans all died slowly of poisoning from the vessels of lead. Promise me you will not poison the Roman Empire. Yes? And Franklin." I didn't know if it were a question.

"Franklin is in Europe, doing finely."

"Your uncle has a much better sense of humor. Much better than Franklin. You, I think, laugh at us all."

It was nice to know Mr. Adams cared, but I didn't know

what he meant. To me, death was a hidden thing. To me, having lead in me meant I had no life. I was death. Franklin was life. I felt I could not therefore live without him, as if it were all a mathematical formula. I am lead. He is gold. He shines upon me and I live. I am as good as gold to him but still, I am lead. And he is gold. He holds the sun in his hands and everything and everyone he touches turns to gold. Except me. For the last five years, Franklin, the Crusader, has languished in his office down the block from Mr. Adams' house, in the sandcastle monstrosity that houses War, Navy and State. He sits with a fresh rose on his desk every day in a high-ceilinged room with a balcony overlooking the White House, with a bust of John Paul Jones on the mantelpiece, maps of Europe on the wall, ocean routes, cigarettes in leadlined silver boxes stamped with the insignia of the New York Yacht Club, a special mix for members, his desk clear, Inbaskets, Outbaskets, tooled Morocco scrapbooks with his press clippings, and the fresh rose, every day. Waiting for a holy war. He works like a nigger, he says, and waits for the greatest battle of all times: the American fleet versus the German fleet. "It will be the greatest war in history, Babs!" Exclamation, exclamation. "We've got to get into this war!" he would cry, barging into Josephus Daniels' office five times a week, nervous, lean, thin-lipped, horse-handsome, chaste, Chevy Chased, limp-wristed, long-riding, graceful, burning, and Mr. Daniels, drawstring tie, curly forelock, little, un-moneyed, uncultured, fat-fingered, pork-pie, patient, South-ern fundamentalist, the Secretary of the Navy, who had removed wine from the officers' mess, thereby offending everyone, would drawl and smile, "I hope not. I hope not." Uncle Ted traveled the country to fan the fires of war by shouting with his lips a half inch from his face and his short arm raised, fisted, swinging over the mastiff head and the fires gleaming in both mirrors of his glasses. "We don't need Mr. Baker as Secretary of War. We need a butcher!" "A butcher!" the crowds responded and hanged their neighbors who wouldn't buy Liberty Bonds. Act sharp. Look sharp. The whole country has its coat off for war, its sleeves rolled up, its jaws snapping, and Franklin, the next Roosevelt waiting in the wings for the leap to the presidency through the good fortune of war, with his vulpine intellect and pince-nez and his jacket off for the press, in his shirt sleeves for the press, smoking Camel cigarettes for the press, looking in the camera's eye for the press the way he once looked in my eyes when he loved me. Franklin crossing this dark century and waiting behind the single rose on his desk for the skies to roll back and let him in. "He's not a friend I'd follow to Hell," Josephus said. "But I'd follow him to Heaven because with his luck someone would probably throw him the key." Franklin has thirsty eyes that are too close together. Under the high ceilings and the maps of the ocean routes and the little golden pinheads of all the fleet he fills with coal and deploys, rests his commission from President Wilson. "Dearest Babs," he wrote when I was with the children last summer at Campobello, "A complete smashup is inevitable and there are a great many problems for us to consider. Mr. Daniels totally fails to grasp the situation and I am to see the President Monday AM and go over our own situation. These are history making days. It will be the greatest war in history." Men have such a sense of history. Franklin's eyes are too close together because they are focused inward, because they are focused on Mr. Daniels' job, and on history—the whore who may make my Franklin a man. Franklin, the *New York Tribune* reported when the U.S.S. *Dyer* arrived in France, "is a young man with energy and definite ideas, as well as a definite objective who can be generous and fair, but firm to his own cause." GOK, God Only Knows—the bromide the doughboys write home on the thousands of postcards I censor at the canteen—God only knows he can be firm to his own cause. He is his own cause.

Franklin went off two weeks ago in clothing he had inherited from his father—a long luggage-leather coat and an ancient Alpine shooting jacket that were already old a quarter of a century ago when his father died. Franklin had his own riding boots. He said to me, to his image, rehearsing, reversing his other self before the silvered glass of the mirror: "I look like an ass." How he longed for a legitimate uniform to wear to the Front. Already, by doing certain favors for certain admirals when Secretary Daniels was out of the office, Franklin has rewritten certain Navy regulations so that when a certain assistant secretary of the Navy boards a vessel, he is greeted with a certain flag (which he designed), a fourteen-gun salute (for which rear admirals wait a lifetime) and a ruffle. Franklin, however, couldn't wangle a uniform. Mama sympathetically offered to have one made up at Abercrombie & Fitch, but Franklin refused, saying, quite nastily and painfully for Mama, that this was hardly the Civil War. Mama has had uniforms made up for the boys and a nurse's dress for Anna.

Letters are already arriving. Franklin wrote at the top of one of his letters "Somewhere in France." Below that he wrote about his trip to Cliveden to see the Astors, tea at Claridge's with Mrs. Edwardes, who was too, too delighted to see him, and shopping at the Army and Navy Stores in London where silk pajamas, it seems, have doubled in price since the war began and he could only buy three pairs instead of the usual six. From Franklin I heard that bullets were bully. The Front was bully. The souvenirs were bully and although he didn't yet have Kaiser Bill's helmet for James, he did have a pencil stolen from the Kaiser's yacht. Almost getting hit with a shell on the ship going across—he insisted on mounting the bridge although he was hardly a line officer, not even having a uniform—that was bully. Franklin must have been a vision on the bridge in his silk pajamas. But when he addressed a group of Marines in his finest Uncle Ted style and offered to swap his passage home just to wear one of their uniforms and one Marine wiseacre took him up on it, that wasn't bully. He was, I'm certain, embarrassed to be taken to task. The Marine and

I are probably the only two people in the world who succeeded in that . . . and his mother, but he can avoid her. Franklin's mission was bon secteur all the way: safe section, furniture in the trenches, dinner at the Crillon, tea with the Countess D'Arcy, weekends at the country estates, with just the faint exotic fillip of danger on the horizon, a shrill shell whistling way off over there while he and Livy Davis, his friend, drank suds or vin blanc in an outdoor café and watched the shells burst in the sky. Franklin fooled someone and finally managed, against orders and his mother's wishes, to go to the Front and he and Livy came back to Paris loaded like Christmas trees with helmets, swords, holy grails and guns. It would never occur to Franklin that his number might be on a certain shell.

IN WHICH I READ FRANKLIN'S
LETTERS FROM THE FRONT

I suppose it is morbid to read the thin packet of Franklin's letters in a cemetery and I will never forgive myself if that morbidity brings on danger for Franklin while he is at war. When I was pregnant with Elliott, I still carried in my blood all the sorrow of losing my baby Franklin Jr. when he was not even eight months old. I'd been wildly depressed through the pregnancy and I still blame Elliott's difficulties on the sorrow that joined him in my womb. Everyone says I am very mistaken, the doctor, Mama. They say my grief had nothing whatsoever to do with Elliott's problems. There was one more, dead, a miscarriage, a shapeless thing that never saw light. I the unshaped who could not shape another. But does one really ever know what prompts what, or if anything at all is truly prompted by mortals? Does character shape event? Does event shape character? When I was pregnant with Elliott, I would lie in the hammock that summer at Campobello and a cat, the same calico cat from the barn, each day would leap into the hammock and knead at my stomach. In the sun, swaying, warm, sleeping, I liked the rhythm of the paws pressing into my stomach and I could feel the infant moving back and forth at the cat's touch. It was very beautiful and I have always since felt uneasy about it. Perhaps it was too strange.

The first time I sat at Clover's gravesite with the letters in my lap, a vagrant budgie, pearl-white with an aquamarine diadem, hopped toward me from the stone skirts of Grief. It had to have belonged to a birdcage decently safe among the dragon plants and Boston ferns and rubber plants of some-one's Washington sunroom. When I did clasp my hand around it thinking to return it to someone somewhere it wobbled and fluttered away, without grace, but away, to perch on a willow branch above me. Later, and many times since, when I'd sat perfectly still, it hopped down to seek odd bits of solace and sacraments and sweetmeats at the base of that statue. Just as I did.

How I envied that woman with her life so cut into her face, so shaped, so strong, so complete against my incompleteness, my shapelessness beneath her. I don't know what was shaping me then. Event? Character? Breeding? Others? Budgie birds, Ouija boards? I don't know. Perhaps I was being unshaped, destroyed. That Franklin left me alone for the first time in our lives . . . had that helped to shape me? The letter from him saying he would join the Navy on his return? A braggadocio newspaper article saying he would join the Navy as a bluejacket? A handkerchief dipped in his tonic slipped into my bosom? A pressed rose from a lonely soldier in the Dutch Bible? Someone studies us and says, "Ah. Yes. And then he left for his mission abroad and when he returned she found his letters and after those letters, she never shared his bed again." It was never that simple.

At night I spread all Franklin's letters out on my comfort-er, drink my Ovaltine and read them over and over again. I accuse him, plead with him, forgive him, rub his back, cry, amuse him, giggle, line by line, space by space, heartbeat by heartbeat. Below my bedroom, tree-shaded N Street is hot and noisy, sleep a rare companion. Around me tiny pale paper roses climb in yellow trellised stripes along the walls and across the ceiling and an old blue Mahal from Auntie Bye's Farmington house covers the floor. Franklin's mother's hope chest sits hopefully with its hammered clasps and cartouches at the foot of our bed. The bed, our bed, is heavy black walnut, knotted and framed with acorns, burls and other bewilderments, as ugly and sturdy as it need be. Upon it, upon me, Franklin hurriedly, dutifully, and deliberately, steadfastly fathered six large children and one without shape. Neither the bed nor I, except in fear, have ever trembled. I dream, when I dare dream, that one day I might tremble. But those are dangerous dreams, the most dangerous, the most melancholy, and I control them. Franklin and I spoke once and once only about those dreams. I was twenty-four and thought of myself as modern. Mama thought me unspeakably rebellious and lacking in grace. I was, probably, all three. Franklin and I stood over three-year-old Anna's crib, Tiny James stirred behind us in another crib. As I had done every night since Anna was two, I had, after Nurse retired, after hearing Anna's simple prayers, after reading her a Bible tale, I had, with the very softest of cotton cord, tied Anna's little hands to the bars of her crib above her head. I don't recall why it was that Franklin had come up to the nursery that night to see the babies, but he had called in a twisted voice and when I finally arrived, having galloped to the third floor, he pointed to the tied hands and insisted that I dismiss Nurse at once.

"Oh," I said lightly, "I do that, not Nurse." It was so long ago. I'd been so certain of myself then.

"You?"

"The child masturbates."

"Monstrous." I felt him looking at me. "How long has this been going on?"

"I first noticed it last year," I answered, not understanding his meaning, "when she was about two." The collection of thick-carved wooden nursery-book characters lined the walls quite unevenly and needed the attention of a busy dustcloth. I moved toward them but Franklin took me by the shoulders and looked very carefully and steadily into my eyes. It was worse than his newspaper eyes.

"Babs?"

Of course he was only twenty-seven at the time and he had already been unnerved when I had come under criticism from the neighbors for hanging Anna in a wire contraption out the third-floor window in winter so she would nap in fresh air. She'd howled and the neighbors came to report me to the Society for the Prevention of Cruelty to Children, which was absurd. "The newest medical texts say masturbation is a condition of, contiguous to, insanity. The beginnings, that is." I slipped from his hands and went to straighten Little Red Riding Hood askew on the nursery wall. I would have to be very careful explaining. "It's perfectly all right, Franklin," I assured him.

"At two?"

"I did."

"At two?"

"When my father left." I was very matter-of-fact.

And Franklin was very still, looking somewhere over my head at carved ducks and pigs above the crib. "You don't . . . any longer?"

"Of course not. It was part of my malady."

"And you think little Anna has a malady?"

"No, nor will she."

"Eleanor, I shall not sleep knowing my child's hands are bound like that."

"Then you shall not sleep."

39

We walked steadfastly from the nursery down the narrow stairs to our bedroom on the second floor. There in small chairs, we sat and faced each other. I sat very straight. Franklin slouched, his head in his hands.

"Why must you control everything the way you do? What kind of tortured valley do you live in, Babs, that . . . that you nourish yourself on your malady . . . and torture others? Your malady . . . what will you do when James grows up?"

"Yes, my malady." Mary Queen of Scots took marmalade for her malady. "I am protecting my child from her own blood. There is a fault."

"Is it sickness to touch yourself?"

"That's correct."

He asked me then the sort of question he has never asked me again and I answered him in a way I would never answer him again, but the subject, unspoken, unmentioned, has pounded like a deaf drummer through the stately rituals of our marriage.

"You touched yourself, Babs? Didn't it make you happy?"

"I have never been happy. It made me mad. Insane, if you will. Melancholic. I had no control. I don't wish that for our children. There is a morbidity in my family, a melancholy of beings, swarms of us, with small heads and hot hearts. The patient suffering from melancholy has usually a small head and a hot heart. We are like that. No one in my family has been happy unless they were insane and then there was no way to determine whether they were happy or not, except by counting the nights my drunken father forced himself upon my mother, by gunshots, by women sobbing behind locked doors, and by what everyone refers to as a riding accident. My father died in a riding accident. Pussie told me a carriage ran over him while he lay in a gutter."

"Damn, damn, damn, Eleanor. Why do you talk like this? Madness is a far cry from eccentricity. I've seen you happy. By God, I've *made* you happy."

I said nothing. He'd made me laugh; I wanted to tremble.

"Babs?"

"I have in me that degeneracy. And my children may. Oversexed . . ."

"Come now. These are terrible exaggerations!"

"Oversexed, melancholic, morbid, lonely. I see it. I see all the dead faces in the living faces and it is my horror and responsibility. And I see it in my own face."

"I don't."

"Of course not. I control myself. Self-discipline. I am teaching that to my children."

"Look, just let the child be. You can't control everything. You're not responsible for everything. Let her sleep as she will. Won't you do that?" Franklin wore butterscotch mules and a tweed dressing gown with a patch at one elbow. He came over to me and put his hands on my shoulders.

"No."

"You're in error."

"If I don't control them, they'll control me. That's what happened to Granny Hall; her children control her and she is still a child and they are . . . unsuccessful."

"Dammit, Eleanor, that's quite enough self-pity. I'll not live under the tyranny of your self-pity; you're becoming an emotional tyrant around here, wallowing in the drama of your childhood. Your moods . . . What is it you are really protecting there inside yourself that you won't let anyone touch? What is it? Such a cold center with such hot fires around it . . . what is it?"

"It's my little hot heart."

"Rubbish!"

I went into the morning room. I need to control myself, I told him silently, so that I don't *want* to be touched. I need to control all of you so you won't touch me. I need to control everything so I need nothing from you . . . so you get nothing from me.

It all had very little to do with whether Anna and I touched ourselves. I knew that even then. It had to do with being touched. I didn't want to be touched. The closer any of them came to me, the less there was of me. I had to control them because I felt violated to the very cells and molecules of my body. I didn't want to become them. Every time I turned away, though, even for a moment, so I could be untouched, something fell to pieces in my household. I didn't love them enough, they said. Franklin fell in love, Elliott fell into a fire, James off the porch when pushed; this happened, that happened while I hid my soul in a corner, one crisis after the other. The kitchenmaid left, the butler threw a pot, the chauffeur smashed the car. I was responsible for it all and when I let go for just that one moment, things fell apart. Yet, if I remained too close, something of me died. And if the doorbell is broken? Leave me alone.

Much later I spoke aloud through the dark deadness to him.

"Franklin, I'm afraid. I am so alone."

"Tell me what to do, Babs. I want to help you." He called from our bed to my sleeping-cot. "Please," he called again without moving.

"If I told you what to do, wouldn't that make me a tyrant?" And then we said no more to each other until morning when he asked me if I were feeling more myself and I said a little and I asked a servant to leave the shutters closed and took my breakfast tray in bed.

Since then I have borne four more children. The second boy, Franklin Jr., is hidden under a tiny, windswept grave in Hyde Park and after Elliott, my middle child, there was that nightmare miscarriage. And then the next Franklin and then John. In all there are the five children. In all, perhaps six for I feel Franklin is just a boy. James is now Master James and eleven and as tall as my ear. Wee Babs John is two. I will no longer have children. Franklin was wrong about the cold center; I was right. My heart is hot; the cold is its vessel. Men think a woman's center is her sex. It is her soul. It is my soul, my lead dead, dead lead soul that never stirs; another dead and shapeless child: my soul.

The new kitchenmaid Ulla told me a story her mother told her about her mother who was expecting and the child never arrived. Eleven months after, two months after the day she was due, she began to drop bits of bones and other things one by one and this went on all year and then stopped. Finally they buried all of it.

And shall that be my end? Finally, they buried all of her, that shapeless woman with a lump of lead for a soul. Until then, she dies bone by bone, bit by bit.

IN WHICH WE ATTEND THE
RUSSIAN BALL

The night of the Russian Ball three years before the summer of war was such a small death for me, bone by bone, bit by bit, shaping me, unshaping me. That night I was brushed and coiffed and decorated with a hundred buttons, a thousand bows and a ten-strand choker of seed pearls around my long neck. I came in swelling with my own beauty. In the two-inch heels I wore, I was over six feet tall and towered above everyone. I love to walk tall and straight beside Franklin, for with him I have never felt awkward. Below us, the others seem small and ungifted. My gown was from Worth's, my heels the newest sharpest last and my shoes dyed to match my gown. Franklin wore tails and was noble and graceful. His color that summer was good.

"Ritzy," Franklin described us. "The smart set." I was then Anna Eleanor Roosevelt Roosevelt. My uncle had been

President, my family propertied enough for generations. We were the American aristocracy and America was finally coming of age. Franklin and I were very much in demand.

Fortunes shifted then with the wind and even though I hated war, those times were marvelously exciting. Everything was an intrigue. The capital was flooded with foreign diplomats, munitions dealers, limping, thin-lipped heroes, the cream of Europe's merchants and ministers begging for American aid. Naturally, Franklin and I had scores of invitations to the best homes, the best balls, teas, excursions. He wore his top hat to the San Francisco Exposition and when he spoke he too was a prince. We were the favorites of the British diplomats. They were favorites of ours. We were invited to join the most fashionable clubs: the Alibi Club, which took its members from the Metro, Metro, of course, Chevy Chase, Mr. Thompson's Fencing Club and so on. I can't imagine why Franklin insisted that we attend the Russian Ball. I hadn't wanted to. Except he'd heard that the Bolsheviks might blow it up and we should show our support for the royalty.

The parquet floor was very soft old wood and the metal shanks of my fashionable heels sank right into the cherry, pitting it, which would have been fitting except that as I looked behind me at the marks I'd made, I blushed a carbuncle red and decided not to dance. I sat, solemnly settled among the gouty dowagers, and there the red-headed emeralded wife of the Russian Ambassador, with the flames of revolution already licking at the feet of her old order and flickering on the diamonds of her stomacher, found and trapped me. I listened for hours as she insisted that Trotsky and Lenin were German plumbers in disguise, that the perfect and holy Rasputin and the poor dear Empress were much maligned ("much aligned," Franklin said later when I told him the story) and that Rasputin's eyes with that glinting cold-metal deep-sea beauty were like my husband's eyes. "I am awestruck with him too, your husband," she assured me as if it would please me to associate Franklin with such decadence. I had heard the Russian people were starving.

Cossack waiters moved through the dancers, Hungarian violinists played waltzes, and when they rested, a small orchestra offered popular music and new dances, which were a little risqué for the royalty but everyone seemed to be enjoying themselves. Men wore jewels and swords, capes and ribbons. Goldfish swam in alabaster bowls, exotic parrots had been stuffed and wired to the palm trees, an orangerie had been built on one side of the ballroom and, on the other, a court of three fountains sprayed ruby-red waters amidst caviar and cossacks and jellied calves feet. I hummed to myself while Madame talked on, and I looked through the dancers for Franklin, discreetly. He came by once to bring me a glass of punch. "Who's to notice if you dance, Babs?"

"If my heel sticks, I'd trip and everyone would notice."

He came back again with caviar on a cracker and vodka on his breath. I wished I weren't such a Puritan. I felt the rigid melancholy seeping into my blood. I was alone. It always happened. I watched him dance away, my mouth slackening, my eyes glazing. This is what happens. This is what happens to Uncle Ted. I've seen him like this before he'd known I had entered his room. This is the anatomy of the melancholy. Franklin came again—I don't know how much later—and whispered so no one else could hear: "Hello in there. Don't be miserable, Babs. Have some fun. Come on. Take the old shoes off."

Much later he whirled by again dancing something long-stepped and lustfully Spanish, a gross mimicry. Everyone laughed as he passed them. He danced by me with his partner, clicking and snapping. She was someone fluffy and un-memorable but her head was thrown back just right and she snapped her fingers in rhythm with Franklin's. Franklin called to me over her tilted head: "Comet Toes? Comet Toes." His lady threw out puffs of cottony laughter. Franklin smiled

46

at me, indulgently, for her silliness, and I called Huckins and went home alone. I knew one of the "Comet Toes" had been "comatose." I knew it.

"I was only trying to wake you up, Babs. You had that look," he explained very late that night when he found me sitting on the floor in the outer vestibule, locked out. I had chosen not to wake the servants. I didn't answer him. He opened the door with his key. "Would it be better if we didn't go to those dances?" I didn't answer that either. In the bedroom I simply closed my eyes. "If we could only have some fun together, Babs . . ." His voice trailed off and he slept.

IN WHICH I WAIT FOR THE
MAIL FROM NO-MAN'S-LAND

The shutters of my house in Washington are closed this summer against the heat. The house is dark. The ugly black walnut, in willful superiority, fills the black corners in great shadowy massive pieces, carved with rats and bats and mythic beasts, all the heavy, doomed Oriental puzzles carved into daises, standing triple mirrors, armoires, chaises of wood, deep-carved in lacy faces and pug forms, intricate and hard, with mother-of-pearl inlay and brass hinges and grinning terrors with lacquered eyes that wink in gaslight. They are Auntie Bye's, my father's sister. Franklin's collections of naval prints cover the walls and his papers most of the tables. Each cubicle of a room has a double sliding door which has never succeeded in keeping out the howling children whose noses always need wiping or blowing, who will come to kiss me good-night with the mucous petrified on their upper lips while I sit in the window seat and wait for Franklin to come home through the dusk. But now in the summer with everyone gone, the house is quiet. Millicent, wiry, very faintly English, delicate and small-footed, who has never broken anything in her life, and young Ulla, the new kitchenmaid from McKeesport, are my only staff. Millicent is training Ulla, who is very rough. They spend the long hot days making potpourri for Christmas presents and mixing winter medicines, so that the upper floors are sweet with the perfumes of violets and rose petals drying on newspapered beds and on the kitchen stoves, creosote and camphor, chloride of iron, corn syrup, honey, stability, the tinctures and oils of childhood, babble and bubble away in mahogony brews in copper boilers. Year after year those smells invade the lower rooms and collect finally in the front parlor in my drapes. Even in winter, I would climb into the window seat, pull the green velvet around me and sniff the camphor still locked into its warp and woof. Even in winter when, with the cold rains streaked along the outside of the window, I press my nose against the pane and my tears warm and cloud the view of the green-black December skies and graceless bare trees scrappling with the wind along our street, that sharp scent of camphor pulls me back to summer. But this summer is different.

Franklin's letters so annoy me this summer. I don't know exactly what it is about them that annoys me most: his foolish enthusiasms for war, the infrequency of the letters, or my own protective concern for him. With Franklin I rarely have control over my responses. I bend like a reed to his every wind. I would rather be an oak tree, tall and firm before him. But reeds, Papa told me, don't break in storms. Oak trees do.

I miss Franklin. When I pull the pins from my Red Cross bonnet in the front foyer and glance over to the marble-topped desk at the green onyx inkstand against which Franklin's blue envelope should be waiting, my heart, like a large iceberg broken loose, wounded, cracking, shifting in its relentlessly blue-cold sea, sinks.

Some days I've met the postman on the street, on the front steps, and he's tipped his hat and said each time, as if it were our private joke: "Well, looks like he's forgotten you again." And laughed.

Too often the letter is not on the desk. The desk was a wedding gift from Uncle Warren Delano. The chair at the desk is a caned and fluted Louis Quatorze we chose in Paris on our honeymoon. But it is all empty now, all quite empty of Franklin. When I remove the hatpins my fingers tremble and I fight looking at the inkstand because I know something has happened to Franklin. There will be no more letters. Ever. He will never come back.

Each evening I sit in my own parlor to look over the day's mail, an efficient business for an official wife, and the tiles of the fireplace dance in the gaslight at my shoulder, green-blue-black frogs and water creatures slither about, their spines raised and taut as my own braced against the horsehair settee, as if they too would escape.

Franklin's shoes are lined up neatly in his closet with their bright little eyes and shiny snubbed noses; his canes and walking sticks—ebony, silver-headed, hawthorn, ivory—wait for their master in the Chinese umbrella stand in the foyer. That stand, a waist-high ginger jar, is the children's favorite hiding place. They always seem to feel, my children, that their destiny is to destroy the house. Master James and Master Elliott would toss out Franklin's canes and stuff in Wee Babs John. Poor John. He would stick his fat dirty fingers through the notches in the china sides of the ginger jar and his howls would echo and bounce against the vast strange amphitheater of depth and holes. And when Franklin would come home and find him in there, he'd announce in his own vast booming voice: "Ali Baba has arrived. Where are my thieves? Ah!" And Franklin, poking gently with a cane into the notches, would pull out a joyous tear-stained child. "Papa! Papa's home!" Usually he and Franklin and the rest of the children would fall wrestling to the floor, the children fighting with each other like beasts to move in closer to Franklin, and I would emerge from my window seat to touch Franklin's arm. Sometimes before he went to the children, I would lay hold of his coat sleeve and speak to him in short sentences hoping he would answer in long ones while he moved restlessly under my words.

I miss his smells. I miss his laughter. I miss the wet wool of his suits when he walks home from Navy, the sweetness of his skin cleansed in the rain, the harshness of the tobacco on his breath, even the liquor after dinners at the Harvard Club, the Yale Club, the Salon, all of his bachelor places, even then. I long for him. You must know that. I long for him and treasure his letters and dream of his arms, day and night. Confidential sources tell me with the best of intent that my longings are not reciprocated. I know that. The knowledge doesn't rid me of my needs. Whatever love is, whatever love isn't, I love. I need. No better, no worse than Ulla with her teapot face and her fat white cheeks and her constant pout and that black handle of hair and the slitted eyes of the Germans, no better than Ulla who has a beau in France who loves her. Letters arrive from him, three and four packs of them, each week. From "Somewhere in France" also. Her beau is Fighting Bill from McKeesport in the Keystone Division and he writes her from No-Man's-Land. Ulla can't read. I read to her. She stands by my chair wringing her hands. She weeps quietly, sniffling, her face turning red in blotches through the rind-white skin. Ulla, I suspect, will tremble.

"Dearest Loving Ulla," Fighting Bill writes in a tedious awkward hand, "Well, Ulla, I'll tell you a little of my trip. Before we left I seen them take a drowned man from the water, he must have been in the water about a month by the looks of him. I seen a whale and a big shark, and one thing that was fun to see was some fish, that would jump out of the water and then back in again, about ten of them all in a row. Another thing that was nice were the Sea Gulls, they followed us over the entire way. I haven't had a headache since I left the US. We would have movies and play checkers and cards and other games. While out in the water I seen another man floating past our ship. I don't know where he came from. XXXXX Your Fighting Bill."

The daily mail from No-Man's-Land: Billy uses far too many commas and writes in long long sentences and says nothing of value. I asked Ulla what the X's stood for and she explained, wiping her red raw hands in her muslin apron, her cheeks the color of her hands. "Kisses, mum. Each X is a kiss."

"The cooties are rotten," Billy writes. "If you know what I mean, darling. They grow in your duds. I had a hot bath in LeMans and it drove them cooties to H.....! Sorry to hear about your boils. XXXXXXX You're my one and only. Your Fighting Billy." Poor Ulla is so terribly worried and lonely.

At first I had Anna, who is now twelve and has a good hand, write the letters for Ulla to Billy. But then the letters were so intimate and distasteful I decided Anna was too young and began to write Ulla's words for her. I had to write things like: "I bet your mama won't mind if we sit in the parlor and crack our chewing gum this time, will she? I saw a drunk soldier and he stuck his hand in my face, isn't that awful?" Once she wrote a poem which I copied from a staggeringly filthy scrap of paper. "No one respects a slacker. He don't deserve a chance. The boys who you should honor are the boys who go to France. To be home with his little girl, would be a treat, tis true, but he cannot see the enemy down the red white and blue."

Bill was twenty-two, Ulla twenty-one. Older than Franklin and I had been when we were courting. "Mind," Billy wrote Ulla when Ulla had discovered that Billy wrote another girl south of McKeesport, "love is a misunderstanding between two darned fools. Except for us, sweetheart."

Ulla talks too much to Millicent about the man floating in the middle of the ocean. Millicent shouts in that thin wiry voice. They are stirring rags for our monthlies with wooden spoons in boiling water. I scold Ulla, who threw her spoon at Millicent. I scold Millicent. "Don't speak about death. It surrounds us." They are hushed.

"Dearest loving Ulla, I'm still in the best of health and hope you are the same. We just got through doing our first hitch in battle. We are now a little ways back of the line, at rest. On July 13 we were all asleep, when the Germans opened fire, on us. The shells fell all around our tents, so we all went to our trenches. We were in them for six days. The shells were falling like hot cakes. They attacked us at 12 o'clock midnight and kept it up all morning, and all the next day and we had big losses and I was on stretcher detail. They still send a few over now, to keep us awake. Some were gas shells and we had to use our masks a lot. XXXX Your Fighting Billy."

Franklin writes that he leaned against a mantelpiece at the Crillon and spoke perfect French to the French press and, underlining and exclamation-pointing all the way, he writes that they were very impressed. He visited the King of England, all alone for forty-five minutes. The King sent greetings to Mama. That is what Franklin writes. He does not write that the Second Division has lost five thousand men, the First more and that another million are still to die. We are at the Marne.

Billy writes: "I seen two men, one a Hun, one a Frenchy, tied up in barbed wire, and they were not men, Ulla, they were skeletons in arm to arm combat and they had their teeth around each others necks. I seen them."

"Doesn't it bother you, Eleanor, that Franklin is off to Europe?" the ladies asked me at Childs where we had raisin tarts under whipped cream after a day of bandage-wrapping.

"Of course not," I said too emphatically. "He is so happy to be doing his duty."

"Really, Eleanor!" They glanced at each other.

"I understand the nurses at the Front are using Army bandages for their monthlies . . ."

53

"Dreadful. Shouldn't we complain?"

"No, no, not at all," someone said to someone. "A gauze manufacturer is now making them up just for ladies."

"No more boiling rags?"

"How this war has changed things."

" 'We shall all wake up,' Mr. Carlyle wrote, 'and find ourselves in a world greatly widened.' "

I sat there wondering if those women thought I was mad, if those women watched me and talked of me, if those women, who knew too much about my marriage, who could slit a man's throat with a whisper, were testing me to see if Franklin had not gone to war but had left me. They wouldn't find out, because I didn't know.

"Don't you think the war has changed things, Eleanor?"

"They'll never be the same again," I pronounced. We slipped on our gloves, white leather, wrist-length, from accordion boxes with tiny gold latches inlaid with wooden violets, and we bade each other good-day. I was happy to do so. The war has changed so many things. The war was changing me. I hoped secretly it would last long enough.

IN WHICH I CONSIDER THE
TEAR BOTTLE

The jealousy I felt wasn't jealousy born from inferiority. I needed to be first, and none of us, neither Mama nor the children nor myself, has ever been first. Nor are the ladies Franklin charms and courts and ballyhoos. Franklin, you see, has no emotional priorities. Franklin is first. Justice Oliver Wendell Holmes' wife said to Uncle Ted once that Washington was a city filled with famous men and the women they'd married when they were young. That isn't the problem. I already was somebody before Franklin married me. What troubles me, why the letters are so horribly important, is the cancerous fear that Franklin will discard me. Franklin was not about to pick up my glass slipper and chase me down N Street after I'd left the Russian Ball. I envied others, truly, and wanted the prince, but there was something lacking in me or not lacking in me that made me less than a Cinderella. Or more.

Not Miss Mercer. She was still Cinderella. Two years ago, before she became a yeomenette and went to work for Franklin at Navy, she was my social secretary. She would come to me in the mornings at ten and sit at my desk or sometimes on the dining room floor, sorting through invitations and thank-you notes, sending greetings, ordering flowers, writing menus and table cards. She was thoroughly competent, dignified, pleasant, a perfect joy. Even when she joined the Navy and stood at attention, statuesque and dreamlike in the crisp uniform, and Franklin walked down the lanes of grass silver-wet with the morning, inspecting all the yeomenettes, Lucy still had that special lost-princess quality about her, the sort of mythic woman one sails with to the end of the night and the beginning of day. She always seemed slightly startled, not offended, just amazed to see someone, like a doe caught suddenly by the hunter's eyes, and then, I could imagine her, perfectly poised, laughter rich in the back of her throat, she would smile and take the hunter recklessly into divine woodlands and thickets on some marvelous moonlit night and they would eat chocolates under a waterfall, never quite real, hopelessly innocent, an escape. And when the magic was over, she would turn at the edge of the woods and say: "You can go no farther. You must go back to now, you a Married Man, I a Catholic, you must go back to your way of life," and she would withdraw sadly and come to my house as a human in the morning and answer my mail and write out cards at my desk, biting her lower lip, concentrating while that lovely sleeping princess, innocent, slumbered below. What was of course never mentioned was that beyond the careful penmanship, the concentration of a girl at her studies, the long swan throat and the coppery warm laughter, Lucy was bedecked with an exceedingly remarkable bosom of which, I believe, to the inverse of her admirers, she was totally unawares; Franklin was not. I had seen his eyes. Poor Franklin. Washington already was saying "Poor Elea-

56

nor." But poor Franklin. It was he who had to eat milk and rice while his heart burned and his stomach tore at him. Franklin would trudge back to being the father, the son, the husband . . . and hoping in the better parts of himself that we too could have fun, could eat chocolates under a waterfall. I knew Lucy didn't belong in my house, working for the pittance I paid. I'm afraid her being there made Franklin feel he didn't belong there either, that happiness lay far beyond N Street.

Lucy's father was the legendary king of Washington: loved, handsome, envied, a sportsman, heir to a great fortune he did not live long enough to inherit. His own wealth was dissipated, he derelict, his wife, Minnie, living on a pension, bitter and demanding. My father had been very much like Lucy's. We had both been Cinderellas except my mother had been quicker to protect the inheritance by having my father declared legally insane. The girls, Lucy and her sister, were reduced to interior decorating and secretarial work, but of course, in the finest homes because they were accustomed to the finest homes and would be invited back in the evening for entertainments. They had both attended a Swiss school and we'd heard that when the nuns saw the nighties of those Southern beauties, they were shocked, confusing the delicacy of the undergarments with scandal. But there was nothing scandalous about Lucy, nothing at all.

Once I'd asked her to bring granulated sugar on her way to our house, and she'd arrived with a tin box in the shape of an Oriental tea chest, packed perfectly and laboriously with tiny sugar cubes and a small tong and tied with a ribbon. "I thought it would be great fun for everyone to take sugar from the chest, as if it were a treasure," she explained, the slight drawl, very slight, the hesitancy that was so gentle.

"I love it. It *is* a treasure these days. That's lovely."

Miraculously even sulky Anna was brought around to repacking the tea chest. I couldn't imagine anyone taking the time. It seemed so stupid. And when Franklin took Lucy on as a yeomenette in his office at Navy, I knew precisely where the stupid single fresh rose on his desk had originated.

"I'm not sure who brings it," he explained to me. "But there it is, every day."

"Well, it must be an employee, don't you think?"

Getting information from Franklin was like pulling a lizard from under a rock, inch by inch, by the tail. You pull and you pull and tug and tug and when you have it all out, there is no head. "I could ask around if you want me to, Babs. But I might embarrass someone by asking, you know."

I knew.

Years ago, Uncle Ted brought me a tear bottle from Egypt. Lucy reminded me of that tear bottle. I was dictating a menu to her, sometime before the yeomenette days, and she sat at the breakfast table writing out the grapefruit, clear soup, halibut with hollandaise, chicken tamales with asparagus, fillet of beef. Her hair was pinned loosely in amber combs and escaped in soft floating pieces around her nape, face, that long lovely neck. Perfectly liquid she was, and graceful, watery languid, soft, her lips always slightly apart, delicate, inviting. My tear bottle can't stand by itself. Someone must always hold it. It has a round bottom to be cupped in the mourner's hand unless it rests in a tiny clay holder, but I received only the tear bottle. At an Egyptian funeral, it was passed carefully from keeper to keeper, filled with tears and then buried with the dead man.

"What is it really like to live with a man as exciting as Mr. Roosevelt? I imagine it would be exhausting. But then you have so much energy," she added, sensing something awry in my eyes.

"One is kept busy. That is the best part." She was a decade younger, slim, unwrinkled, virginal. I had been wide with child or ragged with children every year since my honeymoon. What was it like?

Uncle Ted had pulled me onto his lap at Sag Harbor. In my finest dress I had come from Tivoli, where I lived with Granny Hall, to visit my Oyster Bay cousins. "It's a thousand years old, Eleanor," Uncle Ted told me when he gave me the tear bottle. We had been in and out of the room, eating ice cream from silver trays and running back in to inspect the next box of treasures just pried open. A mummified cat, a cartouche, beads from a noble woman's burial, a mummified young man which brought on the most astonishing howls of laughter from the boys and Alice, who were all finally sent from the room. I was perhaps twelve, perhaps a little more, awkward, trying to play with the cousins, unable to. I adored Uncle Ted. "I knew it was exactly for you, Eleanor. I was delighted when I saw it. I had to trade a pair of silk socks for it, but I knew my Eleanor had to have this."

Its box was inlaid with nailheads, a puzzle which I couldn't open. I was reduced to exploring its sides while Uncle Ted laughed, blowing my hair up and off my shoulders from the force of his laughter. I knew it would be something lovely and wonderful because he was as close to me then as my own father would have been if he could have been. Finally he guided my finger to a flat square of ivory inlay; the box opened and in it was the pearly pink delicate bottle. "It has a message for you, Eleanor."

The bottle was of the thinnest glass, perfectly created. Some of the pink pearl lining was broken from the neck and lay in shimmering splinters, luminous, tears caught by time. "You collect your tears, Eleanor. Bury your sorrows. Your father would not want you to cry."

Dear Uncle Ted with his fat cheeks and his pouting lips and his potbelly and his short little puppet arms and puppet march. Vigorous.

Then Uncle Ted led us all in a pillow fight, Kermit and Quentin and Archie and Ted and Alice, and he fell upon me so hard that the buttons burst on my dress and I went home trailing rags around me, back to Tivoli and Uncle Vallie shooting through the wisteria as the carriage rounded the curve toward the house where I belonged.

I could not imagine how to place a tear into the narrow neck. My tears diffused and flooded and spread across the plains of my face like torrential rivers at winter thaw, into my hair, into my ears, into my hands and seeped through my fingers. "You've buried your tears too long, Babs," Franklin would say. "Let them come." He said it was healthier than having a dream world; it didn't feel healthier at all. By the war, I was tired of chewing my nails, tired of stooping, tired of crying, tired of having Franklin tell me it was healthy to cry when he had made me cry. Tired of Lucy Mercer. Uncle Ted said the Jewish race grew wise through the bitterness of their tears. I did not feel wisdom.

On that day, after I dictated the menu to Lucy Mercer, we picked up the children's building blocks from the dining room floor and packed parapets, fountains, squares, triangles, circles and bridge beds into cigar boxes. I despised those blocks. Franklin brought home boxes and boxes of them— Richter's Comet Building Blocks—and the children poured boxes and boxes of them on every clear spot of the dining room floor. For a short time they would build fantastic mansions and churches and schools, but at the end of the game—a vicious moment I could never anticipate—they would kick over the vast erections and throw the cast-stone parts at one another. It took me months to understand that the children threw the pieces at each other so I would send them to their rooms and be forced to pick up the blocks myself. It also took me a while to realize that while Miss Mercer and I crept about the floor chatting amiably, she too was betraying me.

Lucy came the next night for dinner. She came to avoid thirteen because Franklin was terribly superstitious. "Ask Lucy. She'll make it fourteen. I won't have dinner with thirteen. Bad luck."

And so we ate the halibut and the chicken tamales and the hollandaise and Franklin laughed that night when Lucy told him about the Comet Building Blocks all over the floor. Lucy laughed. Her laughter was liquid, mine was dry and brittle.

"Oh, my boys. My boys have a real sense of history, tossing cities around like that. But their mother just has a sense of horror, don't you, Babs?" He was so entertained by Lucy that night, so delighted, that I managed thereafter always to arrange for Lucy to find herself by herself at the end of the morning's mail, picking up the building blocks and setting them back—it was quite complicated, but then she'd done remarkably well with the sugar cubes—into their myriad of boxes. She had come to the dinner so exquisite and charming with a wealth to her laughter that made every man there feel the poverty of his own life. Soon after, Lucy joined the Navy and worked in Franklin's office.

IN WHICH I ARRIVE AT THE CANTEEN

·

"Madam, Mrs. Roosevelt? We are at the station."

"Ah, the canteen. Thank you, Huckins."

And so began that day in which the walls of my dream world and the walls of my reality bent, slightly of course, as internal events are slight, but momentously. That the walls might disappear would have been the brink of madness, but that I found, at last, a space, a crack, an ambiguity between the dream world and the real world, a place in which I could move safely . . . that was extraordinary.

Under the eagles at Union Station I gave Huckins the Stutz and he drove it over the brick pavement, around the semicircle, toward the marketplace. And I turned toward the cavern of the station and toward the thin brave music from within already swelling and beckoning with its question: "Mademoiselle from Armentières, parlez-vous?" Always that question.

"On the double!" Someone shouts and the shout multiplies itself from car to car as I pass. The faces withdraw. "Double, on the double!" The song is squeezed along by the shout to the last car until it spills out into a ragged crowd of men with eyes still sticky from sleep, knapsacks reeking of Polish sausage and stained with grease, whiskered men, whiskeyed men, sleep-pinked, pale men. All America is waking up and hawking in the sink behind me and singing "Mademoiselle from Armentières" as they follow along to the canteen.

In the tin shack of the canteen, already oven-hot, Mary Patten greets me with a soup ladle and news. "Livy wrote Edith. He and Franklin have been to see Admiral Plunkett and the railway guns and there is influence all through Spain. Plunkett has offered Franklin a commission."

"But Franklin isn't ill?"

Mary's lip curls upward. "You know Livy leaves little out. They went to Scotland and ate oatmeal mixed with scotch."

I like Mary. She is one of three maiden sisters who entertain grandly, insist they neither have nor invite secrets and yet know everything to be known and not to be known in the capital. It is more accurate to say that Mary has no secrets very long. I find her invaluable.

"Ripe shipment today," she whispers as I tie her apron and she mine and the lines of men are upon us and we ladle chowder at dawn.

Our stations are a bank of trestle tables running the length of the shack. Behind us are steel sinks and stoves for food preparation, baskets of sandwiches ready for the ambulance trains farther down the line, candy, sewing kits, cigarettes, coffee, doughnuts and postcards. Washington is the last stop before camp, the last freedom before embarkation. We sell and censor at least five hundred postcards each day. They are so different from Franklin's letters, which are filled with names and places. The doughboys' postcards are not allowed names and places but they spill with passion. Never forget. Wait for me. GOK, GOK, God only knows. Pray for me. I'll be back. I'll love you always. I am your one and only. I'll write to you from Berlin, ha, ha! What do you want for our anniversary? I know what *I* want. Get Scooter to help you with the smudge pots.

This trainload from the West is of city men, from Chicago I guess, for they are sullen, foreign-born and angry with oily skins and hostile hooded eyes and pitted cheeks. There isn't that sweetness of the country boys who call you Ma'am, nor the innocence of their flat faces and bland eyes. Franklin says we'd be safer with this kind rounded up in the Army than loose on the streets. They are hyphenated Americans, he says. I think he means we'll be safe when they are dead. They shuffle along in our line, holding their cups toward us. Only a few even glance at my face as I fill their cups and I don't like their eyes. The answer isn't in settlement houses, I'm afraid, for these men are not grateful and they hate me for being able to give. Something is slicked over in their eyes, missing as in my dream world Kodak of Évian—a blot. Their sergeant, a very handsome sergeant, marches around them, strutting up and down the ragged line, an animal trainer, a ringmaster, watching for a flare-up, more animal himself than the animals, prodding slouches and compacting spaces with a cruel drill stick and whistling between his teeth a chafing "Mademoiselle," an echo, which sounds to me the way the men's eyes look.

"Sharp there, soldier. Pull it in. Pull it in. Thank you . . . say thank you to the lady. Where do you think you are? Home? Pull it in. Pull it in." His song hangs insistent, a vulpine call above the tinny cups and chatter. The women talk among themselves, their voices rising as he approaches, vibrating, and dropping back when he is gone. The sergeant of course should not be whistling.

"He's breathtaking," Mary says.

"Strictly out of order whistling." Through his teeth. Olive

skin, that full sad mouth, heavy brows, too heavy, cutting across a tanned forehead, and shining from mustache to belt buckle to cordovan boots as he moves back and forth, very much the military man, earnest, erect, proud.

The leather strap of his hat cuts through his chin, his chest and shoulders bulge under his tunic and he has the lean power of a stallion brushed on the lines of his face so much like Franklin, but a physical brutality that is not Franklin at all. Franklin is merely verbally brutal. When Franklin is not laughing, I see him sometimes, fleetingly sad and fragile. I suppose it's breeding. Franklin has a delicacy in his face that is almost female, much more so than Mama.

"The most penetrating eyes, that sergeant?" Mary asks. "I think he likes you. He's been *staring*."

I shrug. "All men have eyes, Mary. Few have the gift of penetration. I think he looks too much like an animal."

"Oh, Eleanor, really!"

If I hear another woman say "Oh, Eleanor, really," I shall scream. The women laugh behind us. It is Tessa with her fine bones and bitter eyes who drifts by and speaks into my ear. "I didn't think anyone in our crowd considered penetration a gift. I've always felt it was an imposition, don't you?" Tessa sees too many stage plays and moving pictures in which women are treated like breadsticks, she describes, their souls meant to be broken by love, she says, sighing, and was wildly in love with Ernest Truex until she saw William Faverham. There had been talk about her and the Japanese Ambassador. There is always talk. Little happens. Tessa once told Mary she longed to melt like a chocolate bar in a man's arms.

"Wasn't that the Austrian Countess in the lace cap?"

"And the white satin skirt and chiffon waist, a picture out of *Vogue*."

"Alice wore her flesh-colored stockings again."

"To the Chrysanthemum Show?"

"Yes. And her father was giving out kisses for Liberty Bonds . . . an ex-President. Can you imagine?"

65

"Is he mad?"

"No more than she."

"Just having fun, she says."

"Roosevelts are so amusing."

Had they already forgotten I was with them?

"At the Front? Can you imagine that superb head in the glow of battle?"

"As men, husbands, they are killers!"

It is the Bellamy girl. The sergeant's eyes are indeed on me. Odd eyes, that sleekness. I feel the silk against the nub. I feel like tearing at the skin of my heels. Am I mad? A killer. Has Franklin hurt her also? What does she know about Roosevelt men?

"And the men stayed out smoking an unending time over the Russian situation and when Devereux heard that suffrage passed in Massachusetts he said it was the work of the pro-Germans."

"So we cocained the spaniel's foot, lost his feathers and I . . ."

The voices keep changing, the sergeant whistling, strutting, the men clearing their throats. The sergeant polishes a red apple on the belly of his tunic and bites into it with a great wide mouth and brilliant white teeth. I watch the teeth disappear into the apple. He sees me watching him and I drop my eyes.

"And I went in with the Swiss Secretary and the Norwegian Minister on my right who said to me . . ."

It was always the same conversation at dinner parties. The ladies, waiting for the men to return from their cigars, would chatter idly, dully, not listening to each other, until the men emerged, still laughing from smutty jokes and fellowship, and then we would animate, and then we would listen.

"Ah, yes, Eleanor Roosevelt," a man would bow upon introduction. "I have heard of you. You have four children and move them six times a year."

"No, no, five," I would say. "We go to Campobello."

"I see." He says. "I still suppose it is quite a horror all the way up to Maine, isn't it? All the packing?"

"Yes, the bird . . ." But he would already be looking over my shoulder at someone pretty and lively. "The dog, the parakeet in its cage, arranging the . . ."

"And they are in school?" he continues mechanically.

"Well, there are two at Potomac here in Washington and one at the Misses Eastmans', of course, and then the younger ones are at home but they much prefer to be romping with Franklin's mother at Hyde Park, so they are up there most of the time."

"Then you are quite free?"

"Oh, no, not at all. Neither free nor empty, you see I . . ." He has drifted away.

The women still chatter above the canteen noise.

"When the war is over . . ."

"By fall, they say, and Franklin agrees."

Who is that speaking?

"Yes," she continues. It is a Marine officer's wife, one of my best canteen cooks. I can't offend her. "Franklin hopes to extend his stay in Europe until after the election because he made that horrid little deal with Tammany."

"Eleanor?"

Someone remembers I am with them and can hear.

"What news of Franklin, darling?"

There is a letter from Billy every day. If there is not, a pack of three or four will arrive. Some have money, some postcards, some handkerchiefs, all promises. And Ulla, who knows when I have none of my own, hesitates to bring hers to me. She sees my hands tremble on the thin paper donated from the YMCA emblazoned at the top: "With the Colors." "It would help, Ulla, if you would not cry, dear, while I read. We must be strong." "Yes, mum," and she doesn't cry.

"Franklin's doing finely," I call out. "He's already found a substitute for refined sugar on his oatmeal."

"Really?"

67

"Yes, raw scotch."

They are afraid to laugh. They can't believe that I would make a joke. It is difficult for me to imagine also.

"Dear Loving Ulla, It won't be long now. I still have those old cooties and they go wild simply wild over me. Round my neck, down my back. Holy Gee. But when I come home to you, it won't matter if I have cooties or not, I'm going to hug you so hard you will say, Bill, let me go. Will you say Billy let me go. I hope not. I haven't changed underwear for about 2 mo. They had a big truck there with a big steam heater or oven and you would bundle up your top clothes and they would heat it up to kill the cooties. You ought to see me now. My hair is all shaved off and I'm raising a mustache for sure this time. We captured two Germans. One of them came over and wanted to shake hands so we captured him too. They went to sleep and when they awoke, two of them wanted to pull their pistols but our boys had the machine gun in front of them and pumped them full, all but the one that wanted to shake hands. Will love you only. Will keep my word forever, Your poem makes me cry. Bye Bye. Fighting Billy."

The Washington women know more than I know about Franklin. The sergeant passes by my shoulder. I can smell him above the chowder. He is close at my side. Men from the South smell differently. If the Northern gentlemen smell of wet tweed, the Southern gentlemen smell French. Next to me is a French scent, a spoiled rich musk smell, leather smell, starched smell to the uniform and a sweet perfumed smell that might have been from the tonic on his black hair. He is familiar. Did we dance in New York? No, I would remember.

"And then we went to Childs after folding at Treasury all morning. For sixty cents we had a perfect gorge including the jam cakes they make in the window. Have you been to Childs, Eleanor?"

"Eleanor wouldn't go to a perfect gorge, would you, Eleanor? Is it true you have a chair for Mr. Hoover at your table to remind your family not to eat gobs?"

68

It is true. But it reminds me of the metal seeds planted in me by the planets. I have the chair to remind myself of Agricola, of the long way, of lead becoming silver.

"Eleanor is perfectly correct." Mary defends me. "Perfect gorges are in bad taste. The Women's Dispensary tea was a gorge and as it was official, I think it was in very bad taste. There was not a whiff of hooverizing."

"Haven't he and his wife written a book on mining? On alchemical mining? Aren't they both mining engineers?"

"A translation, darling, from the sixteenth century. Nothing more. Something heavy and drab and medieval and uselessly self-indulgent. Very Breughel, Germanic . . . sub-human."

"Whatever," I say, "Mr. Hoover is saving Belgium from starvation and that's hardly self-indulgent." I close the topic.

They say, "Oh, Eleanor, really." I do not scream.

Next to me is the flank of olive drab. When it moves away just beyond, I allow myself to glance at the sergeant's face for an instant. He leans against the side of the shack under a drape of bunting, under Mr. Creel's poster of the battlefield nurse, and he looks directly at me and smiles. With sharp teeth. As if I am the apple, I go red and I think perhaps he wants some chowder and hold a cup of it out to him but he shakes his head and stands there holding me instead in his glance. Arrogant, rakish, and casual, one gleaming boot against the wall, his hat tipped back off that dark hair, staring at me, quite aware of, quite accustomed to his effect. From somewhere inside his tunic he retrieves a mouth organ and takes up the song once again, in complex chords and counterpoint. The song hovers and I wonder what it is like to be so loved as that Mademoiselle.

I stand very straight. The woman in Mr. Creel's poster has hair like mine, but Franklin hates the poster. "Chaw-bacon sentimentality." He brought it home to show me and it slipped into my dream world as if the slot for it had been prepared long before. There I sit in that great silence between

69

shells, sitting there in Évian under a sky red with rockets and sparkling with stars, sitting there holding a dying soldier in my lap, the sergeant, his head resting on my scarlet cross and his hand reaching weakly for my hair. Franklin said so at dinner parties, so often, that I might hear: "Hasn't Eleanor lovely hair?"

"I die, lady, to see your hair," says the soldier from my lap. "Pull it down. Pull it down." And then my hair would fall softly silken around us both and we would sit there canopied, there in the silence, our hearts laid open, double-time. Oh, how I long to be needed so!

"Disgusting! This poster is a diabolical cross between the *Scarlet Letter* and the Virgin Mary, Babs. We'll have every Catholic woman in America off to the front. . . ."

"Indeed?"

Franklin had looked at me quizzically, understood I meant his Catholic Lucy and ended the conversation by opening his stamp album. I have a penchant for ending conversations.

"Tell me," I address the authentic sergeant against the wall. "What does she look like, this Mademoiselle from Armentières?" It seemed natural to ask him.

"Oh, now, the last one I saw had on an old black bonnet with a frayed crow's feather and a black dress. Leaning up against a doorway she was and chewing on a pork chop. But of course," he winks "she could be a lady, just like you, that Mademoiselle."

"Indeed?" I say to the sergeant.

"Indeed?" He mimics my word, and mimicking, breaks its enamel shell. He shakes sputum from the mouth organ and plays again. I feel it is for me. I don't know why I did then what I did. I am still surprised at myself for having addressed him so easily. You see, the lines between dream world and real world have never crossed. Later, I wondered what it was that had so mesmerized me to enact a daydream. Was it the changes of his music, from joyous quick beats to dreamlike pain, slow and sad? Was it that? Was it that that made me slip across the borders of madness in the WC, loosen the tortoise clips in my hair, pour more rose water into my palms and daub it along my limbs and pinch my cheeks for color? He nods at me through his music as I take my place at the trestle table once again and his music grows faster and happier. Mercury, silver. The men continue to hold their cups to me. I ladle faster, feeling the corners of my mouth stretch into a larger and larger smile. When I turn, once again, to offer him chowder, I am smiling as openly as my face allows and he pauses this time, once again shakes out sputum and then leans forward to take my cup. But instead, in a swift motion I think no one sees because Mary is giving directions to the showers to one man and the women have moved away and are reading postcards along the slicing boards, he reaches up just as I had imagined it in the WC and pulls the last clip from my hair, loosening it, all of it, and dropping it over my shoulders.

"How dare you!"

I leap backward, awkwardness in full dress, slopping chowder, grappling with my hair until he at last returns my clip to me and smiles a beastly smile.

"It needs that," he says softly without mockery, Levantine, sad-eyed. "Indeed." He considers me as I stand frozen and hot at the same moment. My dream world and my real world collide. Found out, the hot wax of the candle I had held over the prince's sleeping form melting and burning on my own hands.

"You know," he speaks slowly. "A lady like you? You got a face like one of those watches? From Geneva?" He speaks in questions but he knows more than he should. "Everything's exposed? Don't get me wrong," he says to soften my anger. "It's a fine face, like a picture. It's just . . . well, it's just so human. Look, I'm sorry. . . . You should be *careful*."

Something moves inside me. My face freezes. Too much has escaped from me. My secrets sprout like chin whiskers on witches. I have allowed a dream, a fragment from my dream world, from my madness, to escape, and it has a form now, a

71

stalking, prancing, handsome, music-making form which turns to me, on me. My dreams? Hasn't he seen them on my face? They have become real. From my dream world, from deep within something out there is happening. This is very important. What is moving? Metal seeds exploding like bullets? Or lust. It is a heavy and oppressive something, tough, not silver from a holocaust but a cold experience moving in me, a child in me, solitary and black, sour and bilious. But felt. I feel it move and it has made something happen.

The sergeant talks with his men, struts around and whistles between his teeth. I ignore him. He leaves, not even looking back over his shoulder. Going home late that night, content to have Huckins at the wheel, we drive under a full moon and I feel a new mix of power and terror. It is an odd mix, but when I look on the desk for Franklin's letter and see only Billy's, the moment of pain comes a little slower and then the mix is gone. I can feel nothing more inside me than the leaden heaviness that has always been there. The rest is gone.

But I had felt it. I had felt something move. It was lead but it had moved. I examined it and picked at it for days. It wasn't the volcanic anger coming up into my neck. It wasn't the pain. Both were still there. I think that it might actually have been the stirrings of a soul, I speak to myself in the standing mirror in the wooden frame on my dressing table. My self says it might simply have been lust. And we both laugh. But it was not madness, that I know. But is it my soul? I ask the lady in my mirror. And she answers that the goose bumps would lead her to think otherwise. Is it my malady? She laughs at me.

IN WHICH MR. HOWE VISITS
EVERY MORNING AND
EVENING

Ordinarily Mr. Howe would come to breakfast daily with Franklin. Mr. Howe is small, vile, vicious, loyal, vindictive, brilliant, brutal and unclean. When he leaned his folded *Star* against the lazy Susan on the breakfast table and the children spun the lazy Susan for salt or malice, he grumbled in his odd journalist fashion: "Keep your digits off." He calls the boys the Katzenjammer Kids and Anna the Princess. Anna despises him and leaves silently revulsed. Mama has told Anna to hate Mr. Howe. Mr. Howe calls Mama the Anachronism. The children scream at him: "Navel cord and belly button. Mr. Howe eats only mutton." And run away when they can. They are always punished.

Now that Franklin is gone, Mr. Howe comes by not only every day but every evening to watch over me and grumbles from behind his *Star* that Franklin has given up his chance for the governorship because he was so "whacked up," his words, about going overseas. He can't understand yet why Franklin went. "That's how you get to be a bridge across the Housatonic, not President. The Marne ain't Santiago, as me friend Dooley would say," he says. He comes to deal in the future like a fortune-teller, that little newspaperman from Saratoga in his high and filthy collars and his three singularly greasy strands of hair combed over his bald head in which he has committed to memory long rumbling passages of Carlyle. He writes poems for my amusement and quotes Carlyle for his own sustenance. "No sadder proof," he quotes wryly, "can be given by a man of his own littleness than disbelief in great men." Half my size and half Franklin's, he chose Franklin six years ago as his great man and chose, for himself, a hero worship which would have put Mary Magdalene to shame.

Mr. Howe has watery eyes and dandruff on his lashes and eats only mutton and Chamberlain's Stomach and Liver tablets by the handful, which tone him up, he says, and cleanse his stomach, he says, and make him feel like a new man but there is nothing healthy about him at all. "I am hated by everybody," he boasts. "I have always been hated by everybody and I want to be hated by everybody," he was quoted as having told a friend, and since Franklin is his only friend I think one must, in that bizarre relationship, redefine the meaning of friendship.

He is a medieval horror, Mr. Howe. A Dr. Cavendish, a weird alchemist working on us, a ghost within us and without us, that little scar-faced smoky man who fell off his bicycle when he was a boy and took gravel in his face, that man is working to eliminate something in us. He sucks on our dreams, on Franklin's dreams, and stokes up the madness in us both. He has a face full of holes and fills his holes with our beauty. "You want to be President?" he asks, says. "Then listen to me." And he builds ship models. He says ships of state; I say ships of death in which he will shrink our souls and push us off burning into a black sky on a black sea. He buys his wood scraps from casketmakers. In Albany he sat by that flickering fire in the three-cornered house, teaching Franklin politics and then, as a reward at the end of their work, in his pneumatic voice, gasping in evil whispers, phlegm from his mouth in ectoplasmic ropes—he has been dying since we've known him—he would read to Franklin, read to Franklin often that one passage from Carlyle the way a mother reads the Bible to a delinquent son. He would read it in the dark. He would read it each time as if we'd never heard it before. And I would listen from the kitchen while their shapes changed and melded into one another before the red coals. He would call me in. I wouldn't answer.

" 'Much wild natural ingenuity in him; cunning rapid *whirls* of contrivance.' Ah-hah? Familiar? 'And gained three battles and very many sieges amid the *loudest clapping of hands.*' How about that? The milk of the coconut? 'Nobody need be braver. Great nature, too, though of hot temper and so full of multifarious voracities . . .' Boss? Listen to this! ' . . . inarticulate good sense withal and much magnaminity run wild.' Come on, Eleanor, I know you're listening. Hear this. It's the bananas."

And I would come in from the kitchen, morally obedient according to Carlyle, and lean against the doorframe of the drawing room, listening with one ear to the coffeepot brewing and with the other to Carlyle's bananas.

"Isn't this your Franklin? Listen! 'A big-limbed, swashing, perpendicular kind of fellow, haughty of face, but jolly too; with a big, not ugly strut, captivating to the French nation and a fit God of War . . . for that susceptible people. Understood their Army also and how by theatricals and otherwise to get fire out of it, whether on the road to ruin or not, he did not care.' "

Franklin laughed at Louis, each time, insisted each time he

hadn't swashed man or beast in years, but each time he would sit spellbound and one could see his shadow shifting with the words of that man before the fire.

I would carry in my tray of coffee and cakes, carry in my carrion to that man, to announce the evening done, to remove Mr. Howe from our lives, but they would go on, tearing and ripping first at Albany and Tammany, then at Washington and war. It was war, it seemed, where a man would/could find his shape and his share.

"A July Fourth parade with popgun rifles to show the Republicans' unpreparedness? A July Fourth parade with popgun rifles to show the Democrats' unpreparedness? Should I order five thousand, boss? They're two cents apiece, boss, and two and a half cents if you get the little flag that pops out. Wooden guns, wouldn't that make some parade? Boy, that would set their ears straight."

"And their noses out of joint," Franklin answered in the same odd journalist words.

In 1913, their schemes brought Franklin to Washington as Assistant Secretary of the Navy and, in jest, I'm certain, Franklin began to call Louis Colonel. Colonel Louis McHenry Howe. Louis took the title seriously and used it on his official letters from Franklin's office.

What Franklin hasn't done well in Washington or hasn't done at all is overshadowed by the flashy headlines Mr. Howe writes and places about the things Franklin does do well or that he has done in Franklin's name. AN EFFICIENT OFFICIAL. FRANKLIN D. ROOSEVELT OF THE NAVY DEPARTMENT. WITH SECRETARY DANIELS ABROAD AND MOST OF HIS BUREAU CHIEFS WITH HIM, THE ASSISTANT SECRETARY OF THE NAVY IS HANDLING FIVE DIVISIONS OF A GREAT ORGANIZATION ALL BY HIMSELF. WORKING FROM EARLY MORNING TO FAR INTO THE NIGHT. THE SHORTSIGHTEDNESS ON THE PART OF HIS SUPERIOR THAT MAKES SUCH SACRIFICE NECESSARY. WASHINGTON, APRIL 3. That was Louis' language. The body of the article was far worse. The nationwide collection of binoculars for the men at sea, thousands of binoculars, none of which was ever used, became a success in merchandising Franklin, and the commandeering of the generator intended for the Hotel Pennsylvania, delaying its opening for many months, was the sort of heroic stance the hero-worshiper molded for his Man of War. Franklin really was doing an impressive although quiet job with labor in the shipyards, with fleet deployment and coal supplies. His name was in newspapers across the country both as a man of action and as a competent administrator. But it wasn't enough for Franklin to have his name known in Kansas. Franklin, burning to be a fit God of War now and strut across history now, left Louis behind, deeply hurt, and ran off to the battlefields Carlyle had promised him. Franklin wrote:

"I have come to the conclusion that there is an awful lot of luck in the game, anyway. The officers of distinct mediocrity, by good fortune, happen to be at the exact point where something big is happening at the psychological moment, and it makes Field Marshals or Presidents out of them. We all have had our share of that kind of luck."

But not my Franklin, not yet. I recall when Uncle Ted was refused the regiment by Mr. Wilson, he went storming around the country trying to convince America to go to war—until he was shot in Milwaukee. "All slackers are traitors," he shouted, and then he was shot. His speech that day, with the bullet in his shoulder and blood on his bulging old-man's tummy, was madness. The crowd was his. "I shall be your hero," he yelled, pushing a large handkerchief into his jacket and a short little arm up into the air. "I shall be your sacrifice!" But nothing happened. He didn't die. He just finished his speech and went home. He was very disappointed, I'm certain. It wasn't his moment of destiny.

Of course Louis Howe had the right idea, but bad timing. Franklin had been expecting that moment of destiny since he first looked into his mother's eyes, and he wouldn't wait. He went to war and left Louis home. Poor Louis, what would become of him? Would he grow smaller? Petulantly, he'd

77

already stopped wearing the tigereye studs Franklin had given him. But he came to visit me, misogynist that he was, he came anyway for a sniff, a word, a blow, a bit of news, from the hero.

I knew very well why Franklin had left Louis home and taken with him instead the intemperate Livy Davis. Livy Davis was a man of his own class, and Franklin, nurtured on those medieval dreams of kingdoms and heroes and romance, was off to see the King. Louis didn't belong with the King. Louis had begun it though. It had been his error to make those promises to Franklin and now the scheme had gone haywire. His puppet, after all, had an upper-class heart and the strings were all in knots and he was in a hurry to be a great man. Poor Louis.

But I can understand now the Louis Howes of the world. When Lucy was a yeomenette in Franklin's one-rose office and Louis chief assistant, Louis, who knew every detail of Franklin's life, must have known those things also, arranged things, condoned things, planned things. He had only planned to drive a small wedge in our marriage, to loosen my control of Franklin, but not altogether, not in a scandal that would ruin Franklin's career, just to shake me off a bit. It had all been very brilliant and very possible. But poorly timed. He does not understand, shriveled as he is, that Franklin, after all Carlyle and Howe and I had given him, might actually give it all up, this God of War, for romance. Louis may have understood the hoi polloi who read the papers, but he didn't understand a man of Franklin's Arthurian class.

Also he does not understand me.

He does not understand that a woman filled with her own lead can be obdurate, can outwink in the nocturnal, that the performed may turn and become the performer, the puppet the puppeteer.

And now he visits me, courting me, which is perfectly ludicrous, and his attentions offend the children deeply. Mr. Howe may lose both Franklin and me now.

So he comes to watch me every day. Some evenings I sit at

his feet, my head against his bony little knees, and he places his vile hand on my shoulder. I sit still. We are both very complex people. He lives through Franklin as I do and we, caged and abandoned, bay at each other, bare our teeth, and smiling, measure each other each morning and each evening for a sign of weakness. What if war, we ask ourselves, or love, gives him the prize first? What will happen to us? And so we calculate each other, he from his world of one-lines, head-lines, deadlines and yellowed sweat stains on his starched collars and I from my world of obligations and wrought-iron gates, faithfully, every morning, every evening. I dream of Louis burning in the fire with his tail burning first, sizzling and shriveling and curling upward along his back to his head, spitting and burning . . . and turning to ash.

IN WHICH THE CHILDREN RETURN AND THE SERGEANT LEAVES

By late September, Mama's harvest was coming in at Hyde Park. Bushels spilling over with apples, potatoes, squash, corn and nuts arrived daily at my doorstep in Washington. I hired a wet nurse for Huckins' second child who was poorly and a new kitchenmaid, which was a coup as most of the young girls with any intelligence at all were in the factories or clerking. So Ulla moved up a peg, on the condition she teach the second kitchenmaid how to bake. But when I advised her of her new duties and increase in salary, she too had conditions, one of which was to go to market with me.

"Whatever for, dear? You aren't ready to be a lady's maid. Not yet."

"I could carry packages."

"Huckins does that."

"Please, mum," she began to cry. "It's for my Billy. I got

this money for my birthday." Ulla showed me a grimy knotted handkerchief retrieved from heaven knows where in her undergarments.

And so I agreed to take her to the Center Market if she would walk behind me and carry my packages until I finished, and then Huckins and I would wait while she shopped at the Busy Corner. I gave her bits of paper with orders on them for peppermint bull's-eyes and pure horehound drops at thirty cents a pound, Little Yara chewing tobacco at fifteen cents—a dime and a nickel, I explained to her—Cascarettes and Red Top matches. She wrapped her hair in buns at her ears which, she explained to me, were cootie garages, a new thing, and I loaned her an old flamingo marabout for her shoulders, which made her feel quite grand, and we were ready to go.

Ulla walked behind me nicely. I turned and she was there, watching with very large wet oyster eyes, reassuring me, one of the cootie garages slipping away from her ear, the marabout slipping off her shoulder in the other direction, teapot-tilting her impossibly. She would tip and dip her head at me and I would walk on but when we arrived at the Busy Corner, she said, "Excuse me, mum," went to the wall on the sidewalk, lifted her aprons, and squatting, watched placidly as a stream of urine poured out from her along the sidewalk and toward the pavement under the feet of passersby.

She knew we had water closets, I reprimanded her. She knew the children would call "fini" to Nurse every morning after breakfast and Nurse would scowl, examine, wipe and flush. She knew that, but she didn't know it for herself. Fighting Billy would teach her when the war ended, she assured me. " 'We shall all awaken,' " Mr. Howe said, " 'and find ourselves in a world greatly widened.' Thomas Carlyle." Henry Adams said he had no use whatsoever for Carlyle. Nevertheless, I waited for the world to widen and I waited for Franklin to come home and I took Ulla's list and shopped for Billy's smokes myself.

I had not however waited with any sort of enthusiasm for

the children to come home, but home they came, wild, spoiled by Mama, and spoiling for trouble with me. Who was it who established the innocence of children? Children themselves? That innocence is merely a form of barbarism. Their hatred is hot and open. Ignorance I can afford them, but never innocence. My horde came home hating school, hating dancing class, long pants, short pants, side parts, Nurse, me, center parts, tangles, combings, each other, brown sugar and above all Germany. Ah, how they hated Germany. It was only war they did not hate.

One day when I was at the canteen, Anna and James, even though nine of the servants were at home, took my sheets, which were very difficult to acquire during the war with its shortages, hung them over the clothesline in the backyard, and without a moment of hesitation, I'm certain, they stuck clothespins into the sheets, into the corners, to hold them tentlike to the ground. And played war. All the children from the street came to play war. What shall always be memorable for me is that before there was an actual war, before we hated Germany, my children and all the children on N Street and adjoining streets had played war with great and real hostility. I have always wondered since about that N Street war. There were no racial differences, no religious differences, no economic differences. The lines were drawn on who took milk from Sheffield's and who from Borden's. When war actually came, Borden's became the Germans, Sheffield's the Allies, and the Roosevelt property, because we took our milk from Mama at Hyde Park, became the battlefield.

I was remarkably placid the day I lost my sheets because that was the same day the sergeant returned to the canteen with another trainload of recruits. "Remember me?" he asked with no manners, no awkwardness, no hesitation.

"I believe so." For months he and I had been in my dream world at Évian, Franklin pale with jealousy and promises, my name in the headlines, my chest filled with love, honor, medals, and, at last, the dying sergeant in my lap.

"I have no one to remember me, lady, and I'm going over. I want you to remember me."

"Surely, there are dozens of girls . . ."

"A lady like you remembers a fellow, it gives him backbone. Please. If anything happens, I'll let you know. And if you ever get to France, look me up, okay?"

He was too dangerous for a dream world. He was very very real. "I won't forget. I promise."

For a while, he played his music behind me and then left, without knowing my name, without my knowing his. It was appropriate that way.

There were days that fall that were inappropriate. Leaden days that had nothing to do with the sergeant but, in a strange way, had everything to do with the sergeant; days of petits fours and tea, gossip and light talk, gorges of ladyfingers, bitter women, ignorant women and pot de crème under chandeliers. "Cruel necessity," I read, "goes before the Fortuna with her awful howl and her molten lead." I don't need someone to melt my chocolate bar; I need someone to melt my lead.

"Doesn't it bother you, Eleanor, that Franklin went to war and gave up his chance at the governorship?" We are at the Powhatan; roses fill large jardinieres. We wear wide, flowered hats and afternoon frocks with chestfuls of beads and pointed shoes and gloves. On our hems there are elastic toddle straps, on our bibs Alençon laces, at our places fried cakes in the shape of butterflies. Tea steams from silver pots.

"It doesn't bother me that Franklin has gone. It bothers me that America has gone to war. It bothers me that Mr. Wilson may be merely competing with Uncle Ted for the next election, that that may be why we are plunged into warfare. It's so easy to win if you can be a hero and since Mr. Wilson is less than a hero in his economic and social programs, he is taking Europe as his stage."

"Why, Eleanor! Mr. Wilson is very high-minded. Mr. Wilson has come out for the vote!"

"For women," someone adds as if I don't know.

Foolish, they will say about me later. "Mr. Wilson is all ideal and little principle." They gasp. Mad, they will say. I go on. They sit with their frog-vague faces, loose-mouthed in their gauzy bonnets. "Henry Adams told me that in three months America out-Germanied Germany. Possibly we're all crazy. Alice Paul burning Kaiser Wilson in effigy to get us the vote and our own soldiers attacking Alice Paul and the women on the streets of America? Isn't that madness? They are trying to commit her to St. Elizabeth's . . . as if wanting the vote, to have the freedom to make your own decisions, is madness. What are we fighting for? Why, Tessa, you can't even receive telephone calls while your husband is at home."

"That's common courtesy, Eleanor."

"I am certain you do not require that courtesy of *him*."

"The vote shall change all of that," she whines in response.

I ignore Tessa entirely. I hear echoes of my teacher, Mlle. Souvestre, lecturing me almost twenty years ago. She is at my shoulder even now.

"Don't you realize," I speak in her voice, "we are operating on who is right and who is wrong rather than what is right and what is wrong? Men don't see that; they see politics and personality. Mr. Wilson has let something loose that he will have great trouble calling back home."

"Isn't it extraordinary to live with a man like Franklin and learn so much," they tell each other, agreeing, giving me the choice either to hang Franklin with my sedition or to show myself an independent and disagreeable wife. Mlle. Souvestre, my old school, the classroom, vanish. Pouf.

And I smile at them and say, "If I want to keep up with my Franklin and take part in his interests, I have to learn. Politics don't interest me in the least. Franklin does." It is somehow, partly, what I want to think. They are satisfied; I am safe. Franklin might indeed be blamed for speaking seditiously to his wife but he could charm his way out of a biscuit without breaking the crust if he were ever accused.

84

"Oh, Eleanor, really!"

"You have learned so much here in Allenswood," Mlle. Souvestre told me as she packed me off to America. I was seventeen. "You return now to a life of contradiction. Live it well. I had hoped you would not meet the conflicts so soon . . . you are still so young." I am twice the age now as when I kissed her cheek and returned to America. I have hidden everything I'd been taught, even the dignity.

"So then you do miss him?"

The ladies blink at me and I at them while I break my butterfly into a pile of crumbs. "I'm very happy for Franklin that he has an opportunity to do what he wishes for his country." And then I pass the tea and pour and sip and sit with my back straight, not touching the chair, just as it ought to be, while the ladies glance in gauzy glee at each other, thinking they have found me out.

Days like that, I could feel the same hot stirring within me that I'd felt with the sergeant. I didn't know where the ideas came from that flowed forth as if given. The more I learned in order to keep up with my Franklin—for that was my pursuit— the more critical of him I grew. There was always the shame and fear that I would drive him away with my newfound wisdoms and sweeping generalizations. It was as if some terrible choice had to be made between intelligence and love.

Well into October, Mary Patten telephoned, squealing out enormous news.

"Oooh, Eleanor, I have the loveliest, most in-triguingest . . . last night a soldier came to the canteen, not from a train, mind you, but just walked on in. And . . . and, he gave Tessa, of all people, a little rough package. He looked around first, Eleanor. Then he said it was from Kilgore, if that isn't a ghastly name. And when Tessa opened it, she swooned for it was a bloodstained Bible, one of those little khaki Bibles? The soldier said, 'Kilgore give it to me to give to somebody called Lady,' and he saluted Tessa. Very rough. Well, by the time Tessa recovered herself, he was gone, really.

Of course, he was more embarrassed by the whole thing than mysterious, but it is mysterious. What do you make of *that?*"

"I'd say the lady's no lady."

"But it was one of us, Eleanor. And we're just going to leave it around and watch to see who picks it up."

"No one will dare pick it up. She'd have to be very foolish."

"Anyone who has made an allegiance like that with a common soldier has got to be foolish in the first place. Or mad."

So I returned to the chaise to lie there with Mr. Hoover's book on my lap, waiting and feeling as I had in the summer hammock with the cat kneading my swollen stomach and the infant moving inside me . . . pregnant with myself. I waited. I didn't slip into the quicksands of the dream world nor into the Griselda blackness of depression, circling down into those horrible whirlpools. I simply lay where I had taken Mary's telephone call and rubbed my forefinger along the fringe of the brocaded chaise longue and felt the wonder of myself, moving within myself. Hot lead? Howling? I had controlled nothing, neither the sergeant nor the Bible, nor the battle, the blood, the saving, and yet he had loved me. I had pursued nothing. I had only dreamed. "A lady like you remembers a fellow, it gives him backbone." "She could be a lady, just like you, that Mademoiselle." I whistled the tune there in the library and listened to myself.

For days afterward, I fought my longing for that Bible. I examined the risks. Each time I went to the canteen, I walked past where it sat on a chest, the blood of the sergeant brown and caked on its covers. Someone, hatefully, had written in black ink on a ragged piece of cardboard propped up against it: LOST AND FOUND. And then one day, it simply wasn't there and I dared not ask who had taken it. But it didn't seem to matter; it had been mine, materialized from my dream world. I could not tell if the world were widening or narrowing, but something had moved, alive, in me, found.

86

EXCURSION TWO
Harpers Ferry, Fall 1918

IN WHICH FRANKLIN
COMES HOME

Then it was the first week in November. We knew that
Germany would surrender at any moment, that Mrs.
Tom Thumb had reached seventy-five years, that
Washington was already too cold, that Franklin had
come home, that Speaker and Mrs. Champ Clark entertained
at dinner on Wednesday evening at the Congress Hotel, that
the Navy League was demanding full and complete surrender,
that ladies of fashion were hobbling and toddling in barrel
skirts of velveteen—tobacco brown is very good—and Jeremy
Muskrat is digging his tunnel and Reddy Fox is going to catch
him any day now and find the carrots. The canteens closed.
St. Elizabeth's needed my services only two days a week now
and I fed lunch spoon by spoon to gassed soldiers on the
porch of the hospital and watched the soup slide from their
loose warrior lips under heads of wild-tossed white hair like
my Uncle Vallie's and read stories and held their limp hands

and wrote notes home for the crippled men . . . the same
sort of notes I found in the beribboned clutch of love letters
Franklin brought home with him in his trunk and has now
under the pile of soft shirts in the chiffonier. He has not
forgotten that I, not the servants, put away the laundry. He
has convinced himself that I am either too stupid to read
them or too honest to read them and that leaving them there
for me to see is an open and honorable act. He has hidden
nothing, he convinces himself, perhaps convinces me. He is a
civilized man propped up inch by inch higher and higher on
his pillows every day as he mends from war. He is quite ill
with two patches on each lung and pneumonia following
grippe. And I? I, as the great Archimedean screw in Mr.
Hoover's book of alchemical mining, the war and I are
winding down to a pit of boredom from which we can draw
up no silver, no gold, nothing that shines, only the lead of
spent bullets, spent lives and spent emotions. I felt it move in
me, but it is still lead. I dream of mines and falling walls and
still cannot take Communion and wake each day with a fear
far more immediate than that of the German's ruining
civilization as we know it, but, fear as I may, the worst has
happened to me and somehow, I am not yet destroyed, not yet
mad. I am, in fact, strangely, curiously, changing, oddly sane.

"There is a land of such nature, my dear Mrs. Roosevelt,"
Mr. Adams told me, assured me, "that if you sow, it does not
yield crops, but if you dig, it nourishes many more than if it
had borne fruit. Promise me you'll read Mr. Hoover's book."

Am I such a land? Are the screams within me the racks and
shackles and iron dogs, manacles, wedges, and red-hot plates,
working by day and working by night to wield the iron tools
on the veins, to dig trenches and carry boulders and tighten
the winches and raise great buckets of leaden evil into the
transforming sunlight? Am I such a land that will someday
nourish?

When Franklin came home, he came home so ill one would
have thought he had sought out the illness. He hadn't

written. Instead, the Department wired me to meet him at the New York pier, which I did, with Dr. Draper and an ambulance. "I need you, Babbie," he murmured, ". . . care of me."

Franklin's eyes were closed when the four seamen carried him up the stairs to our bedroom in Mama's house. Indeed it was as if Franklin had lost a limb in action. Uncle Ted, entirely sympathetic, wired: WE ARE PROUD OF YOU AND WISH YOU A QUICK RECOVERY. LATER, ELEANOR AND I WILL TALK WITH YOU ABOUT YOUR PLANS. Franklin had come home, for his own purposes, wounded, heroic, and wrapped in a tragedy of his own making. With other plans.

"I loved every minute of it," he had written and now he was home with French pneumonia, Spanish influenza, Hun helmets, a broken heart, that indiscreet magenta-ribboned clutch of Miss Mercer's letters which spoke too clearly of love and marriage and which I had finally been able no longer to avoid, and very much shorter sentences in his conversation. I tried to take Communion and I could not. I wrote in my diary: "I have never been so low." I propped Franklin up higher on his pillows each day and read to him.

The house filled with flowers and bottles and venison and old port and new jams and letters wishing him well. Carefully, lovingly, tenderly, tiptoeing while he slept, dutifully, I unpacked for him, bringing him home, putting him away where he belonged. I unwrapped the alfalfa from the entire British fleet in replica, tiny gray wooden replicas that were not toys, nor models, but implements to push across the war maps of the Admiralty. The turrets and guns were uncommonly fragile and as I pulled each little ship out of its straw, I broke off four guns. Since even the fourteen-inch guns were no larger than matchsticks, I slipped the broken guns into my pocket, and lined the fleet up on the mantelpiece from smallest to greatest for Franklin to see when he woke. I placed his ties, his gloves, his six new pairs of silk pajamas, after all, his socks all back into their drawers, his letters into the chiffonier. I must have exclaimed, sighed, said, "Oh!" and he must not have been sleeping. But he continued to sleep, sleep, doze, avoid and when he was feeling well enough days after his return, I propped up his pillows and fed him clear soups and croissants, brushed the crumbs from the bed-clothes and read to him the letters he received wishing him well. And among the letters I read to him was one I had taken from the beribboned pack in the chiffonier. I read it softly. I did not change my voice. He opened his eyes and looked into mine and I into his and he said, "Don't look at me that way." And I said, "Don't look at me that way." And he said, "We will have to talk of this, Babs, when I am stronger." And he slept for days while I tiptoed around his room, read him get-well wishes, softly, while he waited for me to read to him another one of Lucy's letters. And then I lost my nerve and cried, but to myself in the bathroom, and then went bravely on, propping up his pillows, reading him notes, arranging the flowers, feeding him, until he was well and we could talk but there was nothing to talk about except that I said I would agree to a divorce if that was his wish and that I had never expected to feel that the labor I had given all these years would be returned with so little devotion, to which he replied that he loved me and that a divorce was up to me. I said it wasn't time yet to talk about it, hurt as I was, to make a rational decision. We would go on and at the correct time I would let him know when the correct time was, I assured him, tucking the blankets around his neck. At last, our tribe left New York and returned to Washington where Franklin tried from his sickbed to enlist but the war was almost over and Mr. Wilson refused him. Franklin recovered slowly.

The Kaiser may have to face the Bar of Justice, the *Star* reports. Franklin's head is higher on the pillow. He is eating more and he speaks in longer sentences, explaining. The British doubt the sincerity of the new German government, the *Star* reports, and Reddy Fox was startled when there in the moonlight sat Jeremy Muskrat between two rows of

Farmer Brown's splendid carrots. I read the *Star*, Franklin the *Post*. He is not mentioned often, not as often as Jeremy Muskrat for instance. We are reduced to the society columns, which are growing to three pages each evening as the holiday season approaches.

Franklin tried to get his inheritance. Mama would not give him a penny. He asked me for his freedom and I clung desperately to my marriage and scrambled for a footing between the mad and the banal. There was never a scene between Franklin and myself. Hesitantly we agreed to continue the marriage. In fact, to work at its continuance, restoration and maintenance with courage, he said, and a good will, I said. For the sake of the children, he and I and Mama all said.

And certainly he began cheerfully—once he had eaten full meals and sat up for days and moved about the house in his carpet slippers, fragilely—to go to church with us, cheerfully to go to church, cheerfully to help the children with their homework, a placid adoring Anna and her mathematics at his knee, and so on, all cheerfully. But it was oppressively clear to Mama, and to me, and to everyone in Washington, that Franklin was the victim of love and might indeed be ready to sacrifice his career—a tragedy which becomes no less tragic when the hair of the hero who is seeking his timelessness is falling out.

I don't know just what I was sacrificing. I sought nothing. I had no career and I now had no love. I had my sanity, though. I had watched it, cold and strong as it was, an ugly sort of strength. And I had my position and my children and "The Little Stories for Bedtime" from the *Star* and a houseful of rusting beds and long days which I lived through simply by keeping busy, envying the ladies of Washington society who, according to Polly, my mother-in-law's madcap sister, owned delicate silvery instruments in fine boxes and shot something promising into their arms and were often bubbling at teas and parties and races and shoots and country breakfasts. I kept busy. I tried to take Communion. I placed sachets of potpourri and aromatics under Franklin's soft shirts and had the beds painted and went along on paper chases every Saturday morning cheerfully at Rock Creek Park and had the beds painted and dreamed of falling walls and softened my skin with Lydia Pinkham and more Lydia Pinkham for my monthlies and followed fashion and drank Lydia Pinkham for my nerves.

It was Bertie Hamlin who told me the story about the wall. It became *my* dream, *my* house, *my* coffee tray. It became me, an Englishwoman in Hertfordshire near Enfield, who stood with her husband and her dinner guests on the terrace to watch an air raid. The noise was deafening. The sky white and red, but it all seemed terribly far away. When it was over and she could see the moon and stars, they opened the French doors from the terrace into the parlor and nothing was left. The parlor was gone. Two dogs and a cat gone. But the after-dinner coffee tray on a little fumed oak table was untouched and a small mirror over it hung precisely on the wall that stood. Everything else was gone except that wall fronting the terrace. "Only a hole in the ground," Bertie said, "and the wall." I took the mirror and as many cups and the sugar and creamer and sugar tongs and teaspoons and the smoked oak table and all the saucers I could hold. I kept dropping them. My skirts were full as I fell down the hole with the dogs and the cat, and the ashes filled in on top of me and I fell, hoping to catch a glimpse of something shiny and bursting which might be my soul, the vein of silver, the vena profunda, not the lead, something moving on course through the universe slowly. Something with promise.

At breakfast I asked Franklin how it could have happened that one is carrying on with dinner and guests and the usual and behind the terrace doors the house falls in. Disappears. Franklin was so quick to explain in very long sentences the technicalities of vacuums and concussions and implosions and compartmentalizations that I knew immediately why I

94

had clutched the cups and the saucers and carried what little was left of my home with me in my skirts as I fell into the hole.

Franklin, watching my face, controls me with his cheerfulness. Franklin speaks cheerfully from behind his *Post*. Mr. Howe wishes me a good morning and a good day.

"Dear love," Franklin says. Mr. Howe avoids my eyes, my shoulders, our evenings. "Dear love, how I wish I could go with you today. You know how I love Harpers Ferry."

"Ten to one, boss, Katherine Bellweather brings her lazy tongs."

"You're on, Louis."

IN WHICH WE GO TO
HARPERS FERRY

atherine Bellweather, of course, had brought her lazy tongs with her. She goes nowhere without her lazy tongs and everyone talks about it but she enjoys her eccentricity. She has a pair in the hamper, at the dining table, at her bedstand, near her marble bath, which she must enter whale-like and singing. I suddenly do not like her as I sit beside her in the Rolls-Royce. I must like her as it is her husband, the Senator, who appropriates money for the battleships Franklin so wants to build.

Katherine Bellweather's husband has coal mines in Cumberland near the Delano mines and she has her own silver mines in Utah which are quite exhausted, she sighs, so that everyone knows her mines are turning into downtown properties, and she has the Rolls-Royce in Washington. Katherine is older than I by ten years, kinder, more accepting, wider, broader, with an abundant shelf of a chest, fine bones, obedient children, a magnificent four-storied forty-foot house on Massachusetts Avenue, near Alice's, with sprays of peacock feathers over her fireplaces, Navajo rugs, open-mouthed tiger skins and that shocking collection of marbles and Mary Patten says, dozens of expandable lazy tongs that can catch a child's nose or a sugar cube halfway down the dining room table. Senator Bellweather is older than Franklin, richer, more discreet, more content, owns a series of satin vests that are chromatic miracles and an Irish mistress, I've heard, in New York City. People say that Katherine is a natural mother and I am certain the same people say that I am not.

My two boys, Elliott and John, knotted in their charcoal Norfolk jackets, thickening the air with their distress, sit in Mrs. Bellweather's motor car. They had been sullen and surly even to jocular Kennedy, Katherine's man, as he'd swung them into the Silver Ghost, one to each window, with the Thermos hamper from England between them. Little Katy, Katherine's youngest, sits between her Mama and myself on the rear seat, my boys smolder like coals in the center, facing us on fold-down seats, and Kennedy, smart and sleek, drives up front.

We will picnic near Great Falls, along the B & O Canal and then motor on to Harpers Ferry. I will knit. Katherine will sing with her daughter. They always do. I don't know what my boys will do. "You must behave," I repeat to my boys, and Elliott, who pinched my thigh the first time I said this, makes a rabbit face at me, long-lipped, accusing, pitiful and pugnacious. He twists diligently at the yellow Bakelite door lock because I would not let him wear his sailor suit. Even though the District was nipped by early cold, even though I told him the night air had fallen to thirty and showed him the anemones drooping and the leaves of the hydrangeas falling black and straight from their stems like the lead plumbs of surveyors, and the limbs of catalpa clawing at the sky like dead men's hands clawing from the grave, even though. Even though bags and bags of elecampane and glacés and bonbons and caramels from Buckingham's Candy Palace hang and swing in nets behind our heads as threat and reward, even though I promised myself to be cheerful. Even though, or because, the night before Franklin and I had had a noisy row, a regular blowout as Anna would say.

I'd thrown blue willow plates from Franklin's supper tray. I think the children might have heard since the nursery is just above our bedroom, and I threw blue willow plates from the supper tray I'd brought up to Franklin who had come home from the office after his first day of work and retired very early.

"Queasy," he said.

With his sinuses clogged up and his head aching and his liver, he said, like a mildewed mule and his left eye and cheek pulsing. "Working too hard, Babs. All the reports from the Department. As soon as the war's over, the Republicans are going to investigate every cent I spent. I ate a cheese sandwich at my desk today and it's just too hard on my stomach. Queasy."

With a silver spoon from a blue willow bowl, he was eating clam chowder and malted milk, and apple tapioca and victory bread and had Kondon's Catarrhal Jelly snuffed up his nose and ovals of cotton soaked in Kolynos Liquid and stuffed up his nose and Tyrees Antiseptic Powder for nasty, hawking spitting spells and Spanish flu begins in the head and ends in the heart. Now he was eating clam chowder, between swallows trying to identify unidentifiable bits and later he would, with much assiduity, work dental floss between his teeth. Franklin insisted he still had the flu. I insisted he was over it. I insisted, if he insisted, that he follow the government's menu of meals for the sick. He wrote his mother in faithful detail the condition of what he referred to for her benefit as his tummy. I was examining my forehead in the dressing table mirror and rubbing petals from the potpourri between my fingers, picking them from a large blue and white ironstone dish and crushing them on my thumb into ashes. Wrinkles were deepening in pairs at the corners of my mouth. Franklin wanted me to entertain him with word games.

"Katherine called," I said. "She's invited the boys and myself on a trip to Harpers Ferry tomorrow."

"Do you a world of good. Wish I could go. I like Katherine. Come on, Babs, what's the definition of *knapsack?*"

I shrugged and began to rearrange the pins in my red velvet pincushion, jabbing and sticking. A short sleeping bag, I did not say.

"A short sleeping bag. Without the *k*. Get it?"

Nor did I say she'd mentioned seeing you today at Chevy Chase with your golf equipment nor how well and happy you looked nor that cheese sandwiches simply were not on the luncheon menu.

"Nap, n-a-p." Franklin is a very bright man and he thinks through mazes at the speed of bees. Franklin's face was longer and sadder than I'd ever seen.

I walked to the bed. I lifted a plate from the supper tray and he asked me if I knew the story behind the blue willow pattern. I did know the story.

"I know all the stories," I said. And threw the plate against the bookcase where it was caught by the chintz curtains and dropped spinning to the floor. I couldn't bring myself to aim for the wall. Franklin watched with awe. Other plates, filled with and empty of food, followed, spun, rattled and settled unbroken on the carpet.

Much later, silently, I washed my face and examined myself in the mirror and climbed into my bed. I heard him come in. I felt him pull at my hairnet and touch my hair and then my face but I lay very still. Finally I heard him sigh. He left.

We pass the Rock Creek Cemetery. It draws me. I look away. Clover Adams examined herself, also, one night, then climbed the double staircase to her darkroom and drank acid from her photographic solutions and now lies in a new grave. Clover, we heard soon after, had had long periods of melancholy. Women have no passions. For us, we know, there is contentment or melancholy—the banal or the mad. Men of course have lusts, drives, habits, Irish mistresses, baseball, Bearcats, honor. We have our moods.

I knit tightly, binding off stiches at the top of one sleeve and casting on at the bottom of the next. I knit furiously. The war is almost over and still I knit. I cannot stop.

I knit, Katherine sings with Katy in duet, "Oh, Dem Golden Slippers." My dear sons do not sing. Katherine and Katy sing like court mockingbirds. My daughter Anna rarely speaks to me. They sing "After the Ball Is Over." My son Elliott joins in. He sings, however, "Give Me a Drink, Bartender." It is something his father taught him. Liquor is a joke. Father gets drunk at the Harvard Club, the Metropolitan Club, the Saloon and the Salon and then he and Livy and a few close old friends walk down the sidewalks singing. I can hear them as they drop Franklin off and their fair and filthy voices continue up the street while Franklin lets himself in.

"There goes Daddy's train, Mama!" Katy pulls at Katherine's sleeve and counts her father's coal cars out loud as they pass along a ridge above the canal.

Katherine and I talk in the Rolls-Royce over Katy's head. Douglas Fairbanks and Mary Pickford were having an affair all the time they were traveling around the country to sell Liberty Bonds. There is a thin line between patriotism and lust, I do not remark. I think Elliott has succeeded in removing the Bakelite door lock. We talk of the New York Edison sign on Broadway with a light bulb flashing on and off on a silver tray and the proper size of families. I won't have any more. Katherine is not certain. I am for I have moved from Franklin's bedroom, from Franklin's pajamas and socks and gloves and jams and port and bed. I will no longer be Franklin's woman. We speak of things, Katherine and I, things which are fixed, of things which are unfixed, of things which will widen the world. It is no longer easy to distinguish. I have a new freedom now, having relinquished my role as a wife. It is a strange sort of relief, but it feels more like loneliness. I have no one to cling to at night when my dreams frighten me. "It's a terrible world to bring children into." I say to Katherine.

Katherine sighs. Katy counts more coal cars. "I don't even know if there will be a Switzerland to send her to school to."

"A few minutes more, madam, Mrs. Bellweather, we'll be there," Kennedy tells us through the speaking tube.

In the poverty grass along the canal there are cattails in clumps. My boys are very restless.

"Dear Babs," Franklin wrote me last summer when I was in Campobello with the children, "Miss Mercer and I took a motor trip to Harpers Ferry. My liver has been a mule."

The boys scowl and grumble until it is time for lunch and Katherine tells Kennedy to park the motor under the vine-covered cedar at the banks of the B & O. I see the cattails.

"Dear Babs, Going tonight to the Naval Observatory to look at the moon and stars. Ever, Franklin."

I've seen the moon and stars. I've seen the cattails in my house, dried and parched. I had not put them there. I shredded them willfully into my potpourri. It was before Franklin left for Europe that he'd driven here and picked the cattails. And before that and before that. I am shaken by the cattails. I can understand why he has been faithless. I cannot forgive him for taking my faith from me.

The boys scramble from the Silver Ghost. They don't wait for Kennedy to open the door. Little Katy runs after them, her boater hat bouncing along her back, corn-silk hair bouncing at her waistline. I ask Kennedy to follow them and off they go, leaving Katherine and myself to the picnic. We are like two satin pillows bordered by lace ruching, puffed and soft and waiting to make someone comfortable.

Katy's boater reminds me of school in England. I was much older than Katy. We walked in a crocodile every Sunday two by two in brown corduroy pinafores and yellow muslin blouses, two by two, with our boaters pressed down so low upon our foreheads we had to hold our chins far up in the air in order to see where we were going. "That," we were admonished, "is how a lady must walk." And our guide would push our boaters further down over our eyes. Instinctively, we all knew where we were going. I learned truth, history and literature. I learned to think then. Mlle. Souvestre thought I was wonderful, and I she. Most of my pinafored crocodile schoolmates are caught in the war, on both sides, all certain, they write me as often as I write them, of divine right over diabolical evil. We had always been so certain.

My boys shout "Halloo" across the canal to the hills. Thunder replies in the distance, swelling and rolling in from the south. Gray water and sky move sullenly in opposing directions, twisting the horizon. On the low hills across the canal a cold sun slants on barren angular flanks, glints of mica line the folds of the rocks and swallows sit in the cedars. At the thunder, the swallows flutter upward, leaves downward. Gulls move swiftly in flat lines along the canal. The boys return and pull at my knitting needles for attention.

With her lazy tongs, Katherine retrieves cold veal from the hamper, then napkins and salt in silver shakers and oysters in rough-baked pottery and a tub of whipped cream to spread over slices of yellow cake. I pull the napkin rings and spread the linen on the velour car rug. "Just a few more moments, boys." To Kennedy, who stands above them, "Be a good man and take them to wash, won't you?"

Kennedy and the boys march away along a row of cedars. I think of Floyd Gibbons' photographs: carnage in Belleau Wood, horses and men split open like flour sacks between the scorched trees. Eat of my flesh and drink of my blood, there is no such thing as evolution, Mr. Darwin. I am raising sons and Franklin thinks war is a constant.

"Dearest loving Ulla, I am well and hope you are the same. It was a pretty tough job getting the Huns out of the woods but when the US boys start anything they finish it and the Huns had to vamoose. They would shoot at you and you couldn't see them. We took a few villages and hundreds of prisoners. I talked to them in German and it is the same old dope. In the morning the fields in front of us were just piled with dead Boche. We went out and carried lots of wounded Huns back to our dressing stations. One Hun didn't want us to take him in so we left him lay there until evening. Then we brought him in. It was the pain that made him a little out of his bean or he wouldn't of refused to be carried in. They had four ft. high shells in their dugouts and some were connected to wires. There was an inspection and we cut off their suspenders. Ha ha. Also a lot of beer but it was poisoned but he couldn't fool us with it. Love to your mama and papa and Mrs. Pfaffendorf. XXX Your Fighting Billy."

I can hear my boys at the canal. They sing: "Hurrah for the party, hurrah for the feed. Cracker Jacks aplenty, what more do we need." There is so much they don't know and will need. Not long ago there were those simple answers. "To detect an escape of sewer gas in the house," the household book read, written in by Mama with carefully crossed *t*'s, "take an ounce of oil of peppermint and pour it down the ventilating pipe. If you smell peppermint, anywhere, there is gas leaking from the sewer." The reward of labor is love. The wages of sin is death. Have faith. For croup, hang a pomander of rose leaves and spices around one's neck. One has faith, one has virtue and the aim of mankind is to evolve. Pour peppermint on the devil. He will surely retreat. Daughters inherit household books; sons inherit history. I, the sewer. Don't save me. It's the pain. I'm a little out of my bean, too. It's just the pain. It will go away. American girls finish anything we start.

Katy helps her mother spread the whipped cream along slices of yellow cake. There is a chill. When the boys return with Kennedy, one can see only the shapes of the rocks and cattails. The line of trees has been swallowed. My children look more troubled than ever. They come running before the driver's gleaming boots which march out of the fog after them. They are not singing.

"What is the matter, Elliott?"

"Nothing."

"I can *see* something is the matter, dear.

"John?" I ask. Baby John moves away from me, behind Elliott.

"We saw Papa."

"We saw Papa," Elliott repeats softly. "He just drove away."

"What do you mean, dear?"

"He just rolled up the window and drove away."

"Where is Papa going, Mummy?"

"You have a way of steering the course of a conversation, Babs, opening and closing the sentences as you will, choosing the time, the place and the circumstances and brushing off those you dislike. Do you hear me, Babs?"

"I do not and I refuse to discuss it, Franklin."

"Where is Daddy going, Mummy?" they repeat.

"He looked at us and drove away."

"I don't think you are correct, dear."

I have no ventilating pipe. I have no oil of peppermint, no pomander, nothing to protect me. Only my manners which I pull over my head as I fall into the sewer hole Franklin has dug for me. I am the underground sewer, the sower, the reaper, the ripper, the stitcher.

"It *was* Papa, wasn't it, Johnny?" Elliott puts his arm around his brother in defiance of my truth.

"That is quite enough, children. Quite enough."

"And the car was foggy inside and we knocked on the window and he hit his head with his hand and rolled up the window and drove off. He looked sick."

"Now, that's enough! It's time for lunch, not make-believe. Come along." I spread myself on the velour rug. Elliott puts his head in my lap. John pulls at my hand. I am the satin pillow tassled with small blond heads.

"Papa, Lucy, chockablock, Mummy." Baby John repeats Franklin's favorite word. Is it possible that even my children have heard the gossip?

"Papa looked sick," Elliott repeats.

It's so long since I've been chockablock, as close as we could be. So long since I've been kissed and sat upon a knee. My insides are spreading along the ground, split, and I am knitting stitches tightly to hold me together but I am coming apart and holding on in my Hudson seal and muskrat coat, bundled up and coming apart.

Anna has a paper-doll family she keeps on her desk, cardboard cutouts from the *Woman's Journal*. She writes stories about them. "Anne and Paul Fairchild," she read reluctantly to me once when I asked. "This elegant mother and proud father live a comfortable and gracious life with their happy and healthy family. Presenting their demure daughter, Mag, as she is affectionately called, with her marmalade tabby named Nelson wearing an Indian dress." I corrected her grammar. "That means the cat is wearing an Indian dress, not Mag." Anna said, "Sorree," sarcastically, asked her grandmother for an Indian dress, I discovered, in the next mail, and crumpled up Mrs. Fairchild and left the crumpled Mrs. Fairchild like a fetish in the violet-sprigged pin tray on my dressing table. I knew what she meant. Once, when a cactus plant withered and died, she silently, ominously, carried it into my room. I was working at my desk. She silently, ominously, placed the dead plant on my desk, on my papers, and left. "It is all my fault," I wept to Franklin. "Dear Babs," he laughed and pulled me on his lap where I sat stiffly. "You were never a fair child, you were a living stone."

"I can't laugh at jokes about my family. Grandmother Livingston was a woman of character."

"Look, Anna's only a child. Let her make some mistakes. We're all having trouble living up to your ideals."

Two summers ago in a rage of jealousy over the new baby,

Anna pushed baby, wicker carriage and all off the porch at Fairhaven on the Jersey shore. Fortunately the tide was out. I shook sand from the baby's mouth and clothes and Nurse punished Anna severely.

"I have yet to see character in Anna," I told Franklin, still on his lap.

"Give us time, Babs."

And so when a new issue of the *Journal* arrived, I cut out a new Mrs. Fairchild, pasted her to sturdy cardboard and returned her to Anna's desk. How I wished to cut out a new Mr. Fairchild and a new Mag Fairchild, the fairychild of the fairyfather of the River Styx ripping up the laurel in the graveyard. I carry all the stones, living, of those mad people who buried themselves alive and finally died after sending forth their seeds. What were the seeds I hoped would burst in me? More small blond heads that tore me to pieces? How I long to rip up my inheritance—not the real estate or the capital but the blood and the bones, bit by bit, bone by bone.

"Picnic time," Katherine chirps at us all and clasps a roll of cold veal with her lazy tongs.

IN WHICH WE SEE THE
FRENCHMAN'S AEROPLANE

Katherine passes the veal to John who shakes his head and then to Elliott. "Oh, they've found a pair of lovers, have they? Honestly. Children, you must never disturb people like that. Really, Kennedy, I am surprised at you to have let them out of your sight."

We shall blame Kennedy.

"Oh, they clear took off from me, mum. I saw nothing. Heard a car pull away. In a hurry it was."

Elliott spits his veal onto the velour.

"Darling!"

"It's awful and I hate it and I hate Mr. Hoover's starving children from Belgium and I don't care what they eat and I hate Papa."

And I hate Mr. Howe and I hate the silver running from forest fires and I hate Papa also.

"Oh, dear." Katherine sighs. "Isn't this the day the

Frenchman flies his aeroplane?" she asks Kennedy. "Wouldn't the children enjoy that after lunch?" she asks me.

I nod. "After lunch. And only if Elliott eats his veal." How well I know Elliott. He will slip the chewed hunks of meat into his pocket along with the Bakelite door lock. I know him because we are mirrors of each other, reflecting back and forth each other's shadows. He drives me wild. I, him. I pour Katherine's tea into a cup that cannot sit still upon its saucer until she takes it from me and holds it, and then into my own unsteady cup. Shivers overwhelm me. Kennedy offers me a lap rug of Scottish wools, blues and greens, and helps me wrap it around my shoulders. Still I shiver. There will be no tea for my children today. Spots and leper dots of whipped cream crest their lips and noses. They don't look up at me. They don't look at each other. Katy reads Jeremy Muskrat to them with an exhaustive squeaking morality in her small voice. They don't look at her. We go through our lives so well not looking at each other and seeking God.

At last Kennedy rolls up the cabriolet top on the Silver Ghost. I take Baby John on my lap. We all cover ourselves with lap robes while Kennedy packs the hamper, shakes the bits of grass and crumbs from the velour and pours the rest of the tea into the canal waters. In the rear of the car, behind my head, there are three small, round isinglass windows. Franklin is out there somewhere in one of those circles. The fog fills the windows and I cannot see behind me. We don't go to Harpers Ferry, but drive along the speedway and look for the Frenchman and his aeroplane.

John whispers to me: "Don't let Brudder hurt me."

"No. No one will hurt you, darling."

Elliott, who has already used a knife on a tutor, begins to watch me, snake-eyed. To stare at me. I know what they have seen. They have seen their father touching Miss Mercer perhaps with his shirt unbuttoned at the collar and his tie pulled loose and his jacket off. Bully, Franklin, bully for you. Your newest adventure now that the war is almost over? A sewer hole and a car with its windows fogbound and its windshield steaming and a man looking up to see his own little boys looking in at him and seeing, then, himself, seeing them seeing their father frightened? God save you, I pray as we drive along and look for the aeroplane. God save you.

Under the soft shirts in the chiffonier I have found the letters and stood shaking with rage and read: "Meet me tonight, Franklin, if only in your dreams. I love you terribly." I stood still and the veins at my neck bulged with hot anger, not fear, and the blood rushed to my face. The letters smelled very faint, very expensive and I wished to leave just one crumpled on Anna's desk with the Fairchild family.

Before this day but after the letters, I had asked Mr. Howe. "Surely, Louis, there must be a way Franklin can arrange his indiscretions so they are less indiscreet? He planned the mine barrage in the North Sea so well. Can you not guide him in this same sort of logic? Until it all passes?"

"Oh, Eleanor. He won't discuss this with me at all. I'm sorry."

"He's going to ruin his career, Louis." It was a paradoxical warning, one I used often, both wistful and pious, and referred in part to the ruin of my own life.

"And his stomach, Eleanor," Louis said.

"And his family," Mama said later after I had shown her the letters. "I shall speak with him."

"No, Mama, not yet. Give him time. He has made certain promises to me."

"I cannot bear it, Eleanor."

"I can, Mama."

"Yes, yes, I suppose, Eleanor, that you can." She rubbed my arms. I knew she felt them strong. I had won her imprimatur but I had lost her son. I had tried so hard to please them both.

Very gently Kennedy stops the car along the speedway. "There it is, mum, the aeroplane."

The children bounce and wave at the Frenchman. He slouches against his aeroplane perched on the flat field of mustard weed. I have never been so close to a modern machine. It is moth-fragile and thin, papery, far less stable than our river iceboats. The Frenchman is sharp and narrow and small, wrapped in dried cracked leathers. He rubs his palms together in the cold. Kennedy strolls over to inquire if he is taking it up.

"Not in this weather."

" 'Not in this weather,' he said," says Kennedy. "It's a Curtiss JN-4D," Kennedy informs the boys.

"A Jenny!" Elliott shouts and Katherine and I smile at each other over his head. "Aw gee, Mummy, aw gee. We'll come back, won't we? Mummy?"

"Of course. Soon. Definitely."

The Frenchman waves at the boys. They wave back excessively. "Really, Mummy?" I pull down their arms.

"When one says definitely, one must mean definitely." Too many nightmares have I spent waiting for my father to come back, waiting for Franklin to come back, squinting into the clouds for their faces, reaching into tunnels for their hands.

"Come back," the Frenchman calls out. "Come back soon. We fly."

He tips his helmet. It is a leather helmet and he makes only the motion of tipping, an archaic insect helmet with goggles and he rubs his hands together, mandibles. He is something from a moist thicket, something that digs through tunnels, in nasty burrows, not the skies. Must we go deep before we fly? Take me away, I whisper within my stitches, take me away so I don't have to see the steaming windows in the fog and the loosened tie and the lusts and desires, the definites and indefinites and the quivering pen on the register of the roadside cabin, their brave pen writing in our names, so I don't have to feel the forest fire. I'll sit on the wing; I'll balance on the fuselage with one leg up all the way, like Douglas Fairbanks, away. I'll hold on. I won't have moods. Is there a place? There is something I'm looking for. A place where moth and rust doth not corrupt. And thieves do not break through nor steal. That place. Where things endure.

Once on inspection—Franklin in a bowler hat, trying to look older than he was, reviewing the American fleet off the Jersey shore—I climbed the mast to the crow's nest on the battleship. I climbed with Lieutenant Land, Lieutenant Emory Land it was, high over the sea and found no nest. I swayed up there and caught fresh air and shocked my Franklin deeply, he said later, but I found nothing. I looked down upon the other dignitaries' wives who sat folded into deck chairs in rows. Their hats were flat from on high, and feathered, inedible pies of blackbirds and pheasants, night-mare pies with wrinkled fruits and burned-out crusts, with no eyes. When I came down, cautiously, backward, rope by rope, the ladies whose faces looked from below as their hats had from above, said: "My goodness, you certainly are Teddy's child." They were older ladies and weren't certain of the connections. I often deliberately left the impression uncorrected. So did Franklin.

"Come back. We fly." Fly, fly, fly, the Frenchman's promise echoes and drifts over us as the Silver Ghost lifts over mud-hard ruts toward the speedway. "Katherine, dear." I touch her Persian-lamb sleeve. "I need to go home." I claim a headache.

"The veal was rich," she apologizes.

"No, no. I think it's the sudden coldness."

"There has been so much," she agrees. "Kennedy," she addresses the speaking tube above us, "Madam Roosevelt wishes to go home."

My room, my diary, my narrow bed in the morning room, the surveyor's plumb in my stomach that is not veal, nigrum plumbum, black lead, my dressing table draped in Sara's fading chintz, home to Elbert Hubbard's *Little Library* and my limp leather books. If I had two loaves of bread I would sell one and buy white hyacinths for my soul, wrote Mr. Hubbard, with his piercing eyes and his art-for-glory community

111

and his ivory satin cravats. White hyacinths to float on my black lead like votive candles at Christmas. Plumbum nigrum. It doesn't move. Nigrum plumbum. Kennedy turns the car around and points its gleaming nose toward Washington.

"Madam, Mrs. Roosevelt," Millicent wrote in a note left this morning. "The laundry room walls need washing and the storeroom." I have so much to do at home, I wish Kennedy would hurry.

"We *are* in for a bad winter," Katherine says. "The Senator thinks the influence is something dreadful begun by the Germans."

Madam, Mrs. Roosevelt: The light shaft needs painting, the skylight repairing. The storerooms must be freed of moths.

I manage to respond to Katherine. "This is a very cold November already."

And all the white enamel beds and the washstands are covered with white oilcloth to hide the rust.

"But when can we go back to see the Frenchman fly, Mummy?"

"He doesn't fly. That's bunk." It is the first time Katy has addressed the boys directly. "He stands around and watches the plane for the *real* Frenchman."

"When Papa is well. We'll all go together," I say to the little shrunken faces looking up at me like baby birds. Ah, have I a worm for you!

"Has he not recovered?" Katherine asks. "Poor Franklin. The flu and pneumonia. It's just more than one can bear."

"Did you hear Papa's joke? How he got sick in France? He opened a window and in flew Enza!"

"That's quite stupid!" Katy hisses at Elliott.

Her attack so pleases her and immobilizes my boys that the children are quiet for the rest of the drive. Katherine goes on about the influenza in the camps, despicable Bernard Baruch, impossible peg-top silhouettes, awkward toddle skirts and the unfixed future of Switzerland. Kennedy whistles sound-lessly behind his glass. I dream of flying into a hole in the sky, clawing through clouds, buried alive.

"Men are so funny with their machines, are they not?" I ask Katherine, for my dream frightens me.

Katherine agrees. "Kennedy loves to drive. He is so proud of the Ghost. The Senator said, oh, so funny"—she laughs rich and creamy and one knows precisely how Katy's vindic-tiveness will soon be covered—"the Senator says that Ken-nedy will never give up the Ghost." I laugh for Katherine. Elliott is caressing the speaking tube of snaky silk braid, luxuriously twisted floss stretching from Katherine to Ken-nedy through the glass between us all. Elliott sees me looking at him. "A silky wonderful animal, Mummy, with a tufty wool tail." And I cannot tell him to stop. Elliott lives with and speaks with a collection of beaverbeasts on beaverboards, "natural, chummy lifelike," their advertisement reads. They are his friends. I suspect he touches himself. When Franklin was a child he had no friends either but, his mother told me, he so loved the forest creatures he asked his Papa for a gun and went out into the woods and shot one of each and had them mounted to keep in his room. One of each and they didn't talk back or take long strides or criticize or remind one of the definites and the indefinites. "I promise I will never see her again," Franklin said last week. "Definitely. Ever. You must believe me." He had held my chin in the cup of his palm and sucked the blood from my eyes and the ink from the cabin register in Virginia Beach. "I will remove myself from your bed, Franklin," I told him. "I deserve it," he told me.

I would believe him, definitely. There was very little else I could do except put ice packs on my swollen eyes and my linens away again in my closets.

Kennedy has brought us to the end of the speedway. We cross the river. Yesterday when Billy's last letter arrived, Ulla tapped on the door as I was bathing, carrying the letter and warm towels. Fighting Bill wrote "I got a letter from Homer and I laughed till I almost exploded. He wanted to know what I would rather be—a colonel with an eagle on my shoulder, or a private with a chicken on my knees. Well, you know what I told him, I guess. I said, a private with Ulla on my knee. I don't give a darn for war, what I want is love."

"Well, your Fighting Bill is growing very bold," I told Ulla.

"Ah, and he's a different man, now, my Bill."

She left and I bathed speaking to the swan faucets and my knees. "You'll ruin your career, Franklin, with your roadside cabin stops."

"Let's say I was just killing time, Babs."

"Don't you think if you kill time, you'll injure eternity?" He looked at me strangely and his face slid away with the bath water and everyone in the family said as they always had, "Poor Eleanor."

"Isn't it incongruous, Eleanor? Eleanor?" Katherine has been speaking. I haven't heard a word. "You see, one must walk like a Japanese woman. One toddles. Now I ask you, could anything be more incongruous? It's the queerest kind of kittle-kattle. Here we are with our world so very different and the millions of men under arms still ask for all the 'femalities.' "

I suddenly realize that Katherine has memorized last evening's society column. She has no idea that I reply with the lines she misses. "They don't want long strides and uniforms and quick orders."

"That's right. Or independence."

"Whatever, it may be our fighting men will find women doing some marvelous juggling, embracing every opportunity for freedom and work and yet, still exploit all the old 'femalities.' "

"Eleanor, do you think I would be independent if I wore a toddle skirt? Or more female?"

"Dear Katherine, toddle skirts are like electric cars: you can only go thirty miles per hour and twenty-six miles from home."

"You are really the most interesting woman I've ever met. And the deepest."

Katherine can be so nice. She takes the speaking tube from Elliott and asks Kennedy to slow down on the road corduroyed from years of military equipment moving over it toward the capital. Poor Elliott, he shall soon start to pick and pull at himself or me now that he's lost the tufted tube. The sweater sleeve on my lap is finished. I have now bound off all of the stitches. Two every fourth row but I have knit where I should have purled and knots where I should have pearls. Wee Babs John is asleep. I rub his fair head as if it were a worry bead and tell Elliott that we are already at Edgemoor. "We'll be home soon, don't worry." We drive into the streets of the city, over the bricks at Union Station, around, up Constitution Avenue, past War where Franklin ought to be by now. We drive up N Street and the motor stops at my house. I thank Katherine. My boys mumble something and little Katy invites them to come another time. Katherine reaches over to me as Kennedy swings the boys onto the sidewalk. "Eleanor, dear, shall I come in with you? I can send Katy on home."

"Good heavens, no. Whatever for? I have the mail to do and eighteen for dinner."

Her face freezes as mine I'm certain already has.

"Dinner tonight. And I must call Franklin at the Department and have him pick up wine. He walks home, you know. I shall be very busy. But of course, next Wednesday, we'll see you at the Navy League meeting and then at the party for the men at St. Elizabeth's. Until then . . ." I wave to her from the top of the stone stoop.

IN WHICH THE WAR ENDS

Inside, Elliott says he hates Katy. I say as I always have: "Manners first, feelings will follow." And then send them to bed without tea or supper and tell Nurse that Elliott spat food and removed Mrs. Bellweather's door lock. There is great movement and kicking upstairs. Millicent sorts and twists and braids and brushes my hair and locks the structure against my scalp with long-toothed tortoise combs as I think of Katherine with her legs toddled and tied, baaing on her Navajo rug. I don't ring Franklin for the wine. He would have to lie later if he isn't back yet at his desk. I send Huckins out with the lock to the door of the Silver Ghost and the wine list.

When Franklin arrives, I am dressing. I look at him in the mirror. His mouth is a wound in his face. He kisses the back of my neck lightly. "Where are the children?"

I take pressed powder from a Venetian silver compact as if it were poison. "Promise me you won't poison the Roman Empire, Eleanor," Henry Adams had said.

"Anna is at a rehearsal for her dancing class."

"And Franklin," Mr. Adams had added. It had not been a question.

"The boys?" Franklin asks carefully.

I take rouge from a blue Wedgwood tray.

"James and Franklin have a birthday party and John and Elliott have been sent to bed," I say as lightly as he had kissed me, brushing out the loose, soft curls Millicent had so painstakingly pinned and jamming the long-toothed tortoise comb through tight buns. I wear my After the Shower dress, sparkling and sheer and a beaded silk hyacinth in my hair. I have stuck holes in my scalp. Cracked.

"So early?"

"For telling lies."

"I see." Franklin takes my arm and we walk down the stairs.

At dinner over the Maryland crab I speak of my excursion and the Frenchman's aeroplane. I say: "Flying is the nearest to Heaven most of us are likely to experience during our mortal lives."

"And so you want to fly, Eleanor?" Livy, whom I had carefully invited, asks.

"Oh, yes, flying is wonderful. It is entirely a matter of one's own responsibility. No other person can decide for you. Air travel," I go on brightly, so brightly, "air travel will bring about a complete change in landscaping and in the coloring of houses. Houses will be planned with an eye to the aerial view. Many towns will be air-conscious and do much to improve their beauty. I can see poetry written in large letters on their roofs."

"Darling!" Franklin smiles at me so. "You are splendidly, absolutely Delphic. I've thought of aeroplanes only as warships that fly. But, Babs, what of that terrific moral suppository you've offered me all these years . . . that Science will ruin Spirit? What of that?"

Some few at the table tittered at Franklin's rudeness.

117

"Better Science ruining Spirit . . . than husbands ruining Spirit." I cannot bring myself to laugh with Lucy's liquid laugh. I stand and look down at them all. They do not know why I've stood. Then I hold up my wineglass to Franklin, to Livy, to all of them, the candles from the chandeliers sparkling in the redness. "To Flight!" They stand. My eyes meet Franklin's across the table and his lips tremble on the crystal rim of his goblet. Mine do not. However, over the clear soup, he tells the story about the Frenchman who had returned to his lines boasting to his commander that he had just cut off the leg of a Hun.

"My brave man." Franklin is superb in French, not perfect, but superb. There is a difference. My French is perfect. "My brave man. And why did you not cut off his head, that Hun?"

"Oh, mon capitaine, it was already off, his head." And Franklin lifts his wineglass to me. Franklin, belching, apologizes. "History repeats itself." And belches again. He remains elegant nonetheless.

Armistice came the next morning. We all rejoiced. It was false. It came four days later. We all rejoiced. It was false. But we did not know it then. Boys and girls tumbled from the schoolhouses, government workers from the buildings; the bands played, rockets burst. My children filched pots and pans and wooden spoons from the kitchen and followed my servants down the street, banging and shouting. When Mr. Wilson appeared on his balcony, all Washington serenaded him, kissed and hugged and danced around the White House until the White House lights went out and the last band disappeared in the dark down Pennsylvania Avenue and the final notes of "Mademoiselle from Armentières" faded from the street and rolled themselves up in a small hard ball and lodged in my heart.

In the morning we hammered out the bottoms of the pots and pans and swept the confetti from the sidewalk and the war was over. Except for James who came home from school with a bloody nose.

"Dearest loving Ulla, I am well and hope you are the same. I got a letter from you today and was so glad to hear from you. I have another boil on my neck. Do you too? Well, Ulla, we went over the top again. We were all on the front line when the Armistice was pulled off and at 11 bells all firing was to stop, the battle waged on until the last minute and our artillery must of hurled about 200 shells over at the Huns. On the dot everything was quiet. So we got out of our dugouts and walked around. If we would of done that before 11 bells we would of all got knocked off. Well, about half past eleven, I thought I'd take a little trip over to see Fritz, which I did and I shook hands with quite a few of them and we talked about the war. We were happy, but they were happier still. The cooties are biting just now. They said we sure did throw over a lot of shells the last few minutes. Just think, fighting until eleven, and at half past, shaking hands. I could hardly believe it myself. They shot up all their different colored signal rockets at night, and it looked like the fourth of July. At night I was out on post duty and you could hear them singing 'The Watch on the Rhine.' Oh, what a happy day that was. The next day they came over with their brass band and we had some good music. Some of our boys gave some of them rice, meat, bread, coffee, etc. and you should of seen them eat. They said no wonder we can fight for the good meals we get. They sold off all their pistols and wanted mostly all tobacco. They went wild over our bread and tobacco. One fellow gave me a picture of himself and he wants me to write when I get home. To Frankfurt. Which won't be very long. The land in front of our line was all mined and they are exploding all of them now. They are also letting their prisoners go, for today 46 Italians came over to our town and were fed up. I got a letter from Jake and he is well and he says he is near me but I look my eyes out for him. I must go to bed now, so good night. From your true loving Bill."

IN WHICH BILLY BRAUN
COMES HOME

It was not long after the armistice, a month, almost Christmas, that Ulla came to me with a wire from the Navy Department. Immediately I thought it was an error: Billy was in the Army. But on reading it quietly to myself while Ulla stood weeping, it was, I saw, not an error. Something terrible had happened on the transport ship and Billy, instead of arriving in glory with his Keystone Division, instead of marching through the streets of Philadelphia and swaggering home to McKeesport, was in St. Elizabeth's Hospital for the Insane.

"At least he's near," I assured Ulla. But she was wild now with her grief, that impenetrability no word of kindness can puncture. Her life was ending. She didn't know the meaning of battle fatigue, the duration of rest periods; she knew the meaning of the hospital for the insane and she knew that Billy, Fighting Billy, had gone crazy.

"Dripping at the mouth he'll be and slurring and he won't even know me. I saved all the money. He's gone sick." Ulla began then to pull at her cootie garages and out of them drew small wads of money in bills and then at her bosom and out of it drew that grimy handkerchief and threw all three wads on the floor and then bent on her knees to count the coins and bills.

"I'm going home," she chanted as she counted, piling like with like, "I'm going home. If he comes home, then he comes home. I'm going home."

"You must go to see him first," I said from above her. She covered her piles with her hands. "You must have faith, Ulla."

"Going home. Dripping at the mouth he'll be."

"Is that all you've saved, Ulla?"

"Isn't much, is it? I suppose you and Mr. Roosevelt might give Ulla a little starter now I'm gonna be on my own without my Billy," she asked abjectly from the floor.

"One doesn't ask for gifts, dear, otherwise they aren't gifts."

"And how else does a servant like me get it?"

"Of course we'll give you a little when the time comes to go home."

"Well." She knotted up the handkerchief and stood before me. "You better get it ready cause I'm leaving tomorrow." Very rudely, and then she flew off to her room on the fourth floor.

"You can't do this, Ulla." I followed her, sprinting up the stairs after that insolence. "Your contract says I must find a replacement first."

"Oooo, oooo, I can do it." Her voice turned along the windings of the staircase down to me, swelling and narrowing as she climbed. "I can do anything. It's America. I'm going to find a replacement for my Fighting Billy first. Oh, I can do it very well, mum. I can do it very well. And I've had enough of you and your crazy children. The whole world is crazy. Whole world. Whole world. It's Bill that's regular."

By the time I reached her garret, she was kicking at the plasterboard and tearing clippings torn from the *McKeesport Journal* off the wall and only for a moment paused at the worn butterscotch mules by her cot which I knew to be the butler's because Franklin had given them to him. "Oh, this girl can do what she wants, Ulla can. This is America. That's what we're fighting for. To do what you want. 'Over there,' " she sang. " 'Over here. Oh, the Yanks are coming, rum-dum-dum-ming . . . the Yanks . . .' You need money to do what you want."

"You settle down, Ulla. On the bed with you. I'll charge you for the damage if you don't settle down." She fell upon the cot, arching and rearing, gasping, singing, rum-dum-dumming, until at last subdued by the thought of damage charges, she rolled over, lay with one arm folded behind her head, watching me, the ceiling, the other hand stroking her shoulders and thighs while I folded her rough things. She hadn't served splendidly at all and we would be well rid of her. The mules offended me.

I packed her few things, calmly, the letters, the marabout, scraps of clothes and linens, some worn spoons she'd ferreted from me. I said nothing about them except that I wished she had asked for them first and that she must see Billy as it was her duty. She began then to help me, scurrying around the floor on her knees from one corner to the other, to little nests of things I supposed I shouldn't see. Again I said nothing. She had lost so much and I had so much. I repeated that I would take her to see Billy immediately in the morning and we would tell him that she was home waiting for him, baking and waiting for him. Then she lay back on her bed, the salt tears rolling off the teapot face, fatter and whiter than I could remember it ever, and stroked herself again while I cleared her room. When her room was bare I stood at the door.

"I suppose you and the Mister might give Ulla a little starter now I'm gonna be on my own without my Billy," she tried again rather pathetically.

"Of course we'll give you something." I smiled. Insolence is only fear.

"I'll need fifty."

"Out of the question, Ulla. I'm surprised at you."

"Severance pay." She stuck her hand out at me.

"Well, then you will have nothing until I find a replacement."

"Well," she mimicked me, swinging her shoulders and chin. "Then I shall not go to see my Billy."

Much later, when I slipped the five-dollar bills under the door, ten of them, I heard her crying.

The money was drawn inward over the doorjamb.

"Please listen to reason, Ulla."

"I ain't gonna see Billy."

Then she pushed the door open and grinned at me with dry oyster eyes, white ugly oysters. She stood there, holding the slippers, one in each hand, stood there defiant and grinning. I was certain I'd heard crying the moment before. "Well, I ain't your servant anymore, mum. I can say what I please. This is America and I can say what I please. I'm free and I have one hundred and fourteen dollars. So I'm gonna tell you now. So you listen. I'm not staying here a minute longer. If you go off to Europe with the Mister like I heard, you better not leave these children here. There is something really wrong with these children. They don't like you and they got murder in their hearts. Your middle one took a knife to me."

"You're lying!" But I couldn't descend the stairs.

"Them kids are bad kids and they don't like you and nobody here likes them even your fancy Scots maid whose been having a time with I won't say who. Even you better find a way to stay home and mind them kids a little. Loving is what they need and they are not regular. There's no love to spare in this house . . . none at all. Especially the dark one."

"I'll expect you gone by the morning. I will replace all of you, someday they shall all be black. Black! Do you hear me? They know their place!"

The banister swam before my hand but I groped and followed it down.

IN WHICH I VISIT BILLY

The insane area at St. Elizabeth's was a horror of caged porches and sunless corridors reeking and resonating with excrement, loon laughs, bangings, vomit. The staff always brought one or two of the better ones, the ones who had simply been gassed, out to the auxiliary volunteers for walks. But this time I went directly myself into the insane area to see Billy and the doctor who had his records.

The doctor was small with a wide mustache and pained vague eyes that darted here and there off my face. I smiled at him. I made my smile quite as wide as his mustache but there was little response. He read to me. According to his shipmates, Sergeant Braun was normal until Tuesday last week. The ship was coming into New York harbor and he was on deck with his buddies. Everyone was cheering at the sight of the city lit up. The lights had been turned off all over Europe and there was the city, New York, all lit up and live and Broadway and you had to believe in America and what it stood for.

"What did it stand for?" I asked Billy who was standing in a dark and stinking zoo of a corridor with other inmates. One sat in a corner and pushed his eyes open and up with his forefingers. I tried not to pay attention to him for when I did, he screwed his loose fat cheeks and lips into gargoyle faces winking as if I had shared some private joke with him, which indeed I was afraid I might have. Bill was a feisty, narrow little man with a barrel chest and rusty corkscrew ringlets which he snapped out straight, one at a time, as we spoke.

"It stood for freedom, ma'am. Promise. Freedom. We . . . what we fought for."

"I see," I said.

"And then the Red Cross came alongside and fired a fusillade of doughnuts on board. Everybody was scrambling for doughnuts and laughing. It was so funny, them shooting doughnuts at us. And then they come on board to collect for them doughnuts. Well, we just saved the world. We don't have to pay for no lousy doughnuts. So we started shooting them doughnuts back at them. It was still pretty funny. And these two girls who I got to know pretty well on the trip over, sort of nurses they were, was standing nearby me at the side of the ship and acting sort of strange. I mean they wouldn't pick up any doughnuts to throw. So I picked up a couple and gave them some and they dropped them into the water. Not at anybody, just into the water. Ploppit."

"Ploppit?"

"That's the sound a doughnut makes when you drop it into the New York City harbor. Like lead."

"I see." Gargoyles sit on the roofs to carry away the dead. They nest with storks and work together from the rooftops. At times their paths cross.

"That water was dark, real dark. Nobody would give the Red Cross any money, for Chrissakes, 'scuse me, anyway, we

126

was pitching doughnuts at the Red Cross launch which was all lit up and then next to me one of the girls made this little sound. Like a hound when you got something to eat and they don't? You know sitting around a fire and they make that little sound, sort of a growl and begging. So I turn around to see if maybe she's choking on something and she's climbing. She's jumping and goes into the black oily water, and there's only that one splash, ploppit, and then off goes her sister. Right in the harbor. Right in front of the city and the lights. We're home. Two ploppits. Well, I yell and the . . . I yell 'Man overboard.' That's funny, isn't it? Ladies overboard. I don't think no *man* would jump overboard because of doughnuts. Ladies feel different about things, and they start playing lights over the spots but there's nothing at all. They was standing by me and then they was gone and nothing at all. I stood there all night long, ma'am. And I saw this sky turn pink and the sun started popping up bright red and lit up the place in a long streak, right where they'd jumped in, that sunstreak lay on the water and pointed right to the spot. My eyes really started to hurt a lot and . . . I mean the war was over . . . we were home. There were the lights and everyone laughing and they jumped. I mean I had to of missed something. There was something I didn't see. So here I am."

"Well, Bill, I don't have any sense that you are insane."

"Oh, I am, ma'am. I am very insane. I tried to jump into that spot. They stopped me. And I kept telling them those ain't real doughnuts. They're poisoned, I told them. Don't eat them."

"But they weren't poisoned, of course, Billy."

"I thought they were then. Something was wrong. I couldn't tell what. I didn't feel like I was coming home. I felt more like a little porkypine trying to go through a hedge backwards. I'm not leaving here until I find out what was wrong with them doughnuts."

I held out my gift to him. "Ulla sent you some iced lemon jelly and little cakes." He ignored my package and my deceit.

127

"Do you think you might get Doc Woods to let us go sit down someplace?"

"I think so," and I went farther into the corridor to find the doctor with his sheath of notes who found us a small porch occupied by an enormously fat soldier in a striped sweater and shabby white leather gloves. Watching me, he pulled his cuffs over his gloves, then pushed the cuffs up his arms, one after the other.

"Now, about Ulla, Billy. Surely you want to go home and find her. Surely you want to watch her bake and sit with her in the parlor and hug her."

"You been reading our letters, ma'am?" He moved to another chair to see my face clearly in a shaft of sun. I smiled at him. "Don't tell me you been reading our letters?"

"Ulla said she couldn't read," I began to explain.

"She said that, did she? Then how could she be bookkeeping in Howard's Department Store? Ulla went to school just like me. She said that, did she? And you read them to her? And did you write them for her?"

"Oh, Sergeant Braun, she told me what to say. I would write them and I'd give her little bits of money . . ." My voice trailed off. Watching me, the fat soldier wiggled ten gloved fingers at my face. James wanted white patent gloves for Christmas and a Flexible Flyer.

"Ulla's always been a little funny about money."

And Elliott wants a horse, "a Chinese horse what has a dandy saddle on it and a toy watch and a soldier suit." Billy bent over to unlace a boot although he wore slippers. The sun, the dust, someone, the fat gloved man moved and shuffled near us, staring at us, and then stood in front of us and defecated gently into a newspaper. Then he folded his newspaper, carefully, and put it on a shelf, turned and grinned and shuffled away.

"Billy," I said. "This is no place for you. You aren't like him."

"Git, lady, git out a here and don't bring me any more

garbage. Okay? Hey, buddy," he called to the gloved man, "have another sheet of paper?"

I pulled on my own gloves, horrified that Bill would also defecate, but he didn't. He folded his sheet of newspaper carefully into a pointed hat and placed it solemnly over his friend's package. "I don't need your lies any more than I need Ulla's, any more than I need poisoned doughnuts. No more. Now git. And if you see a Keystone boy around, you tell him about the doughnuts. They been cheated. They're just trying to get rid of us . . . all them doughnuts poisoned. They don't want us back in the country, that's what."

EXCURSION THREE
Paris, Winter 1919

IN WHICH I LEARN TO SHRUG

Paris was in mourning but when we docked and Mr. Wilson waved his top hat from the deck of the ship, Paris went wild. Vive M. Wilson! Vive! That moment as the Citroëns of the presidential party sped through the mud and rain, the chain dances, the crying, the weeping, the flowers, the prayers, Wilson was the savior of the world.

The face of Paris looked like my own. The Crillon, once a princess, stood gaunt and gray and hollow; her waiters' bones shone through their skin. Her rooms were cold, her fires damp, her silver laid out empty of food. The Ritz was even worse. The lights that blazed through the nights of my honeymoon were turned down all over the city and although there was still that fever in Paris, it was now a fever of illness, shortage, hunger, homelessness, cynicism. Europe was in pieces. The survivors huddled in the gutters of Paris under a chilling fishnet of rain: Kurds and Serbs and Poles and

Egyptians with scimitar noses and black capes and hordes of women in black veils down to their knees. I saw a woman in mourning clothes picking pieces of stained glass from a pram. I saw young rough Americans wandering the streets with textbooks from the Sorbonne and swallow-tailed diplomats with costive faces sitting at Versailles and fighting for the first two long days over whether the conference would be conducted in English or French. I saw two little boys, bone-thin, hinged, playing with marbles in the Tuileries Gardens and I watched them as they fought and then hit each other over a bright blue aggie as large as an eye.

When I arrived at the Ritz, my drawing room was overwhelmed with roses which I am certain, with the shortages in Paris, had been brought from England by Mr. Baruch, whom I met on shipboard. I was very flattered.

Franklin warned me to be careful. "The man obviously wants something."

"Don't we all," I answered.

"What do you want, darling?" Franklin asked offhandedly.

"Another aide for one. I can't tolerate that Duckworth person."

"Duckworth's a good man. Trenches for five years so I suppose he's a bit off, but if you got some sort of fancy chocolate-soldier type for an aide, I wouldn't have been given a driver also. With a crippled escort, you get a driver. Please don't make a fuss, Babs. That's not like you."

"His eyes roll up in his head. I don't like it. He limps."

"Well, leave him here and go out with the driver. Please, Babs. Don't bother me with it."

Roses and Duckworth arrived daily. As common as a horse trader, a huckster, Franklin haggled with the French over the best prices for American property. When I poked fun at him and told him that peace without victory meant peace without economic victory, he said: "Eleanor, if you had horses, you'd be a better trader than all of us put together. Don't you think so, Livy?" We kept Livy around, a buffer between us. Franklin filled the hotel room with bayonets and helmets and the Kaiser's pencil stolen right off the Kaiser's yacht—I supposed the Kaiser could have more than one pencil—and the women below filled the streets with their bastard babies and their black rags and broken teeth and yellow fingers and lice and disease and stubs of cigarettes stuck behind their ears and pink breasts, warm, cold, and they whitewashed what was left of their walls and scratched in the dirt for what was left of their lives and picked holy glass from their baby carriages.

On the outskirts of Paris, old ones and boys slumped on the curbstones and more women with my face flitted from cellar to cellar raising from the rubble what had been their homes and their gardens. Shells, grenades and skulls rode in their aprons to dump-heaps. And glass, so much glass. Yes, I too lost a husband to the war, I told a silent woman silently. "Yes, I lost my home and lived in the cellar of my despair with weeds in my garden, choking on my fruits, chewing on my wings. But I see you building," I said from the window of my long black Daimler.

One shrugged. Her black shawl hung over a fossil of a face, a baby at a full milking breast, a startlingly pink nipple, rich, poking through the edge of the ragged shawl. She came begging to my window, her hand extended.

"There is no one," she says in French, apologizing, complaining. "We have to live. With men. Without men. We go on." She shrugs and the nipple shrinks behind the shawl and the infant lifts up against her breast and falls with her sigh. "What do they fight for, the men? You can tell me?"

I had no answer. I gave her a handful of francs. She pulled the cigarette butt from her ear and lit it.

"What is there to buy? There is so much to do. God help us all."

My driver asked if I wished to drive on farther or return to the Ritz. I had nothing else to do. We drove on until dusk through broken roads and burned trees and railroad tracks shoveled over with earth, through the places of my holidays, through the places of my honeymoon.

With men. Without men. I tried a shrug. With Franklin. Without Franklin. I was with Duckworth on my way to Mrs. Worth's to order gowns for the next season. I didn't want to have Duckworth with me. Ox-eyed, unevenly gaited, he limped along in serpentine paths to avoid something I could not see on the sidewalk, eyes rolling up in his head. His face was a Darwinian campaign of knobs and boils enmeshed madly in a wreath of ginger beard, sideburns, and hair and stuck with a nose so sharp, so quizzical one knew there were dreadful excesses dwelling within.

Actually, I think Franklin chose Duckworth for me because Duckworth saluted Franklin regularly and attentively. There weren't many regulars who saluted civilian officials. I tried to walk far ahead of Duckworth. He panted and stumbled and rolled his eyes and caught up to me at crossings. At last, I took his arm and we continued along the avenue.

What do they fight for, the men? I have to do my duty, of course, Mlle. Souvestre always told me. "But the great difficulty," she said, looking at me in such a way I felt like a young queen, "the great difficulty, ma petite, is deciding where your duty lies."

Does it lie, I question the bidet in the hotel room, does it lie with the sanity of home and hearth? Does it lie with Franklin's destiny, that palpable creature we both live with, I ask as I am steered again across the boulevard for my second fitting at Mrs. Worth's, past the women on the streets, the prostitutes, the impoverished noblewomen, mad, wild, sexual. Mademoiselle from Armentières sans pork chops is now out on the streets of Paris and the men lean against her arching body in doorways, the crow's feather on her bonnet has a broken spine and her legs are spread. I ask what my duty is. Is that my duty? I have never seen such haunted desperation on the streets and in the salons. Women from fine

136

families seeking men with a fanaticism, an excitement, that equals war. Even Franklin is torn with curiosity, afraid as he is and struggling with the needs common to men, which—since I found Miss Mercer's letters—I had not fulfilled, although I lay in terror each night in the same room, in separate beds now, huddled into a large bony darkbrowed knot, everything on me crossed and knotted, keeping out, keeping out everything he is from destroying everything I might become.

He came to me one night again at the Ritz. I reached to turn on the light and sat bolt upright under a ceiling of amorous shepherds and shepherdesses and grinning sheep painted in pastels, and Franklin sat on the edge of my bed, his head in his hands. Trembling. I think he was trembling.

"Please come to me." His hand was on my hip.

"Do you close your eyes and wish I were she? Do you?"

He bent to look at me. "Your eyes look painted on, like sapphires, like sapphires painted on your face. I've never seen them so blue. God, too blue. Too white, like chalk."

He sat there waiting. His hands were withdrawn into his lap. "I don't ask for much, Babs."

Under the silk sheets clutched at my neck, I tried a shrug. "What will I do, Babs?"

Franklin stood up, over me, staring at me.

I shrugged again. It was slightly looser.

"You are a hard stone."

"Even lead can make the diamond suffer, can't it?"

"That damn book," he sighed, a shiver of a sigh, snapped off my lamp and climbed heavily into his own bed.

The shepherds and shepherdesses and the sheep withdrew into retroussé shadows and the lights from the streets slipped through rain-streaked windows to waver on the ceiling shadows, transversing, veins of silver and Viking winds, and Franklin smashed his fist again and again into the down of his pillows.

Ulla with her oyster eyes said, "In America I can do whatever I please. This is America."

The next day it rained and rained and drummed on the roof of the Ritz, on the roof of the cars, on the cobblestones, and it said we shall all be liquidated. Liquidated, liquidated. Duckworth was late.

"Franklin, why must I have an escort? I know Paris like the back of my hand . . . and a twenty-four-year-old from Surrey . . . really! He never stops talking, he lies terribly and he can't walk straight down a sidewalk."

"Paris is filled with scoundrels, darling. You can't go alone."

"Then let me go with *you*!"

"What interest could there possibly be in watching me haggle over the price of Navy equipment . . . for heaven's sake. Go shopping."

"He has excesses."

"Who?"

"Duckworth. He has the sharpest most quizzical nose I've ever seen and he looks like a . . . a . . . an animal with those gingery fringes all around his head . . . and he lies."

"Please, Babs, don't make trouble. He's a well-decorated hero, Duckworth, and comes highly recommended."

"I too."

"I too what?"

"I am well decorated, I am a hero, and I come highly recommended and I don't want that blabbering child foisted on me while I shop."

"You cannot go into the streets alone. What's come over you? You are so inflexible these days!"

"Then you come with me. I need help trying on hats and I have a final fitting today on three gowns and capelets."

"I have to sell a radio tower."

"And I shall be forced to stay home in this dreadful cold room all day if Duckworth doesn't come."

"Must you whine? It drives me up walls. . . . You can take a car over to Aunt Pru's or go visit your friend Virginia . . . there's a driver waiting if you wish."

The doorbell rang.

"Ah, problem solved. Good morning, Duckworth. There you are, Babs. Have a splendid day. Wish me luck on my radio tower."

"Jumping off it, are you, darling?"

"Have a nice day, Babs. Duckworth."

IN WHICH WE SEE THE LINE

We toured the battlefields for two days, from railhead to railhead, with Franklin leaping from his motor car, the hem of his father's leather coat dragging in muddy potholes as he squatted along a roadside and examined military maps. He and the men had one motor; Mrs. Spellacy, I and my good Major Duckworth another. Bone-cold rain knocked at the windows and hammered on the hoods. Franklin called in obligingly, engagingly; "Ypres, darling. Loos, dearest," as if offering me chocolates, and then we hiked up our skirts, took the Major's arm if the mud wasn't too dreadful, stepped under large black umbrellas held by the drivers, and looked equally obligingly, engagingly, about and across the terrain through field glasses. Mrs. Spellacy, poor soul, finally made the tactical error of saying that the battlefields looked alike and, although she continued to be invited out into the mud and the rain, she was disengaged. No one, not even her own husband, shared field glasses with her any longer.

Once I stood under those great black umbrellas beside the grave of my mother, under umbrellas and broken trees in fog. Fill the cracks with luten, gently cover the tracks with earth. There is no going back, no undoing death. My mother is gone. Understood? Understand. I accepted the field glasses from Franklin and nodded my head with interest and closed my eyes and swayed with nausea because I'd already seen and smelled the sweet-sick moldering flesh out there, the limb-strewn hillocks, skeletons hanging like scarecrows along the rusting barbed wire, their mouths drawn up into a grin, the stick outline of a downed aeroplane, a shadow, a stump, a ragged tree and the endless miles of shell-churned mud. Moths and rust. My mother had earth shoveled over her and the rain turned her earth to mud.

Some men, we were told, hadn't been shot. They had simply drowned in the mud.

"Extraordinary," I murmured and passed the field glasses. I understood this was war and it was a thing apart and it was over, dead, sinking into the bog, and the new order, the new world, would rise like a phoenix from it, revitalized. Even as we drove, the earth swallowed the war. There were moments our driver sped forward to lurch past something we ought not to see. But I saw. I saw skeletons of dead horses like great crushed birdcages and a German boot filled with flesh and a pair of arms folded across a chest but there was no chest beneath the arms, only the arms. One could look away. Six or seven million men sucked under, they said, some still near the top. We stopped for Thermoses of tea and Franklin asked how long it would be before the ground could be planted again and his driver answered rather dramatically, "It is already planted, monsieur."

When Mrs. Spellacy and I chose not to climb from the car,

Major Duckworth began, within the first hours, after muttering louder and louder to himself, to counterpoint Franklin's comments.

"Due respect, madam, it's more like ten million."

"Really?"

"Suicide Corner, Babs," Franklin told me through the window, gesturing toward the fields. "Isn't the trench system amazing? Remarkable."

"Due respect, madam, even with covering fire, no matter what we did, seven thousand died every day anyway in the trenches. Without taking a step outside."

"Bapaume, dearest. This was *really* the place."

"Up to the men, madam, the war would have been over Christmas, 1914. That's when we had the ad hoc truce . . . just climbed up and over and traded snapshots and Woods smokes, we did. I picked up a pipe . . . felt like a fool puffing on a pipe—little too fine—and our officers were up in a doodah. Told us never again to call our own truce. But next year, one of them merry Welshmen did. Got himself into the rum ration, he did, Christmas day and off he went . . . got shot from both sides. Bim and Bam. Officers wanted the war. They loved it. Just like him . . . uh, in due respect."

"Babs, Arras. Shredded willows. My God! Look at the tank."

"Muckety mucks, they felt different about war than us. We just queued up at Victoria Station all patient and docile like a queue for the loo. And we knew we had gems for officers because they had the spirit of the ancient race in their fine breasts and they'd all been to Sandhurst and knew how to sling a camel on a transport, knew where the tush teeth were in the sides of the camel's jaw, knew that blood is the sweet wine of youth. They get out to the Somme, madam, where we shall all soon be, and they're still memorizing the chapters. If we play the game . . . by the rules . . . we win. Just like a little Olympics. You win; we win. Take our turns, follow the rules. Be a good sport, mate, no gas, mate. Nobody thought it would last. We would have dug our trenches deeper. Nobody thought the ancient race would live like rats for five years."

As we drove from one battlefield to the next, Franklin unfurling one military map after the next, I found it increasingly difficult, the more of the trench system I examined, to comprehend the numbers of it. I tried. Yes, all those men churned into those fields shimmering now in liquid sun. Yes, and many more shells. Yes, more than four years. A new kind of warfare. Was it I who had sighed and sighing said, "Ah, War, all those men." All those men, swallowed. Trenches like vines; men like grapes. Where are the larks? I was trembling and swaying under the black umbrellas. But where will my mother be? Where does my mother go?

"Better watch the sediment in the bottom of your wine bottles, ladies and gents," Duckworth mumbled as we settled back into the motor. "Better watch it when you drink French wine." Our escort was not happy.

"And this is where they first used tanks. See . . . there's one over there. Over there, darling."

"Oh, my. Grand."

And was it I who had once said war was passion? The war I saw in the mud had nothing to do with passion. If war had anything to do with passion, it was just another bit of baggage in the knapsack, like the peppermint bull's-eyes we sent the boys for constipation, until someone had the grace to say, after shiploads of bull's-eyes, that the problem was quite the contrary. Well, passion was just as useless as peppermint, just another slug one sticks into the machine of war. But you can't tell where the gas is leaking from, Mama. Throw out your household books; throw out your bibles. Nothing works. Neither passion, nor poetry, nor prayer, nor bull's-eyes, nor Latin conjugations. "Up we'd go and over, madam, and between shells it sounded like an examination room for the fifth form. Everybody's reciting anything they know. Bam. This is the Slough of Despond. Bam. To be or not to be. Bam bam bam. Just keep dropping into the mud halfway through

143

their times tables. Fourteen times fourteen equals. Bam. Only thing that worked was smelling salts. And rum. Rum helped."

In a notch between two low banks on a road raised across marshlands, our cars came to a sudden stop. It was an old road, with bits of brick and rough stones, covered and covered and covered over centuries and finally paved. The stumps of burned trees along it were thick and twisted, braided with age, hazel and hickory. We stepped out to examine a deep pool in the road through which the driver refused to drive.

"You see, it is impossible, sir."

"Oh, try it, man." Franklin slapped the driver on the back. "We'll be hours before we get to Paris."

"No. No." From somewhere the driver found a large rock, struggled with it over to the pool. "Listen, sir." And then dropped it in. There was no splash. We could hear nothing. Weeds which looked too much like seaweed waved beneath the water.

"Take a cork, F.D. See what happens." Livy was on his knees looking into the pool.

"The water isn't flowing; it's stagnant."

"No, there are pools all around . . . see what the cork does."

"Which way is the sea from here . . . oh, look."

"Watch that pool over there."

Within moments, the cork appeared just to our left in another pool.

"You see."

"Livy, look at that. It's all floating to the sea. Everything's moving. Extraordinary. Under the hills."

"Well, let's find a place to turn around. Driver. On the map . . . here, we can bypass the circle around Richebourg. Strange feeling . . . everything moving beneath our feet. Strange, isn't it?"

I felt a sharp pain in my chest.

"You're looking at a survivor, madam. Duckworth, the

144

Hero of Attrition Hill. That's me. My regiment, madam, at full strength was eight hundred men. We never went over full strength and we have thirty thousand names passed through the regimental history for the last unpleasant event, as they say. Thirty thousand passed. You want to hear about war? I'll tell you about war. Oh, I'll tell you about the trenches."

"I think perhaps that's enough for now, Major."

"Sorry, madam. I do get a bit queer about it. Sorry."

"Don't worry. It's perfectly all right. It's just enough for now."

"It's going back and hearing your husband . . . with due respect."

"Perhaps you ought to have requested to be relieved?"

"Oh, no, madam, it's worse walking with you in Paris. I keep seeing corpses on the sidewalk."

"Dear man. I thought you wouldn't step on cracks. I thought that was . . ."

"Corpses. I know they aren't there, but I don't step on them anyway."

"I'm sorry, Duckworth."

"It shouldn't last much longer. I'm not the only one."

"It's the old world passing away," I assured him. "There's a new world coming. This is war and it's over now."

"Yes, madam."

I repeated and repeated and repeated "and it's over now" until we turned off the road to Richebourg. It wasn't over.

"Remember Richebourg, darling? When you first realized . . . ?" Richebourg—1905. I remember. "Franklin, I feel so sick Franklin—but I'm not sick." "Do you think it's something else? Oh, I hope. I do hope so. Darling. Dearest. If I'm to be a father then I will insist we see no more damned churches!"

IN WHICH I SEE THE END
OF THE LINE

There under the remnants of a ruined church a crowd of soldiers stood well within the area restricted by a hastily scrawled sign: NO LOITERING IN CEMETERY. The soldiers stood as I did over the shellhole made by a late-blooming bomb, and stared as fixedly, as morbidly frozen as I, into that shellhole in the little civilian cemetery.

It is very difficult to report with innocence my own innocence after losing it. I can no more imagine the state I was in when I went to Europe than I could have, en route, imagined my state on return nearly two months later. There were many things I had always believed. I had believed that one could reach out to love and beauty; that the world was in a state of progress; that through the unfolding, opening, evolving, the world was moving toward something more divine, more realized, less painful than the day before, and the duty of each of us was to enable, to bear witness, to contain, to be a part of the process upward. One had only to climb on board to believe, hitch your wagon to a star, be ready. Not as a leaf falling unchanged each autumn did man move; man moves spiraling always upward to some misty mountain peak . . . but I already give myself away. It is not easy to report innocence with innocence, for after I stood, leaned, nearly collapsed against the No Loitering sign and Franklin ministered to me with smelling salts, I could no longer believe in a meliorating universe. I had heard that the trenches were just too much to comprehend, too much, but as I stared into the singular horror before me, I knew my innocent incomprehension was done with. I looked into open vaults and graves, into a pool of greenish water with bones and skulls and spongy bits floating in that pool, bubbling and rising as water flooded in with new nightmares from the graves, bubbling to the surface in the pool and in my throat. It wasn't war. It was a civilian graveyard. Deaths in peace. Rest in peace. Life was death. Death was life. It was the other side. Only I standing above it was fixed. The unconscious was unhinged, the eternal was unhinged, the whole dream world welled up like a rusty button from a Civil War uniform in the rose garden. There is no end. There is no eternal or there is an eternal and it returns, eternal turning. I was my own wall. There were no other walls. All those things we've covered over so thinly with screens and grates and manhole covers and manners, they are all loosed now and rising from the very trenches of my brain. Whole landscapes shift, railroad tracks go nowhere, are covered with earth and become seas of mud. Nothing endures. Nothing is fixed. Not even the past. Not even my lead. I looked down into the unconscious and it didn't recede, eye sockets and butcher pieces drifting in a world of dreams. No Loitering. You also, Eleanor. You also. Each and every one of you. It was at Richebourg, close to the line and there was no line at all.

I could hear the grinding shifting noises of the rocks, far below the edge of light and the dew of the grass, far below where the dragon who shuns the sunbeams waits in the cavern of the metals. Shall I drown in my own acids? The fixed is unfixed; the unfixed fixed, congealing, dissolving, congested, digested and spat out.

I had been nauseated like this here, on this spot, on my honeymoon when new life welled up in me, acid and ungiving, vomiting up those juices here in Richebourg and now the caverns below the earth are vomiting up their juices and I am dizzy and swaying once again over this spot of foul air and the vinegars of fermenting bodies and vapors. There is a land of such a nature, that if you sow, it does not yield crops, but if you dig, it nourishes many more than if it had borne fruit. I am such a land. Inverted. The haunted catacombs of Richebourg vomit back at me; the eternal returning. I am part of that pool. It holds me. It clasps me by the great coiled serpentine braids on my head, by the filthy hems of my skirts it holds me. I have returned from the black and rusted russet mud and seen the flash of white bone on its crest and now I come to the green pool. Mortified, black; killed, white; promised, green. A middle-aged Alice in Wonderland with everything topsy-turvy and in my belly a loaf of lead, in the furnace of my belly a loaf of lead and I want instead a cake of silver, pure silver, stamped, with the handprint of God on its back. Or Franklin's profile on its front? Ah, we shall waken and find ourselves in a world greatly widened, I have been promised. This wide? This deep? Every vein has two out-crops, Mr. Hoover says. One to the daylight. One to the strike. I have let go of the daylight and taken a nighttime way, I, stepping over the dead in my long dark cape and my great russet coils with my face distorted by pain . . . I take the nighttime path. Here, at this moment. A death that is not death converges on a life that is not life and something is redeemed. I am no longer ambivalent. The lead is the child I must bring to life.

"Prince Ralph," Livy whispered tonelessly to Franklin. *"The Pool at the World's End."*

Franklin responded: "I read that! Where he goes to have the wounds of war healed." And then he remembered me. "Are you all right, Babs?"

"In a moment." I wasn't. My chest was tight with pain and my face flushed.

"You see? This is precisely why they don't want women at the Front. Come on, let's go. This is really too much. Major, my missus. . . ."

Poor Livy. He was green with fear. Major Duckworth took me to my motor and put me in near Mrs. Spellacy who had not been to the cemetery pit. Excusing himself, he returned with the largest and silliest dried sunflower I had ever seen and, with a salute, presented it to me for my bonnet, a gesture so insane it steadied me.

When we arrived back at the Ritz late that night, and Livy found his rooms were gone and he'd been given others, he lost control. Created a stir, as the British would say. Actually he screamed at the concierge and stamped his boots and banged his fists on the desk for his original rooms until, at last, Franklin shoved Livy into the cage elevator and we heard him rattling in fear and fury as he was lifted toward his new rooms. Franklin smoothed the flustered hotel staff, but in the morning when Livy discovered that it was Mr. Baruch's party that had taken his rooms and when Livy strolled by and saw the famous Jew with a pretty manicurist at each hand, a bootblack on one end and barber on the other, Livy carried on in the parlor until dinnertime about Jews and Polish dwarfs and the end of the white race.

I had no idea I was already ill. That night and the next and the following I burned with dry fever. And when the fever and the redness and the dryness of my face and hands slipped away in a warm bathtub, I rubbed from my ankles and from my heels and my soles, thumbfuls of dead skin, dead white ashes of myself. I am different. Something has happened. I stand looking through the leaded windows into the rain on the silvery streets and the rain shifts in double images

149

converging and diverging as I move from my center back and forth before the circles and squares of the leaded glass.

Lead makes a diamond soft. Even so, lead is silver gone wrong. Even so, silver is a prisoner of lead. Even so. How is it to be freed? The fixed is unfixed; the unfixed fixed, congealing, dissolving, congested, digested and spat out. I cried after my fever, dissolving, bewildered. I put my shoes and Franklin's shoes outside the hotel room doors for polishing and hope there will be elves to attend the birth of my soul. For that birth will be a lonely way, the longest way, through all the terrible stations of my lead.

IN WHICH I CALL ON
MR. BARUCH

When I called on Mr. Baruch to tell him about the pool in the cemetery and thank him for the armloads of roses and a Chinese pheasant, of all things to find in Paris, he was very sad, too sad to tell. We sat huddled by the fire, I in my purple wools, he in a black greatcoat, the fire hissing and puffing but never bursting into a blaze. Mr. Baruch forced the fire with bellows, open-close open-close as he spoke, the soft white long hands of the Jew feeding air to the fire, pouring water in the cups of earth for tea. Fire, earth, water, air, but it is porcelain, this cup he offers me, white porcelain. It ought to be pottery, luten, earth. No, not yet. The parts aren't ready yet. The lines don't transverse yet. But something is different in my head . . . my thinking is faster. Is it the fever? Is it that I saw the pool? The inner turned outer; the outer turned inner. I am part of that pool. What else am I part of? He leans forward, this emissary of the President's, this man of millions, and confides in me: "Europe wants its revenge. And we can't force their hand by moral strength . . . which they laugh at . . . but it is the only strength Mr. Wilson will allow us to use."

"Don't be silly. He may say moral force but he knows better."

"Then he isn't telling us the whole truth, is he?"

"He's waiting for you to use force."

"And so are the Europeans. But he won't use military force. And even if he did, military force would keep the dogs off only as long as we left a standing army over here, policing all of Europe. Can't. But they think the Germans are subhuman . . . Clemenceau is intractable . . . and I am being maneuvered to satisfy this country with this treat, that country with those spoils; nitrates and oil aplenty for America in case there's a war again. Everyone's already lining up their ducks for another war. And everyone wants souvenirs. Rumanian oil fields for instance are the prize this week." He collapsed the bellows and laid them in his lap. "I don't like to use economic force . . . it makes war all over again."

"Come, come now. You must know by now, Mr. Baruch, that money is immoral only if you do immoral things with it. If money can keep the peace, let us spend all we have." I clapped my hands together and then felt terribly childish.

"How direct you are. If only my wife were so direct. We could talk."

"It's quite new for me."

"Delightful. Would you like a corner of Alsace-Lorraine or the mining rights to Russia?"

"It looks as if Mr. Wilson wants you to use economic force but that he doesn't want to know about it . . . so you needn't feel guilty that you are going against his ideals. He may have two sets of ideals. You see? Now, my husband wants a football, only a football—the ones that were kicked about in the trenches."

"God, I wish he were Clemenceau . . . I would find him four thousand footballs. Clemenceau wants heads on platters. Mr. Wilson is willing to give in at many junctures because he figures if he gives a tad here and there on the treaty, they'll buy the League idea and then the League can rejudge all the tads he gave away. Gamble. Big gamble."

"You're doing that also, though, aren't you?"

"Not the way he is. It's like talking to Jesus . . . excuse me. I'm sorry. You see, Mr. Wilson thinks he's the first man to come along in the last two thousand years who knows anything about peace. You can't tell him anything. You have to believe him . . . I do . . . God, I do, but you can't *tell* him anything. Clemenceau tried. Wilson said he wanted a permanent peace. Over and over. Finally Clemenceau, old as he is, leaped up and shouted at him: 'All right, we can make this a permanent peace. We can remove all causes of war. All right.' "

"Really?"

"Wilson turned white. Even that sham Lloyd George was nonplussed . . . what does *nonplussed* mean, Mrs. Roosevelt?"

"Baffled, perplexed. Can go no further, at a standstill."

"Oh, well, plussed." Mr. Baruch laughed. "Lloyd George jumped up and down." Then he stopped laughing abruptly and rose from the hearthside to walk around the parlor. "The old Tiger was after Lloyd George's throat too. 'We must first give up our empires and all hopes of empire,' he shouted. 'England must get out of France, out of India, out of Africa; America out of Puerto Rico and the Philippines . . .' "

"Oh, my!"

" 'All must throw away their keys to the trade routes and surrender their spheres of influence. Are you willing to pay these prices? No?' And then he jumped up, hit the table once again. 'You don't mean permanent peace. You mean war!' He said that to Mr. Wilson."

We were both silent then—Mr. Baruch pacing the room with his truth, I before the weak heat of the fireplace. There was no belief in peace. Only revenge. Sweet revenge, sweet as the smell of burned flesh in the wet air, sweet as men on crutches and women moaning in cabarets and children in black. "M. Clemenceau was a child when Louis Napoleon took the throne. I think he must know what he's speaking about."

"Yes. I think he does."

"And so?"

"And so I find oil and nitrate for America and make certain we get the oil fields and plenty of German tonnage in our bags and all the free markets we want . . . except we don't give any free markets away. It won't be a fair-minded treaty because one doesn't dare to be fair-minded. It's a waste. The whole business."

"Despair is not worthy of you, Mr. Baruch, nor is complacency."

"Nor of you." He sat down and took my hand. "In Hebrew, *Baruch* means 'blessèd.' Knowing you, I feel closer to my name. I feel just a tad blessèd, knowing you, Mrs. Roosevelt."

"You must see something in me that others don't."

"They will. They will. You're what we call a long shot. That's Wall Street talk."

"Well, I too have a secret for you. Since I've been in Paris, I have been learning to shrug." I lifted my shoulders. "A one-shoulder shrug . . . and a two-shoulder shrug and then, my pièce de résistance, a shrug . . . like so . . . with a smile. Do I shrug well, Mr. Baruch?" I had retrieved my hand.

"Madam, as far as Baruch is concerned, in all that generous frame of yours there is not one real shrug." He bowed and I thought about Moses and Abraham Lincoln. "This was was such a waste. This peace is such a waste."

"No. No, Mr. Baruch. You and I have learned, haven't we, that we must work—spend our lives to uphold the dignity of man and self-determination. I'm afraid what you have seen and have had to back away from, Mr. Baruch, dear Mr.

Baruch, is that the world is entirely interdependent . . . that we are all brothers."

"Another time."

"Even if we fail . . . we must bring that message to the people."

"To know that . . . and to know how low human nature really is . . ."

"Terrible."

"Dear Mrs. Roosevelt." Mr. Baruch again took my hand, standing above me. "My family is coming over and I've taken a house outside Paris. Won't you come and meet my children and my wife?"

"Oh, my, we're leaving so soon . . . I have so many relatives to see still and shopping to do . . ."

"I understand . . ."

"I want to . . ."

"Of course."

It was such a shame Mr. Baruch was a Jew.

IN WHICH I VISIT AN
OLD SCHOOLMATE

With my Aunt Pru tut-tutting miserably all along the twelve-mile drive from Paris to La Celle Saint-Cloud and Major Duckworth up front with the driver, we passed in the net of driving rain, through long avenues of broken poplars, through towns, their edges softened and rounded by shells and their people gone. The fields were empty of cows and sheep. Here and there, smoke floated in wreaths from a stone chimney and a lonely cow was tethered to a stump or to the front door of a cottage. We passed the luminous heights of Saint-Cloud and then cut through the woodlands, down through Garches with its cluster of prerevolutionary cottages, and then on to Virginia Littlejohn's chalet which stood on the border of the royal woods between Versailles and Saint-Germaine, the haunts of Louis and Madame Pompadour. Virginia was, as she had been in our schooldays at Allenswood, still talking about pets and herds. She'd grown up in Kensington, married, divorced, written a slim book of poems about Delhi where she'd never been, belonged to an arty set in Paris but was in no way herself artistic. She was tweedy, long-legged, wore heavy country shoes, a moth-holed sweater. Her house was freezing, her ashtrays filled with cigarettes, her tables with Socialist magazines. I assumed Aunt Pru came along to protect me from Virginia's politics.

True to form, Virginia apologized immediately for her cow. "Kerry Cow is making her nasty noises. You must forgive her. She lives unhappily beyond my hedge now and can't wander in her best places and she and that *brute* of a donkey whom I have never seen—he's gone wild now—have it out at each other all day long."

Her chalet was just as she had described it in her letters over the years since our girlhood. Everything was reached by a wooden staircase and balconies which ran around the outside of the house, so that one entered the first-floor bedrooms through the French windows from the balcony and the second-floor garrets in the same manner. The balconies overlooked Madame Pompadour's woods, the Seine and the tethered cow tied to a pear tree just beyond the kitchen gardens. The ground floor contained a dining room, a drawing room and the kitchen. In the kitchen a skulking, ratty pug named Charles Horse sent Virginia into further apology for her animals as she laid out a sparse tea on Sèvres china.

"They aren't at all like your American dogs . . . American dogs are always all over you and perfectly silly. French dogs now are small and nasty and antisocial. Although one can't blame Charles Horse. French dogs are like the French I'm afraid. They actually avert your gaze whereas most dogs I know, have known, are social and seem to relish humans. Don't you think so? Tea?"

We were perfectly exhausted from following her about the house and listening to her battery of animal lore. Virginia

157

had always been very shy and had always talked too much. She lit a cigarette and Aunt Pru, sniffing, settled herself in a window seat far from the side-chairs Virginia and I chose. Virginia smiled indulgently. "Aunts." She orchestrated her own words with the smoking cigarette in little circles at shoulder height, toward me, away from me, thrusting, withdrawing.

"I haven't seen many cats or dogs in Paris at all, Virginia."

"Well, what's left, of course, is shifty-eyed also, slow but with wily wits. Peasants. Like the people. Of course the dogs and the cats . . . the most trusting ones went into the pots long ago and the remaining have . . . uh, lemon, Eleanor?" She ignored Aunt Pru who clearly wished to be ignored. "One lives longer if one learns not to trust."

"I hope that only applies to dogs, Virginia. But, now that we've blockaded Germany, if this is what happens to animals, the ugliness, can you imagine what the eyes of the German children will look like after five years of war and starvation? Mr. Hoover reported to the Red Cross that three and a half million German children are already subnormal. You can imagine what the children whom we have starved will look like . . . that demented look nothing can ever feed. Franklin says we're making a terrible mistake to starve them. They'll be the next army."

"Does he say that?" Virginia stamped her cigarette into her Sèvres saucer. "Do you recall, Eleanor, at Mlle. Souvestre's, it was possible to have your father send extra money so you might have bacon on your plate each morning? The rule was finally disallowed, after our time, but do you remember the hatred and unhappiness bred in our hearts because our fathers for some reason—either shortage of funds or a desire to breed stoicism—sent no bacon money? Do you remember how we felt about the girls who had bacon? That smell each morning?"

"Dear Virginia, I believe I must have had bacon . . ."

"Oh, yes, of course, but then you were American. How

silly of me. Still, they were wonderful days, weren't they? Mlle. Souvestre taught me how to *think*."

"Tut-tut," Aunt Pru addressed her teacup.

"Oh, I too," I agreed readily and Virginia's teacup paused midair, that almost indiscernible second and then was set down softly. "I understand," I was quick to add for I could feel the blood rushing upward to my cheeks, "that the men in Germany are fighting for turnips in the streets. Killing each other."

"Men would, wouldn't they? German men are so silly. That's why they lost the war. Americans think Americans won the war. The simple truth is that the Germans lost it."

Aunt Pru was smiling beatifically into her saucer, and I knew her cup, although it had been empty for a very long time, was indeed running over.

"Do explain yourself, Virginia."

"Yes, indeed," Aunt Pru added. "A claim of that nature involves an enormous amount of courage." Her voice quivered with animosity.

"Well." Virginia took to striding round the room. "There was no progress, I think, until the Germans . . . oh, by May of 1918, had simply won too much. After they broke through the Fifth Army, you know. And they began to raid the wine cellars at . . . oh, wherever it was, and drag silk curtains back to their trenches. And it was then, when the Germans had run out of steam, that you Americans arrived. Perfect timing. You would have been slaughtered a week earlier. Of course you did bring the war to an end." She raised her teacup to Aunt Pru. "But everyone wanted to stop by then except those who wanted to win. It was such a parody because we all knew the war would never end and at the same time we were all perfectly convinced England would win."

"You do mean 'paradox,' don't you, dear?" Aunt Pru called over.

"No, I mean exactly what I say."

Aunt Pru clucked away. I continued to say "Well" periodically into the silence about us. I didn't dare look at Aunt Pru. Unfortunately we had another ten minutes before our driver would return. Virginia bent forward to me, whispering: "Poor old thing, is something wrong with her dentures?"

I executed a fine shrug. Both shoulders and vacuous eyes. "But of course, Virginia, you do know the Allies won . . ."

"Don't be goosey, Eleanor. Whatever has happened to your *mind?* No one won. War won. It always does. Always. And I shall never again have anything to do with men, for men are war. Never shall I be touched by one, support one's career, live for one. Never. Not so much as a cup of tea shall I give to one."

"Men perished in the war."

"Ah, but that was working class. The managerial class . . . they are responsible for the war. The working class has small hopes and strong beliefs. The upper class has great hopes but no beliefs whatsoever."

"Is not hope a belief?"

"Hardly. It's a vicarious pleasure, hardly a conviction. But let me go on." We had no choice. She lit a second cigarette. "The men who control the marketplace controlled the war. The others were always just fodder for the management's projects. Men are born to slay. Now," she paused again and I so wished we had only spoken of pets and herds, "now, I want you to know I'm happy. Some people—" she jerked her head toward Aunt Pru, "say I'm not. But I am. Eleanor, I have taken a woman to love. That does shock you, does it not?"

"No, not under the circumstances. But that's a subject obviously we could dally over for hours, and it is time for the motor car, so we shall save that for the next time, shall we not? I must meet Franklin and our dear friend Livy at the hotel at half five and have a supper ready for them, in their rooms. So then, God bless you, Virginia."

"God's a man, Eleanor. All that's rot."

Of course I never saw her again. In the motor car, I thought I had been fairly deft until with great authority Aunt Pru

160

pronounced very slowly, majestically, "This is for insulting England," and drawing the Sèvres saucer from her arm bag, laid it in her lap. "And this," she placed the teacup precisely on the saucer. "This is for insulting America. And the teaspoon for insulting my family. Dreadful woman. Dreadful."

Duckworth pulled all of his ginger fringes over his face and hid behind them until we dropped Aunt Pru and her war reparations at her apartments.

"With due respect, madam, your auntie is nice and nimble."

"Hush, Duckworth."

"Was the lady all that bad, madam?"

"No, no." I answered thoughtlessly. "Bitter, avant-garde. Very very avant-garde. Doesn't believe in war *or* God *or* men and loves women."

Duckworth was thoughtful. "Due respect, madam. She and I would have a lot in common."

"Oh, no. No, Duckworth, how funny. No, no. Not at all. Not that way."

"Oh, ho! That! Why, I should have pinched me a teacup myself."

IN WHICH MRS. WILSON
AND I VISIT THE WOUNDED

Mr. Wilson said he didn't want to starve the German people. Mr. Wilson insisted that the German people themselves weren't responsible for the war; M. Clemenceau and Lloyd George and others, just as Mr. Baruch said, thirsted for revenge. "In England," Lloyd George apologized privately, to Mr. Wilson, "my people are stoning dachshunds and with a general election on the immediate horizon, my people expect me to insist on the harshest of measures." Everyone else, particularly Clemenceau who made no apologies, wanted a blockade to force Germany into accepting the treaty. It was agreed that since all the Germans fought, all the Germans would starve. Mr. Wilson studied the maps of Europe. Mr. Wilson prayed. Germany starved.

The newspapers of Europe were about to turn on him. He hadn't brought peace without victory; he was being too idealistic. The papers couldn't decide what they wanted either. They turned first, tentatively, on Mrs. Wilson. She hadn't been to the Front or the hospitals, how could she know what the war had been like? Out of loyalty to my country, I took it upon myself, after having had a nice tea with Mrs. Wilson at the British Embassy, to invite her and Aunt Pru to visit a British hospital—in Neuilly, I think it was—and to my delight, Mrs. Wilson accepted. I invited Franklin to join us and although he was impressed with my coup, he declined. If he came along, he said, it would look political. Otherwise it would simply be women's charity—a remark I found insulting. Nevertheless, I was as pleased as punch with myself when we picked Mrs. Wilson up at her apartments and drove, with an escort and a press car following us, out to the hospital. People cheered along the road.

Mrs. Wilson was no one's favorite in Washington. She was short and plump and painfully corseted so that everything extra seemed to be stuffed up into her bosom and her chins and cheeks.

Just before we all left for Europe, Sommerville-West, the aide at the British Embassy, had apparently told a joke about her in public and she, highly incensed, had him returned to England. The joke was: What did Mrs. Wilson do when Mr. Wilson asked her to marry him? Why, she fell out of bed. Remarks like that can undermine the best of relationships between countries. It was also very clear, troublingly clear, that Mrs. Wilson had undue and unwarranted influence on the President's decision making and on his relationships with foreign countries. Since we'd all been served by her when she was Mrs. Galt of Galt's Jewelry Emporium, we found her current Dowager Empress Act sickening and un-American. But she did carry herself well that day in Neuilly, at Red Cross Base No. 1, with great courage and dignity, and by the end of the day, no matter what else I thought, I had a new respect for her strength, if not her judgment.

It wasn't until I visited at the hospital, until the actors

163

climbed wearily onto the stage, that the mud took life, that War unfolded for me like a bleeding lily. Mrs. Wilson had wisely requested that our party not be trailed by every nurse and doctor in the institution, saying we would want only two nurses so as not to create any more of a stir than was necessary. The two nurses assigned to us, starched and prim and pretty, led us to a ward of amputees. Of course, we were shown every deference and the ward was spit-and-polish clean, but the sense of having stepped into a madhouse was as clear as it had been when I visited Billy at St. Elizabeth's, except these men, most of them, had no faces, no lips, no noses, no mouths, no eyes, no chins.

Where other things ought to have been, they had great plaster lumps. "Left me chin in the mud, ma'am," and from somewhere behind an empty chest as I stood over a bed came a gurgling sound like laughter, a gleeful piping.

It was, obviously, a great moment for the men. The wife of the President of the United States stood above a bed and, laying a single dramatic red rose on a form of white plaster, murmured "Honorable wound."

From within the plaster, a hand reached out and up and snatched at the official hand. She drew back as I did, but her hand was tightly gripped. It was as if something else were inside the plaster. You come across a lobster within a shell, under a rock. And something suddenly reaches out and holds you. It was awful.

"Come closer," he was whispering to her. "I want to tell you what happened to me." Around us, the other men who could, lifted up on their elbows, listening.

"You see, my brother was making his bit of tea in the trenches and I was coming across the duckboards to visit with him as I had a package from our mum . . ."

"British," I pronounced for no reason to Mrs. Wilson as if, not American, we could somehow remove ourselves from him, but Mrs. Wilson couldn't remove herself except with a real wrenching which would have created headlines across the world. I felt very sorry for her and would have come to her aid but the poor fellow to whom I had spoken at the next bed also had a tight grip on my arm. I thought perhaps Duckworth had set up this prank . . . but it was too serious and Duckworth would not have allowed me to be hurt, which I was being at the moment.

Of course it was a prank, but their truth lay in the hollowness and rattling laughter. "I'm quarter man," my patient whispered. "And three-quarters shell. Hah hah hah."

"And he was making his tea, Archibald was, bit of it, and Mum had sent over some jolly biscuits so off I go over the old duckboards with some of those nasty mortars whizzing by my ears, here and there but it was daytime and I was down low and blimey if one didn't drop hard somewhere up front of me. Thought nothing of it, I did, and then just as I am coming round the zigzag to my brother's place, there they were: three of Archibald's company looking down over the hole and there were bits of old Archibald splashed up against the parados . . . and there . . ." he wheezed and coughed, which was genuine and horrible, ". . . and there and there under the old duckboard was my brother's eyeball. Bright blue it was, right under the old duckboard. Alas, my poor brother."

Through my heart, I felt a thin barbed thread, a bloody floss, pulled back and forth, and in my bowels my parts were constricted as the thread caught in my heart. Cobalt blue in the mud. Back and forth. The ward broke into gales of laughter, chortling, whistling, roaring, those who could, wheezing, those who wheezed, bubbling, some of them just bubbling. "You'll crack your plaster, mate."

I've seen it, I thought. The two boys in the Tuileries have it now, in the dirt among the marbles.

"Under the duckboard it was. Bright blue." Which brought on new roars and wheezings.

"Cheeky beggars!" Nurse yelled at the men. "The whole lot of you! Gormless!" She started to cry.

"Ah, stuff it and let him have his time."

"This is the President's wife, of America!"

That brought on new torrents of laughter. And those that could chorused: "Alas, my poor brother." The nurse in tears ran for help and the boy holding my arm whispered in words like a fog: "Listen, madam, no one won."

"What is it?" I asked. "I can't hear you, son."

"No one won. Tell them. The war won. Tell them. Had its big feasts it did. Ate up ten million and left the bones and the bits in the mud. You tell them."

"I will. Yes."

A squadron of nurses and staff flew into the room to release us. And it was over. The boy's fingerprints were scarlet on the white of my own flesh.

We left to their laughter, lifting up, bubbling up like black blood from punctured lungs. Those smiles along the barbed wire? Those skeletons one after the other with mouths drawn up into a grin? It was the same grin drawn up in the faces of the men who were without mouths, who whistled when they laughed. Alas, my poor brother. Alas.

"But where are all those bodies, Franklin? One cannot bury ten *million* men in a narrow strip of land. The neat rows of markers all going up and down in straight lines . . . they aren't even real, are they?"

Franklin had inches of paperwork before him and the skin was black and drawn under his eyes. "I don't suppose. I do hope the British didn't get themselves organized and put the markers in alphabetically."

Under them are the same green pools with the bits shoveled in, bits of things plucked decorously from the mud if they seemed to be human. "Where are all the rest of them?"

"The rest of what, darling?"

"You aren't listening, are you? Where are the rest of the bodies, the parts, the people?"

"I don't know, Babs. How in the world should *I* know? Ask your Duckworth. Why ask me?"

"My, you are testy tonight. I only thought . . . you seem to know so much about the war. . . ."

"Well, you're pushing me and I don't like to be pushed. I don't *know*."

Duckworth told me the rest went to the Tallow Factory at Eatapples. "Perfect French dining, madam, light the candle and pour some wine, fe fi fo fum . . . et cetera, et cetera."

Eatapples remained as much of a mystery as ever, although I did discover that Eatapples was Etables, an actual word on a map, and sometimes Eatables. I went home to America not asking any further questions, not discussing what I saw or what I felt, the floss through my heart too bloody, too awful. I couldn't comprehend the immensity of it.

"Dear Billy" I wrote. "I have found out something for you about the doughnuts. The problem is, I believe, that we didn't win the war. Of course, neither did Germany. The problem is that War won. Most sincerely, Eleanor Roosevelt."

EXCURSION FOUR
Boundaries,
Spring through Fall 1919

IN WHICH GENERAL PERSHING
COMES HOME

"What is this clutter, Babs? Can't you have someone remove this clutter? There's no room whatsoever for my models."

He is looking for a smooth surface but every flat plane in our home is filled with flowers and Comet Building Blocks and notes and records and letters and reports.

What am I to do? I had gone at Christmas before our European trip to ask Uncle Ted, stricken and swollen and dull-eyed in a hospital bed. "Uncle Ted, what am I to do about Franklin? The woman. He is so unhappy. What am I to do?"

"Promise him his career. Keep him from being bored. That's what makes us fools. The intolerable boredom stirred only by the arched eyebrows of our equally boring women. The lines of those brows are the spades of our graves. And we revenge ourselves upon them and upon our fathers by becoming heroes. The only freedom we have between naughty and nice is war."

I have seen him with his ships. "Clutter, Babs, what is this clutter?"

"It is our lives, Franklin. That is the clutter."

"You see, Uncle Ted," I explained as a nurse entered his room with medication and he waved her imperiously away, a brave last act. "You see, for Franklin, nothing is ever allowed to interfere with what he thinks is important to him."

"Yes," Uncle Ted answered blandly. "That's correct."

"When a man becomes a hero, Uncle Ted, then are his thirsts satisfied? His debts paid, his parents put to rest in their places?"

"Do you mean, my darling niece, to ask me if Franklin will stay home once he has advanced his career satisfactorily?"

"Yes. Will he?"

"We are just boys, you know. Just boys." Uncle Ted's voice softened, dreamily, drifting into the Veldt, the Amazon. "I ruined myself by going to South America on this last hunt. I'll never be well again. But it was my last chance to be a boy. Just one more time."

"Is that what he wants? To be a boy?"

Uncle Ted seemed surprised I was still there. "Why, he wants to be a hero. A hero out there, a baby at home. He wants his mother to recognize him as a man but still care for him as an infant. He wants to die of his wounds but complain of his tummy-ache. He wants to take his father's place and die a hero so he doesn't have to be his father. Quentin has taken my place and died a hero and I'm the old dinosaur, terrorizing silly nurses. Urinate in the snow, scratch your initials in the sands of time. That bullet in Milwaukee? I was the madman, not the madman. I was so tragic and then so embarrassed that I didn't die. Oh, the zest is gone Eleanor. I'm an old man."

"What shall I do with Franklin, Uncle Ted?"

"You want to keep him with you, don't you, dear?"

172

"Yes."

"You love him?"

"Terribly. He is my life."

"Women are so strange."

"Please, Uncle Ted."

"Make him President. That should keep him home for a while." And then he turned his face to the wall and although I held those pudgy swollen fingers, the face that looked so like mine I would never see again. "Eleanor, don't forget, Ted Jr. wants to be President also. Don't let Franklin get too nasty. He can be so competitive. Do what's right."

I always wondered if Uncle Ted actually was a great man or just very, very noisy.

In New York on Fifth Avenue, eight buxom ladies with silver crowns on their heads and white oxfords on their feet stretched an American flag between them and marched four on each side with tears running down their cheeks and perspiration down their arms onto the flag. People climbed on the black tops of cars and on the roofs of trolleys lined up along the parade route and swarmed eight and ten deep on the sidewalks and hung, clusters of them, office workers, from the windows and the balconies of the buildings and everyone, hundreds and thousands, cried, shrieked, sang, cheered and tossed carnations to the marching soldiers. I had never seen so many carnations. A thousand loins quivered, a hundred thousand loins quivered, horses' loins, Pershing's loins, generals' and privates' loins, lady loins, everyone's loins quivered at the immensity of the moment, at the joy of the great hero, his horse sweating, prancing, horse nostrils bursting with the nascent honor of the lionized loinized man riding him, horse rectums bursting to the thrill of the parade, defecating, ploppit, all the horses on all the white carnations under their hooves, beating carnations into dung and weapons into plowshares and white oxfords into brown until the entourage of old men on high wheelers, the old soldiers with their fool bicycles with the enormous wheels, pedaling along over the pastiche of love and manure, petals and war, their eye-high wheels twisted and wound with red, white and blue strips of crepe paper, medallioned with clumps of carnations, pedaled through the mash and lifted the clumps of it in widening circles onto their high wheelers and then whipped it off and out onto the knees of the crowd bringing up the rear.

When the parade was over, the sweepers in their metal helmets and white uniforms came along in a formation of push brooms, behind the high wheelers, and Black Jack Pershing and his horse went off to Washington, where the General was presented with a hand-carved regency desk twice the length of his horse and invited to address Congress.

Franklin reserved a seat for me in the balcony so I could hear General Pershing speak.

There is General Black Jack Pershing speaking to Congress. He has not brought his hero's horse and he looks quite small. The other heroes in Army uniforms sit in a bank before him and behind him the President of the United States, Mr. Wilson, flickers like a dying candle. They sit, the heroes, basking in the first circle of Congress. In tiers and banks sit the lesser men and in the balconies the mothers, wives, admirers. I am all three. I see my Franklin there on the floor below me. He is third from the left of the podium, on the outside, but in the first circle. He sits simply with his vest and his pocket watch and his pocket-watch chain hanging from his lapel to his pocket and his superb head and a finger on his cheek and two fingers across thin lips, legs crossed at the knees, stretched out, limply noble, arrogant, the hero of the Chevy Chase Club, the Harvard Club, the Saloon, the Salon, a hundred thousand supper parties, the Brooklyn Navy Yard and the Arlington Flats where I hear they have been seen also in a car and a cabin in Virginia Beach where I hear she registered in my name.

Franklin is losing his hair, I see from above, and his hope, I know, and his leanness and his thrust. He presents himself as older, stable, content, but still he looks so awfully hungry. There are people who avoid him, invitations we do not receive. Franklin has spoken for the League since our return, but Mr. Wilson hasn't spoken to him. Franklin burns with that terrible hunger of his as he watches General Pershing's sharp little jaw jump up and down with mighty phrases. Franklin, the doughnuts are poison, Franklin.

He watches the lesser generals, his eyes floating like a pair of gray vultures, sweeping along the clusters of golden eagles and epaulets, the scrambled eggs on their hats, the venerable swords and beards and medals. I see on Franklin's face that hunger for power which I have seen before on all the men in Washington as they watch each other burn up in the cremation they call career. Franklin burns brighter than most.

And I? I am not immune to General Pershing. I watch him and dream also. Have I not dreamed of Évian? Have I not dreamed of the sergeant? Have I too not dreamed of triumph? Have I too not dreamed of fame?

Under my barbarous feathered bonnet stuffed with birds shivering and shaking I wait for the General to look up into the balconies and sense the fire in my face, aglow, as I look into the face of the hero. "Come here, child," I imagine. I go to him with violets. "Come here and I shall with these hands of history, these very hands which strangled the Hun and cut off his suspenders, I shall pat your dear and courageous little head." "Oh, general, I don't give a darn for history. All I care about is love," I say as I lean over the balcony under the gleaming glass roof and see that Franklin is sulking.

It is because the General has just said, "As for the Navy, where would we have been?" Congress cheers as the General dips his head stiffly and swiftly toward Mr. Daniels and the admirals but their smiles are as icy and salted and bitter as the North Sea because the Navy had not fought. The German fleet, surrounded by the eminent British and American navies, sat in the eerie ashen calm of Scapa Flow and those barbarians, those heinous criminals, I have heard it said by

Franklin and the Navy men, those Huns who had not the courage for a sea duel, pulled the plug and sent the most magnificent battle of all time down the drain. The oceans closed over. There was no blood stirred. It was not the act of gentlemen. It was, that battle, what each Navy man had coveted as his heart's desire, that final smashing, sinking, full-speed-ahead, exploding, bully, burning, screaming sea duel and now we'd won the war to end all wars and never again would there be a war at sea. Criminal. Heinous. We never used the fourteen-inchers that can smash a hostile fleet at twenty miles; the twenty-two-inchers from Watervliet are still in their crates, untried. The admirals sulk and Franklin still waits to hear his own feet clicking up the stairs of paradise in the vast halls of the sandcastle of War as he runs to the map room ramrod and burning and slippery because no one else is there to give the order when the wire comes in just as it had come in when Uncle Ted was Assistant Secretary of the Navy and sent the fleet to Manila and became President because his boss was out of the room and he acted.

Franklin is waiting to act, to dance himself up the stairs, to a place, a space, an opening in the marble. He amuses himself watching Pershing. He watches himself and amuses himself. Later, strutting in our living room with sharp little teeth and the little chin up firm and high, arms swinging like a windup toy, Franklin will imitate Pershing and then imitate Franklin imitating Pershing, a mirage, a mirror of mirrors, shimmering. Poor Pershing, man of few words, clearing his throat, nervous and stumbling over the barbed wire and minefields of ideas like bravery, justice, and honor while the reporters record his terrors and errors for history and everyone else in the room is waiting for him to make a fool of himself.

"As for the Navy, where would we have been without their convoys, their cargoes, their transports, without the North Sea mine barrage?" I can see Franklin stiffen. The barrage had been, he said, his idea, and he had fought uncompromisingly for it. "Although the Germans actually lost only six or eight submarines in the mine barrage, that one barrage, that one magnificent idea, is probably the principal reason for the German crews' demoralization, for their mutiny. The fleet may have been lost at Scapa Flow, but the truth is, the German fleet was lost because of the mine barrage in the North Sea. I salute Admiral Belknap." General Pershing dipped his little chin toward the Admiral. "I want to thank you, sir, for that mine barrage." Franklin's face closes.

"What is this clutter, Babs? There is no place for my models."

There is no model for his place except the White House.

That evening, after General Pershing's speech, the boys and I picked up Comet Blocks and *Congressional Digests*, old maps and new letters from the floor of the morning room and far into the night Franklin, on his hands and knees, had it out with the German fleet afloat on a nine-by-twelve fringed Aubusson sea of beige and blue chrysanthemums. He lined up the *Intrepid*, the *Invincible*, the *Indefatigable* and the *Valiant* and launched an incorruptibly brave flotilla against the Germans while the *Eagle* and the *Argonaut* zigzagged from torpedoes beneath the Aubusson and I realized that the only difference between my madness and his ambition was a set of small gray wooden ships, four of them missing artillery, and, au contraire, the only difference between his madness and my ambition was possibility. It's funny, I thought, watching him creeping about the floor. I submerge like the submarines and he deals with me like the battleships, zigzagging all over the place.

The morning after General Pershing's speech, lightly I told Franklin that Uncle Ted thought he should be President.

"When did he say *that?*"

"Just before he died. Before January."

"You waited all this time to tell me something like that?"

"Oh, Franklin, we were going to Europe. You were so busy

177

with your radio towers and all of those transactions. I thought perhaps he'd tell you when we returned from Europe . . . it was too late."

"Babs, is that what he said? That I should be President? My God, if you'd only told me. I could have gotten him to make a *statement!*"

"He was very ill."

"He really said that, did he?"

"In a way."

"You must tell me precisely."

"I don't recall precisely." I began to giggle between words. We both began to laugh politely between words, sheathing them.

"Perhaps he really didn't say that and you're . . . and you're telling me that to please me. And that's why you didn't tell me in the first place when he was alive."

"Really, that's ridiculous. Give me *some* credit, darling."

"But he did say that?"

"Yes."

"In what context?"

"We were discussing your career," I trilled in operatic tones, still lightly, still offhand.

"My career. Oh, Babs!" He pulled me to him and swung me in circles while my toes avoided the toys and ships on the morning room floor. "Oh, Babs, what would I do without you? Where would I be without you?"

"Do be careful, Franklin, your models."

"Yes, oh, yes." He lifted me over H.M.S. *Trafalgar* and H.M.S. *Conyngham* sunk and sacrificed last night in the fringes. He is a leopard ready to take large bites of marble and men and me in his triangular grin as he measures us all in victorious mouthfuls, this man who fattens himself on the credulity of fools, and this woman, Anna Eleanor Roosevelt Roosevelt, who, having neither horses nor charm nor radio towers to trade, fattens herself on the credulity of Presidents.

IN WHICH BILLY COMES TO
CALL WITH A
LETTER FROM PARIS

What had illumined my life at Richebourg cast even longer and deeper shadows on my life in America. The summer after the war, one night, near midnight, Franklin and I returning from a ball, left our motor car in a rented garage and walked the short block home, arm in arm, under the catalpa trees juicy with bloom, under the gaslights, I wearing the three ostrich feathers of the Roosevelt family in a tiara, Franklin in top hat. Our shadows stretched before us and behind us, shrinking before us as we left each aura of light, looming, growing behind us as we entered another, past and future, the flat cardboard cutout Fairchild shapes we were. Only for that brief direct moment under each light did the shadows disappear and then we would move on, once again, still, the cardboard family from my daughter's desk. There was something in me of Mrs. Fairchild, something strangling, implanted, inherent, loathed. There was something in me very much like Mama. And that something, that wall, I treasured quite as much as I loathed.

As we rounded the corner our street was ablaze with searchlights. Every house had its doors and windows thrown open, crowds of neighbors in their nightclothes stood before our lawn and policemen moved toward us with wooden horses for barricades. Tucking plumes and top hat under our arms, in horror Franklin and I ran the distance home. Running, all I could see was the house in Hertfordshire with its one wall standing and the rest gone and me falling into the hole, clutching the coffee things and the smoked oak table. That was all I could see: the one wall still standing.

But all the walls of my home stood. My children were safe. My house was whole. Mr. Palmer's house across the street from us was not. Its windows were blown in and he was outside wandering on his lawn, the Attorney General of the United States, in a red silk bathrobe, pulling its lapels together across his throat again and again and muttering sentences which contained, oddly, thees and thous.

The damage had been done not to Mr. Palmer's family or to Mr. Palmer but to the arsonist, poor inept soul, who had himself been blown to bits by his own device. If Franklin and I had left the ball a few minutes earlier, if the arsonist had gone to our house across the street or used a larger fire-bomb device, we could have all been murdered. We were very upset.

Franklin stood in his cutaway tapping his cane on the brick pavement while Mr. Palmer went on in fragments about anarchists, America First, thees and thous, and who's going to pay for this and saving the country. Of course it didn't disturb us that Mr. Palmer was a Quaker. It just seemed odd that he had kept it so hidden. And it seemed odd that this man arresting thousands of other men for sedition and shipping them home to Germany and Italy, any place but America, was a member of a sect that believed in speaking out. How odd he should deport all the aliens, him being one, in a way, himself. There were bits of blood and bone on my front steps and bits of red cloth sprinkled among my hydrangeas under the searchlights. We went inside to our children.

"Well, it doesn't surprise me that Palmer's connected to America First. But I never imagined him to be a Quaker. Did you, Babs?" Franklin asked as we pried our wide-eyed children from the front windows of the second story and put them to bed. "Just imagine. Well, I still say any man who attacks another man on the grounds of his political beliefs or his religion is acting in a manner both un-American and wholly un-Christian."

I didn't know if Franklin meant Mr. Palmer or the anarchist. The anarchist was no longer wholly anything and certainly not an American.

"What's America First, Franklin?"

"I only know enough about it to know Palmer shouldn't be connected, that's for sure."

In New York I had seen the horses on Wall Street fire-bombed by anarchists. Tripe, guts and blood escaped from their bellies like a thousand breeding mud-demons creeping into the gutters of America and up onto the marble lintel of the House of Morgan, the dray wagons splintered on the sidewalk. I saw those horses and the shattered windows of Mr. Palmer's home and I saw the bloody bones and pieces of the anarchist all over my own front steps in that strange rain of hatred and I knew war had come home with us like roaches in a steamer trunk. Bits from Richebourg on my doorstep. The unconscious, unhinged, welling up now in my neighbor's yard, and on my doorstep, and my son James found a bone. The other children were jealous and fought with him as he rinsed it off in the sink and took it to school the next day. Did anyone find the anarchist's tie? Had he worn a tie when he went to bomb the Attorney General's house? Did he feel like Franklin felt when he went to see the King? All alone for forty-five minutes. And did he wear patches on the knees of his corduroy pants when he knelt to light the fuse? Everyone is doing his bit. I could hear Duckworth. Do your bit, mate. Do your bit. Don't drink the wine. And the bits were in the hydrangeas. "Melting pot," Franklin said last month to the American Women's Legion of the Great War in the New Masonic Temple. "Melting pots that don't melt." "I believe in the gospel of love and force," Vice-President Marshall said, after which Franklin spoke, after which General Pershing, who declined to speak, received an ovation. "I believe there are too many hyphenated Americans in this country," said Mr. Vice-President Marshall. "I believe first in praying for men, and when that is not successful, I would grasp them by the neck and put them in jail." After which there was community singing and a tableau of Liberty in which four women representing East, West, North and South wore brown crepe paper and Mrs. South, an orange tree, had papier-mâché oranges hanging from her under outspread arms like tumors.

The morning after the bombing of Mr. Palmer's house, while policemen hosed the street and sanitary squads in white uniforms and helmets scrubbed the sidewalks and housefronts, Mr. Palmer's General Intelligence men knocked on doors and assured us that the bomber had been, according to the hydrangeas, the mailbox and the light posts, a white male of foreign extraction.

"Hyphenated?" I inquired.

"Very much so, madam. All over the place." The GID man answered and I closed the door.

We were relieved that the bomber had been a white male of foreign extraction. That sort could always be deported, extracted, but the black males from Foggy Bottom could not. War was with us still. For a month already the people of Foggy Bottom were rioting and on Saturday nights soldiers and sailors were going down there and pulling darkies from bars and on Monday mornings from trolley cars and beating them with clubs and gunstocks. No one knew why. We were all afraid of some catastrophic retaliation. When the soldiers left Foggy Bottom, the darkies, who now had nothing else to do, turned upon themselves and fought with each other all week long, burning their own homes. And when Billy Braun came to call in his Army uniform two days after the bombing, I knew War was still winning.

"May the Lord be with you, Mrs. Roosevelt."

"And with you, Billy Braun."

"It's Billy Brown now, Mrs. Roosevelt. A real American name. Billy Brown." He shook my hand. "I . . . can we talk someplace private?" His hand was damp. His grip powerful.

I took Billy into Franklin's library. "Wow, your mister sure has enough books. Does he read them all?"

"Oh, he'd like to. Someday when he's out of politics."

"I know what you mean." Billy Brown removed his hat. Through a layer of grease and tonic, red kinky curls snapped up one at a time. Billy edged into Franklin's fireside chair, placed his hat on his knees. "Well, I sure liked France a lot. Sure glad to be home though. Nothing like America."

"It *is* good to be home."

"I hope Mr. Roosevelt never gets out of politics. We need a he-man like him up there with all those crazy fools running around destroying this country. He's a good man. You're both darned good people. I've got to . . . uh . . . look, I want to show you my certificate." Billy passed me a legal paper. He had been certified sane.

"I'm so happy for you, Billy. I am very pleased."

"Well, I wanted you to know but that's not . . . uh . . . I'm not bothering you, am I?"

"No, no. I was just putting away my linens."

"How come? With all these servants? Excuse me, I guess that's not my beeswax."

"I just like to."

"Well," he settled further back into Franklin's chair, "I always say folks should do what they like, no matter what. That's what I believe in now. Freedom."

"Billy, you *are* feeling well now, aren't you?"

"Oh, I am. I really am." He leaned forward. "It's the country that's in trouble." He searched my eyes. I nodded reassuringly. "See, I belong to this private group, America First. I'm a speaker. I go all over the country. And I report personally to Mr. Hoover."

"Wonderful man. I'm reading his book on mining."

"Uh, no, this Hoover works for Mr. Palmer. GID."

"Mr. Palmer's a neighbor."

"I know."

"Oh."

"Well, look . . . uh, so I report to Mr. Hoover. I report about aliens who seek to undermine the very foundations of American beliefs." He laughed at himself. "That's part of my speech. They say I'm a real crowd-raiser."

"I'm sure you are. I'd love to hear your speech."

"Oh, well. Well, they say I do okay. I'd . . . God knows, Mrs. Roosevelt, if you could ever find a way to come hear my speech, it would be the proudest moment of my life. I mean that—the proudest moment. Look, I never forgot how you brought me iced lemon jellies and I never forgot how you fixed up that stinkhole . . . excuse me . . . for us veterans who was shell-shocked and got us cleaned up and got us recreation rooms and decent food and got us separated from the crazies. So, I'm real . . . well, you know how I feel about you, I guess, and that's why . . . well, that's why I brought you the letter from Paris." He touched his vest pocket. "You're good people, you and the Mister, and I don't want to see you getting into any trouble. I know you didn't mean what you wrote in this letter."

No one won. War won. Ploppit. Billy has a document saying he's sane. Bill has a document in my own hand, from the Ritz, saying I'm not. "Oh, Billy, dear sweet Billy, this is all so silly. That was just an emotional reaction."

He shook his head, very sadly. "I know that. Look, it's

what happened to me with the doughnuts. I understand. Don't think I don't understand. That's why I want to help you."

"Help me?"

"I just can't turn you in, Mrs. Roosevelt. A little letter like this can make real trouble for you, for the Mister. I know I should turn you in but I just feel so bad about . . . I mean, well, we all have weak moments when things just aren't too clear and I know a lady like you . . . look . . . here, take it." He stood and put it in my lap. I didn't touch it.

"Oh, Billy."

"God, Mrs. Roosevelt . . . I mean . . ."

"I'm sure you did the right thing. I'm sure you did. Don't you worry about it."

"You know how I feel about you, Mrs. Roosevelt."

"Yes, Billy. And I feel something very special for you and I can see how courageous you had to be. I see that."

"I should go."

"Billy, do tell me when you'll be speaking. I'd love to hear you speak."

"I'd be real proud, Mrs. Roosevelt."

"Really proud. You say, really proud, not real proud."

"Thank you. I know how busy you are . . ."

"Well, if I can. I take the children to Fairhaven this summer but if I'm in the city, I could come by."

Billy opened a rich leather appointment book. "I'm not due back in the East until fall. Hoboken, September fourteenth at two in the afternoon. I'll send you a letter."

"Oh, no, no. You mustn't do that."

"Well, you just come down. You could sit in your car, I guess. I usually speak outside. And I won't let anything happen to you. I mean, there's no danger. I'd never let anything happen to you. I mean, we all make mistakes."

"Billy." I squeezed his very damp hand. "Thank you Billy, you are very sweet and very brave. I'll try."

"Well, I'll look for you. Really proud. I'll remember."

I watched Billy walking down my steps and up the street. Even though it was all a tempest in a teapot, I burned the letter. Of course, I never mentioned anything to Franklin about Billy or America First or Hoboken, but I did begin to imagine conversations with Franklin which began with just guess where I was today and Franklin leaning forward on every word, asking questions, terribly excited, even suggesting that he go with me another time to hear Billy speak. "You've found something very important, Eleanor. Very important. That is very important information. Now tell me, did he say anything about candidates, anything about political parties, about who is behind this? Is it really most of America? Or is it just a small group? Did you see anyone we know?" Franklin and I would talk on and on. "And what do you think, Eleanor? What do you think is the attitude of the American working class toward the League? And what do you think is the attitude of the American working class toward the Wilson administration? Do they seem to be organizing into strikes? What do you think they want, Eleanor? I am so curious, darling."

Mr. Adams said it isn't enough to be curious. Would it be enough to go, to actually go and listen to Billy? No. People have bombs and guns. I don't belong there. I can't endanger the lives of my family. Billy may be crazy. I am still Mrs. Fairchild. Franklin would be furious.

IN WHICH I ATTEND THE INTERNATIONAL CONGRESS OF WORKING WOMEN

If anyone else had invited me to the Working Women's Congress, I'm certain I wouldn't have accepted. But it was Dorothy Straight who called me because I was an official wife in Washington and had a second language. Occasionally she used Social Register matrons for her projects and we were always thrilled to be invited although none of us ever did more than pour tea and donate money. "I'm giving the opening tea, Mrs. Roosevelt. There are women from every part of the world and I think we are going to use French, but I do need Spanish. Do you know of anyone?"

"Lily Polk has Spanish but I don't know just how well she can mix. I worked at the Henry Street Settlement . . ."

"I'm afraid you'll find the congress very different. It isn't charity in any way, but I know you can handle it. Please come. And ask Mrs. Polk. I do need Spanish."

Lily and I decided to dress simply and leave early. Basically, when one is mixing, one asks about children, husband and home, offers little information, much sympathy and listens very intently without, of course, becoming involved. But Dorothy Straight was correct: it was very different than Henry Street.

I didn't know any of the American women Dorothy was working with. They all seemed frighteningly professional. Two were actually lawyers and one, although far below the class of the lawyers, ran the Women's Trade Union League. Dorothy was very busy and inaccessible and since there was no receiving line nor anyone arranging introductions, nor a tea table, I had no choice but to plunge into this group and that group and found myself, each time, ignored. Buzzes of anger and laughter, stray bits of language, the scrape and pound of heavy shoes on a wooden floor in a rented hall, hundreds of women, Oriental, Slavic, Continental, fold-up chairs, a strong scent of perspiration—I was not comfortable. Lily sat stiffly in a chair at the side of the hall.

"Caps. I make caps." "Men are worms." "Vampires," someone responded. "Born killers." "I do boning on them corsets." "Lace, fifth generation in lace." At last I found a Bulgarian woman in a heavy brown wool suit, very square, very plain, who stood alone, and I descended upon her with my halting German. She nodded at me, encouraging me, patronizingly, smiled roundly and moved away as quickly as she could. "I bone corsets." "I make caps." "In the morning I make believe I married a duke and I live happily ever after all the time I work the machine until the mill shuts down at night." "And what do you do, Mrs. Roosevelt?" "I have five children and I move them six times a year. You see, we . . ." One cannot play croquet with a flamingo for a mallet. Lily found me and said she was appalled and would never accept another Dorothy Straight invitation no matter who she was. "Dangerous. Dangerous for us and for our husbands. We should not be in places like this. These are anarchists."

"Oh, that's ridiculous. I wish you would understand, Lily. Things are really *changing*."

"And what do you suppose anarchy *is?* I've called for my car, Eleanor. If you wish to leave with me, I'm leaving."

"Oh, I don't think so. I'm very curious."

"Good day, Eleanor. You are making a big mistake."

"The problem," Rejeanne, the lawyer, explained to me, "is not what their family situation is, but the conditions of work. These women work. Speak to them about work. I'll walk around with you. Ask them what they do, what problems they have working and what they want."

"You're very kind, Rejeanne."

"We need you, Mrs. Roosevelt. We need all the women we can find to help us. To help each other."

"It is extraordinary . . . all these women . . ."

"They're finding a voice. So you must speak to them and listen to them." Rejeanne waved at Dorothy Straight and I realized she had been assigned to me. It didn't matter. I liked her very much. She wore a loose woven dress of wools with Navajo geometry on the bodice. She was small and burning with energy. I'd never known a woman lawyer. I never imagined there were women lawyers. Franklin would be fascinated.

He wasn't. At home, the first night of the conference, Franklin and I dined alone. Except that a white bisque bowl sat on a length of blue blind-stitched silk between us and was filled with red Delicious apples from Hyde Park, Nora, our cook, had again made a meal for which we needed no teeth. Franklin scraped kernels from the ear of Mama's corn with an enameled fruit knife and dropped the kernels into his bowl of warm milk and sugar. Steaming casseroles of oysters in cream sauce were at our elbows. I would have to speak with Nora. The distance over the blind-stitching from Franklin's end of the dining room table to mine had never seemed greater.

"Pleasant day, darling? No, I don't suppose. All those she-males shrieking. It must be a bloody circus, Eleanor."

I could feel my eyebrows drawing together. "Well, some of their ideas . . . seem . . . very curious . . . and I certainly am appalled by the hatred, appalled . . ."

"So then they do hate men?"

"Not really. If they were to examine themselves. . . . There were some men there, in fact. I think I saw Mr. Gompers."

"That's surprising. I understand he doesn't want women in the unions at all."

"I know. I suppose he was spying."

"But they do hate men?"

"I don't . . . I can't really say that. They transfer the hate over so quickly from the system to men in particular, this sweatshop boss, that politician."

Franklin grew very thoughtful, corn poised over his bowl. "I would have been eaten up alive."

"Oh, Lord, no. Ladies love you."

"Don't be naïve, Eleanor. Those women prefer each other."

"You don't mind that I go, do you, Franklin?"

"Mmm. No. Can't do any harm. But I think you should tell them that it isn't men, it's the system."

"I suppose." I tried to soften my eyes, release my knotted eyebrows.

"Well, of course it is, darling. Just happens the system is run by men."

"True. And the women do wish to change the system."

The corn was reactivated. "Who doesn't? Even we evil politicians. Look, Eleanor, don't be naïve about these things. Women in the system won't be any different than men or . . . or monkeys in the system for that matter."

I hesitated, watching the kernel plop into the milk. Ploppit. "Women, these women," I said finally, gently, softly, "don't feel they can change the system unless they first change men."

His knife paused over the ear of corn. "Hah! What's wrong with men? Short of castration, which is a delicious phrase, isn't it, short of castration? Short of castration, how would they change us? Leave our beds?"

"From some of the talk, well, from some of it, I don't think they think short of castration. They think men are born to slay, that men cause war. I don't know what they really want. But some of the ideas they have could be applied as a whole to society . . . if they could only stop shrieking and carrying on so. They want to turn everything upside down and that's wrong too. After all, why should men cause war if they have to die in it?" No one had shrieked. Condemning manners was a trick I'd learned from Franklin, my master at many games, who would openly admire a woman's shape and then damn the coarseness of her mouth. Ah well, the coarseness of her mouth is hardly a matter of interest, nor the shape, nor the clothing, nor her bed companions, if I may be so bold. Some of the women were as coarse as one could imagine, with a brutal, beaten hardness. Some were soft and lovely. Rejeanne was lovely. Her companion, Caroline, who came to meet her after the meeting, was perfectly elegant, stylish, small and porcelain. All were fiery. It seemed wiser to entertain Franklin with their spread-legged poses and heavy suits and maroon ties and cigars and ten-pound shoes and how they looked openly at one another in ways I have seen men look at women. I chatted on and on, condemning, and told him everything he wanted to hear so that I did not have to hear him make the connection between his empty bed and the women who loved each other. I was not clever enough.

Franklin leaned back in his chair and gazed at me. "I'm curious, Babs. If these ladies who dwell, shall we say, between sexes, are such a sorry lot, why do you go?"

"I'm . . . Dorothy needs me there for my French."

"Dorothy's getting to be a bore. Ever since she lost Willard in France . . . all that money. If the Paynes and the Whitneys knew how their heirs were spending their money, they'd roll over in their graves. Ought to marry again. All of them."

"Dorothy is bright and courageous. We all make mistakes.

191

But the other women there . . . don't you think they must hate themselves, you know? They . . . well . . . you must consider their backgrounds." I started to chew on my tongue but stopped immediately.

Dinner was over and I knew, in Franklin's mind, I had joined the ladies who sucked on cigars and lived with each other. What I didn't describe to Franklin was how the women hugged and kissed and cried and walked arm in arm and held hands and sang songs I'd never heard but everyone knew. I so wanted to weep and laugh and sing with them. They were like soldiers, with a spirit of love and fellowship I had only seen in wartime.

"Of course it feels like a war, Mrs. Roosevelt. Because it is a war."

"I see."

"A worldwide war. On men."

"I see. But I'm certain it's the system. If women were to take the place of men in the system it wouldn't make any difference," I attempted.

"Oh, my, for one thing, Mrs. Roosevelt, we'd probably let men in. No, it's a war on men . . . on men the way they are. If they could only be more like women . . ."

"Now, don't scare the lady. It's a war on the system."

Rejeanne invited me to supper whenever I came to New York. "We're on Fourteenth Street during the week. You must come. We have such fun, Caroline and I. And you know we edit the League of Women Voters' newspaper. We do the reports on legislation. You really must come."

"Well, I will . . . I would love it . . . if I'm free."

"Yes. Free. That is the problem, isn't it?"

"Genevieve," I heard behind me, around me. "Whenever will you be finished with my copy of *Jurgen*? I have it promised."

"Did you get to Becket this weekend, darling?"

"I stayed the entire week."

"No! Imagine a week with Violet in Becket! How lovely for

you. You needed a rest. I've never seen anyone working so hard in my life. How lucky to be all alone with Violet for a week. And the porch? Is it done?"

"Fell in. Next weekend is work time so bring your hammer. Everyone's coming up. Felicia's about to have her pups and she needs all the support she can get."

"I've finished the Marie Stopes. Do you want that instead?"

"Haven't the stomach for her."

"You're wrong," someone added. "She's very important. Very. Politically. America First is already burning copies."

I asked Rejeanne later about Marie Stopes. She told me I must read it. "Everything from childbirth to masturbation. Too much treacle but very honest. Basically what the world's up in arms about is that this madwoman says women should have . . . deserve . . . can have . . . sexual pleasure and it's their husband's duty to give it to them."

"Good Lord."

"And sexual pleasure . . . well, one can have it without being involved in childbirth, so there are long chapters on contraception. On how not to have children. You see . . . it really is an extraordinary concept and the book has already turned England topsy-turvy."

"Well, English women are far ahead of us anyway." Oh, how I stumbled for a response.

"If you'd like, I can bring the book tomorrow."

"Not if you aren't finished with it . . ."

Rejeanne giggled. "Oh, Lord, *we* have no use for it!"

I didn't dare ask her what she meant.

When the congress was over and resolutions passed on issues of equal wages, shorter hours, child labor, maternity aid, health care and union membership, the women cleared and lifted stacks of the fold-up chairs from the great hall floor and the American women taught the foreign women simple square-dance calls. Promenade and gents to the right. Do-si-do and hold her tight. In French, in German, in Spanish.

One very small woman, Rosie, no more than twenty-five with a face like a white raisin and a half-tooth, black and broken, midmouth, touched my arm and asked me to be her partner. "You wanna be the gent or the lady?"

I apologized for my tiered skirt, which was much too complicated, finally removed my hat and my jacket and kicked off my shoes, took my place in a line of self-proclaimed gents and danced with the women, avoiding columns, avoiding tripping, tripping, laughing, swinging from one to the other, forgetting myself and who I was and being, for that night, one of them. It was quite wonderful.

Rosie was so light I lifted her off the floor when I swung her. "Whew," she said at the end when I set her down. "You learn fast. You're strong."

I looked for Rejeanne but couldn't find her. Rosie told me she was from Seattle and lived with the Wobblies. Some of her friends had been hung.

"Hanged, dear," I corrected her without asking who her friends, the Wobblies, were or what was lacking in her diet or her childhood that her face would be so lined.

"Hanged, hung, feels the same. See this?" She pointed to her broken tooth. I really wished I could find Rejeanne and perhaps have a cup of coffee with her on the way back to her hotel. "Wounded in action. I'm organizing in Fall River now." The tooth was raw and blackening in the center of her mouth. "You know why I don't bob my hair? Because I need it long in case I have to be dragged up the sidewalks again . . . and to hide rocks in."

"Really? Rocks?" My hand moved up to my twisted and piled hair.

"Rocks." Rosie nodded. "You have a family?"

"Yes. I love them very much."

"Didn't say you don't, did I? We gotta give up loving. Love's no priority in our line of work."

"But what you're doing, fighting for others, that's certainly loving."

194

"I mean loving one person, one family. That has to go."

"I still don't agree."

"Well, maybe we got a lot to learn from each other," she concluded magnanimously.

Before the congress was called to an end, I invited Rosie and some of her Trade Union friends to my Washington house for tea. I have a little silver Mother Hubbard bell which I ring to call the servants. It's always at my place. Sometimes the servants stand behind screens and wait, but for that tea I preferred them out of the room. With each tinkle of my bell, with each gleam on the silver sherbets and each crème on the three-tiered Meissen candy dish and each ring of crystal on the Marie Thérèse chandelier over our heads and each trace of carving on the wainscoting of the dining room and the silver brackets of the gas lamps, with each of the things of my life—my curiosities—the bonds I had felt at the congress unravelled. My servants were skittish and slow and finally insolent. I could hear them laughing in the kitchen. At last, when a young girl with unruly hair and blue-white skin, a lacemaker from Puerto Rico, spilled her tea and I rang for the servants and they didn't respond because they didn't hear me over their laughter, the lacemaker and I both flushed.

"I am very sorry. Very sorry," she insisted, patting the spot with a napkin.

And I comforted her. "Don't worry. It's nothing. I have dozens of other tablecloths like this."

Anger flashed in her eyes. "My family lives for many months on the pennies we get for weaving such a cloth as this."

The tea spot spread. I imagined, as I stared at her and she at me, how many hours of that woman's life my tablecloth cost, and I, for all my honest sympathy, was ringing for my own servant-women who were also probably underpaid and equally resentful, who did not yet dare to carry rocks in their hairbuns, who belonged, more than I, with the women having tea. I did understand. I did not see the women again. I never called Rejeanne for supper. I had nothing more to offer than curiosity. It had been a dreadful and awkward mistake. What I was embarrassed me. To compound matters completely, as the women left, my two eldest children dropped bags of water upon their heads from the second-floor window.

Rosie sent me a scribbled note from Ohio weeks later thanking me for tea and saying that I was all right. "All the girls thought you were really all right."

IN WHICH I GO TO HOBOKEN

nclosed in my Packard, with the doors locked and one window opened only a crack, I watched an army of workers march along the trolley tracks down the main street of Hoboken toward the docks. They wore black suits and black peaked hats and their faces, from drink, I think, were pink with pleasure as they marched, steel-nosed work shoes hammering on the bricks of the street and the men sang "Goodby-ee, goodby-ee. Wipe that little tear, baby dear, from your eye-ee." A shapeless song in shapeless suits and I had to drive along slowly behind the parade of other limousines and open cars. I could see Billy Brown in his uniform standing in an open car before mine and waving exuberantly to the thin crowds along the streets. A banner on the car door identified him. BILLY BROWN'S COME TO TOWN. Businessmen, I supposed, merchants, manufacturers, small-time bosses and royal orders of royal groups I'd never heard of, rode in other cars hung with other signs and banners that read: AMERICA FIRST! In Hoboken, the people knew Billy Brown. I slumped as low as possible into the seat of my car so that my head rested against the horsehair and couldn't be seen from outside. The march stopped. The cars slowed. The steel hammering of the men's shoes died down, reverberating a moment beyond its own time, and the lines of cars curved around the workmen and toward the meeting point where the docks began and the trolley line ended.

Billy climbed a loading dock and shouted into a megaphone. "America First!" In one voice, the workers shouted back: "America First!"

"My name is Billy Brown!" he shouted, "and I've come to town." The men cheered again, on signal, I suspect, from another black-suited man standing next to Billy.

"I've come to tell you the kind of trouble this country's in. I want you to know while we're working hard to put America's enemies behind bars—and I don't mean the kind we like—there are some so-called innocent women walking the streets undermining the very foundations of this great country of ours. And doing just as much damage as the anarchists. Except they're too sly, those women. Sneakier than the men we caught. In twenty minutes we will witness right here on this spot exactly what should be done to the women from the following organizations: Oh, I forgot . . . and I get this from the War Department . . ."

Billy stuck one foot forward, held his list before his face and read. At the top of the list was the League of Women Voters, at the bottom the Women's Trade Union League. "I say," he shouted, "these women are poisoning this country. In networks, in conspiracies, in red spider-webs, and Billy Brown will tell you."

Had he seen me that last week visiting Rejeanne's hotel after the Working Women's Congress? Had he peeped through her windows to watch me reading the legislative reports she wrote for the League of Women Voters? Had he been watching my house when I had the Trade Union women to tea? What did he know? Did he know I had new friends? And borrowed scandalous books from them? Was I being watched as if . . . as if . . . I smiled into the horsehair . . . as if I were effective? Was he actually speaking about me? Could it be that I, that my friends, really *were* able to turn the country upside down or even right side up? I concentrated on every word.

"Why are these women backing welfare measures? They say they're benefiting a class of people. They lie if they say so. It's all a part of the German propaganda to break down the United States Government. These women are paid by the Huns and fattened on Bolshevik ideas while our brothers are still dying over there at at . . . uh . . . Archangel. Fighting the Bolsheviks at Archangel. These women want to take away your jobs, take away your tools. Why, they don't believe in marriage! Do you know what that means? I won't say what they do believe in because we have ladies present, but I'll tell you this much: they believe in immediate passions."

Well, he certainly wasn't speaking about me. How could he be so comical and yet so dangerous? There was a sense of expectation in his audience. Every few minutes the men turned to look up the trolley line and then turned back to Billy. Again and again I watched the heads turning. "They don't believe in no future life; they don't believe in children, in punishment for sin. That's the kind of women who are telling you to give up your freedom. Who are telling you how long you can work each day, who are telling you to join unions. That's where your un-Americanism comes from. America means freedom of choice. Well, these women are telling you WHAT TO DO. They think women should make the same amount of money men should. That we should pay insurance into some fund so if some Dago stops work because his wife's having her tenth kid . . . *we* gotta pay for *him*."

"Billy Brown! Billy Brown!" The workers cheered in a body, they stood and cheered for him, stood and cheered, the men in black with their faces florid on their day off.

"I say get rid of these women who are poisoning the country. We found a way to get rid of the men, now let's find a way to get rid of the women!"

They were the miners searching for my silver; they would take it from me, poisonous men who wanted my silver before it was born. "Billy Brown! Billy Brown!"

"Thank you, ladies and gentlemen."

There were no other women to be seen.

The man who had been beside Billy examined his watch and pointed up the trolley line. Two trolleys rolled slowly toward the dock.

"Here they come!"

The anarchists were wearing ties after all. One by one as they stepped from the trolleys into the sunlight on the pier, blinking, faces flat and numb, hair well combed, nails clean, I'm sure, they were all wearing ties. What have you done that you are anarchists? Have you forgotten your manners? Are you Bolsheviks or Huns? I can see your faces under a flashlight by my hydrangeas tying that last stick of dynamite, your fingers trembling with fear and hatred. Now you carry a valise and a gunnysack. Why didn't your mothers teach you to behave? You dress up to go home to Germany in disgrace in your corduroy pants and ties and nice jackets. You are decent and clean and we line you up in cars like cattle and ship you home now that the war is over, now that Germany is a bucket of ashes. Well, we don't want you anymore; we don't want any more trouble here. Do you realize one of you could have murdered my entire family with your fire bombs? So go home.

The workers stand in a solid square between the dock, between the pier, between the boat, between the fatherland and the trolley car. I think they're disappointed. In the light, the anarchists are too clean-shaven, too fat, too thin, too familiar, their shoes just as steel-nosed, their hands just as worn, too familiar to be proper enemies. The workers sing to the anarchists.

"Goodby-ee, goodby-ee. Though it's hard to part I know-oh-oh that I'll be tickled to death to go-oh-oh. So don't cry-ee. Don't sigh-ee. Why there'll be a silver lining in the sky-ee."

Yesterday you were obedient workmen. Today you are the people who wrap bombs in packages and paste labels from Gimbels on them and ship them to the leaders of our country. You are criminals. My son came home with the anarchist's bone and the anarchist had no bone nor bits left. We kept the bone in the pocket of my son's knickers. My son who hates liver, my son who hates veal. We keep our bits rotting in our pockets like amulets and call the hyphenated Americans the names we should call ourselves and kick them out. Done our bit, we did, thee did. Done our bit.

"Goodby-ee, goodby-ee. Wipe the tear, baby dear, from your eye-ee."

Are you leaving your wives, your bank accounts, the Easy Washer half paid for, your children? Why did they choose you? Did they find you because you didn't march in the Edison Liberty Loan parade four years ago or you didn't paste a flag decal on your lunchbox or you still called it German measles instead of liberty measles and the company doctor who signed the death certificate for your children turned you in? And turned you out?

My husband is so convinced that Germany has a future he has a corporation with very grave papers stamped and engraved, investing in German marks. Indeed, graved and ungraved, marked and unmarked. Mr. Howe devised the corporation and there are a lot of biggies in it also. Well, we can't have bombers among us. Or those who act like bombers or even those who look like bombers. So go home. We have to get rid of the Socialists and the anarchists. You understand that of course. But I don't know if Huns are Socialists or if

Bolsheviks are anarchists. Alderman Beckerman and Becker-
man Alderman were duly elected to the New York State
Assembly as a Socialist and duly unelected as a Bolshevik, so
I suppose that makes sense and Eugene Debs is in jail and Mr.
Wilson, who believes in freedom of speech, doesn't want to
hear a word about Eugene Debs. And Hun money is used to
support the Bolsheviks in America, right? Right. While
German troops are fighting the Bolsheviks in league with the
League of Nations who told them to do so at Archangel
because the Russians are threatening the world. The Russians now? They are so far away. There are such shifts these
days, one can hardly keep up. Every child old enough to be a
member of the Junior Red Cross for Christmas Club hates
Germans and every gang of boys who joined the Yellow-Dog
League and sought out spies—your own children—they all
hate Germans. Did your eldest son turn you in? We encouraged your children to turn you in. We were encouraged to
turn you in, out, upside down, inside out. The pool is in
Hoboken under the pier. "Goodby-ee, goodby-ee. So cheerio,
chin chin toodle-oo-oo, goodby-ee. Wipe the tear, baby dear,
from your eye-ee."

We are sorry we hate you. I feel the string drawn through
my heart as I look into your unformed faces. You should have
changed your name to Brown, right? And attacked Bolsheviks and Dagos and women and cigarmakers. You could have
stayed in the land of the free if you had hated properly.

Right? Right.

The steel-shoed workers turned from the trolley car and
split into two rows along the docks leading to the boat, and
the deportees were directed to pass through the line.
"Though it's hard to part, I know-oh-oh there'll be a silver
lining in the sky-ee. So cheerio, chin chin toodle-oo-oo-oo,
goodby-ee, goodby-ee." And as the men sang, the anarchists
walked silently through their lines to the pier. The men who
didn't sing spat in the faces of the anarchists, so that I couldn't
distinguish the tears from the saliva, the saliva from the tears.

IN WHICH I JOIN A PICKET LINE

Because of the racial riots at the edge of the city, Aunt Dora and Aunt Polly had to turn back to Tuxedo Park. They would be late for the party. Their chauffeur had been struck in the head by a stone but Jack Astor was driving in and would give them a lift right to the Waldorf. They were terribly sorry.

Mama was upset. Lord Grey cannot be kept waiting. What shall we do? Franklin assured her that Lord Grey could be kept waiting. He had, after all, survived waiting all these months for Mr. Wilson to see him. Mama didn't think that was amusing at all and thought it dreadful of Mrs. Wilson to act so high and mighty as to disturb foreign policy and to insult Her Majesty's Ambassador. Franklin assured her again that we would all have our chances to make amends that night at the party and if the party worked out well, Alice would charm Lord Grey, Lord Grey would charm Alice and then perhaps he would charm Senator Lodge and Senator Borah and who knows, perhaps all of the anti-League group would then sit down with the League group and affect some sort of compromise and then Mr. Wilson would finally see Lord Grey and America would join the League of Nations.

"Not on your life, Franklin," I advised. "Not with Sommerville-West back at the Embassy."

"Oh, it's a chance. Wouldn't it make a great coup, though?"

"And what part would you play in it if such a meeting did come about?" I asked pointedly, nastily, jealously, I think.

"If I could bring the factions together," Franklin finally admitted to me in the car, "it could mean an ambassadorship."

"Just don't lose sight of the fact that it is Aunt Dora's seventy-fifth birthday, Franklin. Do pay some attention to *her*." And to me, I didn't say.

When the doorman opened the limousine door, I descended onto the sidewalk to look directly into a picket sign: ONE DAY IN SEVEN. EVEN GOD RESTED. The doorman and two policemen lifted the woman with the sign and set her down roughly behind a flaming garbage can and then bravely shielded Franklin and me so that we might pass unmolested up the hotel stairs. It was a bitterly cold night.

"Charmaids," the doorman apologized. "Insolent lowlives, lawbreakers. Very sorry."

"Very sorry," everyone said as we walked into the lobby. "We'll be rid of them when the guests come if we can."

Mama arrived a moment after we had, fuming at the hotel for allowing the demonstration and then at the concierge for folding the napkins in fans rather than lilies, as she had told them quite distinctly to fold the napkins in lilies. "Everything will be so stupidly awkward, Franklin. We should never have tried to surprise Dora, Franklin. I know my sister. She hates surprises."

The tables were in blue and white with Mama's double set

of Limoges and the eighty napkins, after all the waiters had been summoned to refold them, were in perfectly resplendent lilies. We sat in red-velvet gilded chairs waiting for the guests to arrive, and the ice sculpture not to melt—it was Aunt Dora's favorite polo pony, dead now, whose tail Franklin had stuffed, framed and hanging over his bed. Through the arched windows we could watch the street activity, the women walking back and forth, patiently, holding their signs to the windows for us to see.

Lord Grey appeared at the doorway to our banquet room, tall and courtly and nimble-footed, spinning his ferruled umbrella and waiting for someone to take his coat and hat. He wore the thick blue glasses of a man going, as destiny would have it, quite blind. Franklin practically scurried over to him on all fours. Alice arrived with Nick and did, of course, immediately charm Lord Grey who positively pounced upon her and demanded from her, and she promised him, a list of every book she had ever read, neither of them meaning a word of it.

Mama had been correct: it was awkward waiting for Aunt Dora and Aunt Polly because we wouldn't take our tables but sat instead in stiff little groups, chatted, milled about, sipped sherry and generally did not throw ourselves into the evening except for Franklin, who took his place beside Lord Grey and kept it steadfastly while Alice held forth about how terrible it was that the nation was leaderless and Wilson a dead man and Mrs. Wilson making the decisions of state, that the government was neither a democracy nor a republic as intended but a necropolis. I wandered over to the windows to look at the strikers. How fortunate they were to do what they believed in. Sommerville-West arrived just after Lord Grey and with him a young lady in a daring gown within which she carried between her voluptuous breasts a little gray pet spider monkey. The roars of masculine laughter burst behind me each time a tiny claw or a head poked out from her décolletage. I thought it was in terrible taste. Before me, the women with cracked knuckles and red, broken faces marched diligently. One made a Queen Anne's fan by waving her fingers from her nose at me. Lord Grey, who clearly did not understand the indecorous laughter about the spider monkey, came over, glanced out at the strikers, a vision he could only see in the most hazy of shapes, cleared his throat and directed the waiters to pull the shades and curtains. Alice, jealous of the lady with the spider monkey, grew utterly outrageous and magnetized the group by quoting lines from the new Marie Stopes work. Everyone was very "amoosed," as Franklin pronounced it. "You are so amoosing, Alice."

"That book happens to be very important," I said unamoosingly. "For women. Not men's women, of course. . . ."

Alice pounced on me. "Eleanor, darling, what other kind of woman is there? But don't tell me you've read it! Franklin, how could you allow our Eleanor of all people to read that terrible book. Oh, Eleanor . . . never!"

Ass.

"Probably Mama gave it to her," Franklin roared. Everyone roared and Mama hit Franklin's sleeve with the lower loop of her rope of pearls. She loved being shocked by Franklin and would grow wonderfully imperious and offended.

"I want to hear nothing of that woman's book. Nothing!" Mama huffed. Which of course was permission for Franklin and Alice to go on. The voluptuous lady sat in a little chair and Sommerville-West, standing above her, reached down to pat the head of the monkey as it protruded from its nest of cleavage. I don't believe the lady said very much all evening. The tiny claw scratched across her chest. I wondered how it felt.

"That was the funniest book, Aunt Sally," Alice said, Sally being the familiar name for Sarah. "Her language is ridiculous."

The spider monkey stuck its head out, very bravely now, peeked about with bright little eyes, bright little vacuous eyes, and ducked back into its nest once again, quite confused I'm certain, by the crowds.

"Why, one should string Mrs. Stopes up for her syntax alone . . . on her own rubber goods. Swing her high on her own rubber goods." Sommerville-West joined the conversation.

"Really, West, your own countrywoman."

"Franklin, where is Dora? Can't we call? Oh, where is she? Do you think they found more racial riots?"

"Just relax, Mama. They'll be here. Her pony's turning into a large flat snake though. Alice, you haven't actually read the book, have you?"

"I? Franklin! Of course not. But you do know," Alice took Lord Grey's arm and he looked down at her uncomfortably, not certain who she was, "you do know, Lord Grey, that the lady had the audacity to tell your own Lloyd George that if the world used her rubber goods, he would have no more problems with the world. As if rubber goods would solve the problems of the empire."

"Cutting out the cancer of Germany would solve the empire's problems," Lord Grey spluttered.

I waited for an opening and found a small space. "As you know," I spoke over other voices, "the book is trash. I've read it. But the concept can free women, can reduce populations, can solve the food problem. Mrs. Stopes, as unacceptable as she is, is correct. It is Malthusian but far better for it gives women a chance for sexual happiness and self-determination." My voice was horribly high.

"For *what?*" Mama ballooned with anger.

With far less effect I could have thrown my corselet into the punch bowl.

"Really, Eleanor!" Franklin puffed with the same adder anger as Mama, an anger that had once immobilized me. "Really, darling, must you always spoil the fun?"

"I'm *very* serious. And I think she is absolutely correct about solving some of the empire's problems by making women happy. We are half the population. Furthermore, if you'll excuse me, I find the room suffocating . . ."

"If you're suffocating, consider the poor monkey," someone said behind me as I walked out with as much dignity as I could muster.

"Personally," I heard Mama saying. "Children are the object of sexuality. Mrs. Stopes is a threat to the sanctity of marriage and the family and I think, Franklin, you had better keep your wife away from those labor conferences . . . and her perverse friends."

I retrieved my coat, walked out of the Waldorf to the picket line on Thirty-fourth Street and stood next to the small fire in the garbage can while the wind ripped around the corners and down the valley that was Thirty-fourth Street, twisting and binding my chiffon skirts tight about my ankles and strafing my face. Some of the charmaids pushed their signs at me but I held my place, assuring them calmly each time they advanced upon me: "I am with you. I am with you." Once the doorman moved toward me to protect me but then he backed away toward the warmth of the hotel entrance and stood watching at the steps, rubbing his hands and catcalling half-heartedly to the charmaids. "You're mad, Gussie, you'll lose your job. That's all. Lose your job." When someone from the hotel staff ventured out, the doorman called loud insults. "Trouble-makin' lowlives."

Within a few minutes a young woman came to stand by the garbage can and warm her hands one at a time, shifting her sign, and coughing horribly into a handkerchief. Examining me carefully, the jewels, the ermine, the golden shoes, waiting for me to be frightened off, she reached into the garbage can for a roasted potato, extracted one and ate chunks of it, skin and all, her eyes on me. Her coat was without buttons. One pocket, almost entirely off, was held by a diaper pin. Her knuckles bled, her thin legs swam in galoshes and her teeth were gapped by disease. "I'm Kate," she finally told me, and offered me some potato.

208

"Oh . . . oh, no, Kate, I'll be . . ." I mumbled, swallowing words. "I'd just like to join your picket line for a while."

"Faith, would ye now?" and without further question, she relinquished her sign and spread both hands over the fire.

"You don't mind, do you?"

"Hell, no, lady. You're protection far as I can see. Hey, girls, she's okay, let her in," Kate called to the line. "She'll keep the cops off."

I wore ermine and chiffon and my mother's jewels and my hands were covered with carbuncles of rings like boils on my fingers in the places where the charmaids bled at the knuckles. Where I had diamonds they had calluses; where I had rubies they had blood. "Kate," I asked, delaying, frightened. "Will the doormen bother me?"

"Oh, them? They're okay. They want as many hours' work they can get. We got kids at home. Go on, now, lady, do your bit if you mean it." She prodded me gently with the potato. "Can't learn it all at once, now, can you? Off with you. Nobody's gonna lay a hand on you."

And so I marched around with Kate's sign, stopping now and then to warm my silk-gloved hands over the fire. Franklin opened the glass of an oriel window. A wrought-iron cage bellied gracefully at the bottom. "Do you want to take the spider monkey out for some fresh air? He tells me his lady is wearing cheap perfume."

I ignored him.

The second time as I passed under his window, he called out: "Babs, this is too funny."

"Hush, Franklin."

"Have you any idea what will happen when Mama sees you? She'll burst. Can I get you cocoa or something . . . it's bitter cold."

"Yes, that's a marvelous idea. Order up cocoa and doughnuts for everyone and do have them sent out on trays. That's marvelous. See if they'll send out silver trays."

"You are so funny, Babs. Was it what Alice said to you?"

"I feel for these women out here. I can't sit in there eating paté with this suffering out here. I don't belong in there."

"Come on, lady, move on, will ya?"

"In a moment. In a moment."

"You're not exactly dressed for the occasion out there. We'll have to get you some new clothes . . ."

"I'm bored with it in there."

"Who isn't?"

"Franklin, come out and join us."

"I can't. You know that. You're freer than I am."

"Move on, lady, please. You're holding up the line."

I moved on. When next I passed the window, Franklin and Sommerville-West stood looking down on me.

"My wife," Franklin was explaining to him, "wishes to remake the world after her own heart."

"Very noble," he nodded at me. "We can't be too conservative and accomplish things. If the world is to be destroyed, better that people like us with the right thinking, destroy it our way, than the others. Very noble of your wife," he commented sourly and turned away.

"Well, darling, I can't say you're going to be the hit of Aunt Dora's birthday party."

"Go back, Franklin."

"Babsy, you know I can't join you."

"What makes you think I can do this any more than you?"

"I do respect you, Babs. I really do. Just don't make a fool of me. Don't do that."

"These women work seven days a week and most of them have children." I waved the women on around me. "This has nothing to do with you."

"Just wait until Aunt Polly and Aunt Dora arrive and see you parading about in the Delano jewels and your ermine. Oh, 'tis about to be jolly. You've certainly outdone Alice and the monkey lady."

"I don't mean to be entertainment for you . . ."

"Move on, come along, move on." A policeman harangued me. I was a little frightened.

"Well, stay in the shadows, won't you, when they pull up, Babs? It's going to be really bad." He shut the window and pulled the velvet drapes closed.

I did slip into the shadows when Jack Astor's car pulled up and it was terrible because Kate caught sight of Mama's two sisters done up as queens and, growling, moved toward them from one direction, just as a society photographer from the Sunday rotogravure section moved toward them from the opposite direction, camera ready. Aunt Polly and Aunt Dora left the car and stood on the sidewalk for a moment, just a moment. Their straight old monolithic bodies were draped in French velvets, their snowy curled heads were topped with diadems of rubies. Ormolu, wainscoting, balconies and latticework, parchment buildings, wrapped in the fortunes of the China trade. I would inherit those jewels. Diamonds to the waist, emeralds to the elbow. Franklin's aunts had dusted their faces with white parchment powders and redrawn their lips in heart shapes of red and stenciled new eyebrows in thin arched blacks. Just so, ah, lift your chin, Aunt Polly. My side of the family is mad. Look directly at the camera, Aunt Dora. They pulled their fur collars away from their faces and stared with bright little vacuous monkey-eyes at the photographer's box. In full frame of the lens, at right angle, Kate spat in Aunt Polly's face and then in Aunt Dora's face. Their hands flew, fluttered, parchment butterflies, monkey paws, clawing, to their geisha faces, to their jewels, to the anchovy curls around the diadems. And then Aunt Dora and Aunt Polly remembered who they were. I could hear them and Mama, the third sister, reminding me in the same voices. "Eleanor, remember WHO YOU ARE." And I could see frozen on their faces those words, frozen just below the thin surface of their foreheads like the leaves from the hazel tree trapped in the ice pond in winter. Remember who you are. They remembered

211

for that one click of a moment while the photographer took their picture for the newspapers, while they smiled, while Kate spat her catarrh and her hatred at them, clearing her throat again and again and spitting the sickness of the whole country up at them while the camera focused and clicked and the ladies held themselves together for the photographer and clutched their tiny silk purses and pursed their tiny red lips and lifted their dear brave old chins while Kate's sputum fell upon their faces. It was over in a moment. Kate reached around for a hot potato from the garbage can to fling at Franklin's aunts as they moved forward, out of the frame, and I yelled, "Kate!" and pulled her away, the potato still burning in her hand. It rolled from her hand and off into the gutter. I don't think anyone ever noticed me for at that moment the splendid doors of the Waldorf swung open and the entire Roosevelt clan standing before them, shouted: "Surprise! Surprise!" and we all walked in together singing "Happy Birthday, Aunt Dora, Happy Birthday to you." The picket line was dispersed immediately by the police and Kate was hustled off.

Franklin looked quickly at me, I at him. We said nothing. This elegant mother and proud father live a comfortable and gracious life with their happy and healthy family. Mr. Fairchild wears a white suit for golf and has a collection of canes and gas masks. Mrs. Fairchild is as sweet as the water in French Lick Springs and sees that everyone has all the Cracker Jacks he needs. With no surprises. None of us likes surprises. We like to be surprising. Cracker Jacks aplenty, what more do we need?

I didn't ruin the party nor did the party save the League of Nations. Alice, Nick, Senator Lodge and Senator Borah eventually poisoned the nation against the League. Lord Grey and Sommerville-West never were admitted to the White House; the lady's spider monkey, Mama told me, summarily died of exposure from the cold, and the charmaids, either those or others, were back at work at the Waldorf, seven days a week. We were, none of us, very effective. In the White House, Mr. Wilson, one side of his body paralyzed, leaned on a blackthorn stick and limped in darkened halls. His mind was still good; his heart was broken. Honorable wound, Mr. Wilson. Honorable wound, Aunt Dora. Honorable wound, Aunt Polly. Oh, how long the shadows were between what I knew and what I was. I have to go into the pool to get out of the pool, but God help me, how deep must the pool be? How sharp the claws of the dragon?

EXCURSION FIVE
The Campaign Train, Fall 1920

IN WHICH I RIDE
THE 1920 VICE-PRESIDENTIAL
CAMPAIGN TRAIN

Most of my hours on the campaign train were passed watching cows from a wing chair in the drawing room or on my knees in my stateroom crying into my trunk because by the time the train had cut across the belly of America into Colorado and was on its swing back through Missouri, I knew America believed in nothing but itself and my husband was fashioning himself after America.

"Irritable. Irritirritable!" Franklin declares the mood joyously from one length of the Pullman car to the other. "Let's play poker." Ladders crawl up my last pair of black hose and perspiration down my spine. Mr. Sullivan, whose teeth click upper to lowers as he deals the cards to Franklin and the gang, has spilled last night's kidney gravy on his country clothes and they seem to be his only clothes.

Why I was brought along I can only surmise. I was as anxious to be included in the final and fourth swing across the country then as I am now anxious to be off the train once and for all and never smell kidney gravy again as long as I live. I suppose Franklin brought me along to attract the women's vote but as far as I can see there is no women's vote and I am in no mood to attract anything.

"Why don't you make yourself happy and go home? I know you're miserable."

"I may eventually be useful, Franklin."

It was my duty and I remained but I could see no point in the campaign, in my presence, in votes for women.

My world widens and my bed narrows as we flee from our past through this enormous unaccountable country and I splash tepid water on my face and I dress and stand next to Franklin and shift from one foot to the other and smile as I receive dozens of long-stemmed roses from shabby wives along the route. I long for my sectioned ebony tea tray and drink steaming black coffee from cracked crockery mugs delicately traced with a repellent brown stain as the train lurches forward and rocks from side to side. The coffee sloshes perversely away from me as I dip to it and toward me as I lean from it.

"Louis, I cannot bear politics. I am tired of cows. My feet hurt. I cannot sleep and I am constipated." I do not tell all this to Louis. "Louis, Franklin seems unscrupulous." He assures me that Franklin is merely thinking a hundred thoughts at the same time, some of which contradict others of which, he says. I seem to think only one thought all the time. I regret confiding it to Louis, but the alternative confidants are Christ, who, in the Ozarks, seems less and less available, and my trunk. "I can't bear politics. I am tired of cows. My feet hurt. I cannot sleep. Mr. Prenosil, the AP man, wears his clothing too tightly and I am constipated."

Our car, the *Westboro*, is a standard Pullman, eighty-two feet long and nine feet wide, narrowing between the staterooms to a foot-and-a-half corridor. The eight staterooms are at the back. Each of them has an overhead fan, two berths and one facility. At the front of the car is what Louis and I have dubbed the Swamp with its sofas and chairs, a gaming table, a public facility. In the center is the lounge with its high-backed wing chairs, blinds, curtains and filthy windows, and at the far rear, of course, the observation platform with its little fencing, its gate, its awning and a photograph of Mr. Cox stuck on the door and curling up at the corners from the sun. I have no feeling about Mr. Cox except he is an instrument of Mr. Wilson's and is losing both his hair and the election in clumps.

In the night I can hear every noise every man makes and in the morning every cough and groan and hack and sour stomach and rancid joke. I can hear the chunks of ice dropping into the glasses of bourbon. I can hear the cards slapping the table and the coins clinking into piles and I dream I am Jesus on the temple floor. I can feel whispers and sense my name. Shhh, here she comes. Close the door. Jesus, close the *door!* A few have, kindly enough, chosen to absolve themselves in the morning at the sink of the public facility forward. The walls of the *Westboro* are paneled in mahogany; the body of the train, however, is that cosmetic metal which only looks like wood but heats up like an oven and inflates every sound and sorrow until I am smothered.

Mr. Sullivan across from me in the lounge area has a mouth like a hungry goldfish. His lips roll back and he swallows his words. He is overly solicitous to me and his pants rise three inches above his shoes, his hairline seven above his eyebrows over his very broken nose which is why he breathes, I suspect, through his mouth and through his teeth, which are separated by quarter inches of pink wet space. He also advises Franklin. I do like Mr. Lynch, our old friend Tom from Poughkeepsie, who disperses funds, whom Franklin calls Mr. Lunch. Mr. Lynch has a ruddy little sharp-nosed cat face and is perfectly self-reliant with that British sort of efficiency that is always on time but on the wrong day. Nevertheless, although Franklin will be in debt over his head at the end of this hot little jaunt, I do like Mr. Lynch. He never complains.

Mr. Prenosil, modern, smooth, young, bald—I believe his head has been shaved—resembles a newt. His clothes are too tight for his muscular shape and there is something subterranean, slippery, unfinished about him. Mr. Sullivan, poor soul, has a face like a hambone. I have seen him drawing closer and closer to young girls in the dark places between gaslights until he disappears while Franklin speaks. Mr. McIntyre has a deep sensitive face and heavy thick hair. I do like him except I always find him watching me. Mr. Camalier, the secretary, weighs two hundred pounds and has used fisticuffs on little Mr. Howe. We seem not to be with him as often as with the others. He goes off by himself a great deal and comes back with tiny bits of river fossils and flowering mosses. Occasionally we have with us Mr. Early, the advance man.

"Didja catch that lady today shouting something about Johnson's grass and the railroads? What's that all about anyway, Frank?"

No one knew.

"Did you see her? Jesus. She had a face like a toilet bowl."

"Betcha a quarter her mother had a royal flush."

"Mr. Lunch," Franklin said, "find out what the story is on Johnson grass, will you?"

I had no idea what they were speaking of. I smiled lightly from my wing chair. If I could fly, I would fly away home. The men made bets all day. "Betcha you're wearing the worst tie in Oklahoma." "We aren't in Oklahoma." "Then you owe me five bucks." "Har, har, har." Between platform stops, schoolhouse speeches, firebarn rallies and at the end of the endless campaign days which begin at seven in the morning and go too often to ten or eleven at night, the men raced to the front of our car, to the leather couches and leather chairs and sinks and stalls and pallor of cigar smoke where they played poker until one or two in the morning, while Romeo, the porter, dozed, read his Bible, moving his lips as he read, hopped up to fetch more bourbon and waited out the game so he could sleep on the leather couch up front which was his right according to the contract we made with the Pullman people. I complained too often about the injustice to Romeo.

Franklin finally snapped: "If you want to find a way to be effective on this trip, Eleanor, forget Romeo's nap time and speak to more people on the platform instead of fading off behind the flag."

Louis hovered about Franklin. "Look, boss," he tried, "we turn the trick on them next time around. They think you're expendable? Okay, next time around, you nominate Smith. He'll never win. Not yet. You see those faces out there? They wouldn't touch a Catholic with a ten-foot Pollack. Nominate Smith. He loses. 'Twenty-eight you move in."

"I'd say 'thirty-two."

"Whatever."

"What do I do in the meantime? Tread water? Romeo, wherefore art thou with the bourbon? Groggy-grog time, gang."

"Franklin, to me shifting issues at each station stop is simply without morality."

"Morality? Come off it, Babs. It's no more than changing your ammunition. Number-four shot for ducks, number-one shot for geese, number-seven for plovers. The gun doesn't change; neither does the hunter."

"Bad, boss," Louis pronounces softly.

"I like eight for plovers, seven on rails," Mr. Lynch adds blandly.

And I leave to cry into my trunk. Ladybug, ladybug, fly away home. Your house is on fire, your children are gone. Louis whistles aimlessly between his teeth. We are sitting at some nameless siding at a flat, placarded painted clapboard someplace in America the name of which passed me by as we pulled in to wait here for another train to pick us up, but the name is written in triplicate on the itinerary the men are studying.

"But what do you *think* America is, Franklin? You should *tell* these people. You must bring the issues to them and educate them."

The coffee sloshes in the mugs. Franklin breaks a doughnut and dunks it. The men look away from me, annoyed, embarrassed. Franklin mutters and moves his hands into contortive tricks which are supposed, for he has done this before, to be a spider with hiccups doing push-ups on a mirror. Bully, Franklin. For the first week the men on the team were very chivalrous and considerate and spoke at length of the women's vote because there had been four hundred women delegates at the San Francisco convention and Harriet May Mills had actually been appointed to the National Rules Committee. But none of them has had much to do with me, really, except of course Louis, whom they also avoid. I had been on the train only a week when Franklin, standing on the observation platform, overspoke a ten-minute speech by fifteen minutes. I sat in a fold-up chair behind him and pulled finally at the hem of his jacket but Mr. Prenosil reached out quickly and, far too forcibly, wrenched my hand away from the jacket so that Franklin turned to feel an even greater yank and stumbled on his words. The train was pressed to make up almost fifteen minutes to its next stop and although I have sat through endless meals of coffee and sandwiches with him and the others, I have not spoken to Mr. Prenosil since.

"For God's sake, Eleanor. He's my AP man. Do you know how I had to *fight* to get him? So what if the train's late?"

"No man has any business to be that familiar, to come between husband and wife. The people who are deciding your schedule should have cut your speech short. I think we are being treated much like a pair of dancing bears dragged out so the curious can see us. What we say, what we do, doesn't matter one iota."

"Oh, stop fluffing about so. It's hard work. The gang's a good one, they're all under tremendous pressure, and it makes absolutely no difference to me if the train is late or not . . . that's not *my* problem. If I have something to say to the people, by God, I'll not have a woman pulling at my coattails."

"You were just going on."

"What I say doesn't matter. What matters is that I do go on. There were a few people listening this time. It's very difficult, Eleanor. You might try it someday. Believe me, you'd sing a different tune if you had to risk yourself as I must."

"Thank you, no. This whole trip to me is . . ." I sought for something I'd heard from the newspapermen and found it. "This whole trip is like a tour of a sewer in a glass-bottomed boat. And I do think that referring to Mr. Harding as Mr. Hardly is quite beneath your dignity. Common."

"And your dear cousin Ted Jr., trailing us and telling the folks I'm a maverick and not part of the Roosevelt family . . . is that not common?"

"As you would say yourself, that's politics. And you would shrug or do your handtricks, wouldn't you?"

"I don't have any time for baiting. I have speeches to write."

"We both know better."

I heard him speaking to the gang later and left my stateroom to sit with them. There was so little room anywhere on the train and the fans barely moved the air.

"What blows me out, boys, is that each of those lumps of putty out there has the same amount of votes I have."

"That's America, boss."

"Jefferson was right after all: the elite must run the republic. God help me if I'm ever equal. Okay, let's go over the issues, Early. What do they want to hear in Missouri?"

"Over here, we do the flossy bit, Frank. Law and order here. No issues Cape Girardeau. Twelve-oh-five noon at Sedalia, then Kokomo at ten fifty-six." Once I memorized

Hiawatha because my father was going off on a trip and, leaving, said, "Nell, when I come home I want to hear all of *Hiawatha*. Every word." I was seven. I am thirty-six and I hear the broken poetry of the names of American towns and there is no substance worth memorizing. "Kokomo at ten fifty-six. Madisonville at noon. Bowling Green at ten fifteen." They speak in codes, these men around my husband and I have understood the code but not the message. "Ten for the League. Labor is nine. Repeal, five. Ten, five and nine are out for Kokomo. Shoes and Germans. Red, black, brown. Too many Irish here. Federal soldiers' bonus? How about a satire on the Republican fund along the Ponzi lines? There is nothing in the Covenant which says Ireland can't have its independence. The Covenant provides, to the contrary, protection of territories from external invasion. Boston wants to see the boss in fighting togs, more boasts and not the apologetic tones used by some Democratic speakers. High cost living knotty problem. Offer something."

"I can't think about that or Boston yet."

"Bryanites are dissatisfied with League question. Germans don't want ten. In Marion, refer to Germans as small hyphenated disloyal group who don't want League and were disloyal during war," we are to say in Marion to the blacks. "Avoid eleven, they can't own land. Stress nine and blink five. Eleven very important over here. We can get them on eleven. Romeo, more smokables."

I ask, "Oh, dear, what is eleven? I've forgotten eleven. No, no, no, no. Don't let me disturb you." I laugh my laugh and I cannot stop it.

Like priests, they pause, fingers pointing to crosses on a large inked map. "Farmers," someone answers, and looks back at the map. I have interrupted their ceremony, have I? Their train of thought. This is not a train of thought. It is the Twentieth Century Limited, at lease the car *Westboro* is, and we ride it, thoughtless and limited, across the country into the dark century.

"Oh."

I wait.

"But shouldn't you somehow *tell* these people while you have the opportunity what America means? I've seen their faces. There isn't a light in one of them. Of course they are hostile and ignorant but if they were educated, I know they'd be quite reasonable."

"We just put them through a war, dearest, and then lost the peace. They have reason not to trust us."

"But they did believe . . ." I continue.

"Yes."

"They ain't gonna believe in nothing for a while, Mrs. Roosevelt. We just gotta tread water and keep the name up front a bit."

"Politics ain't religion."

"Well, I don't think it's poker, either. These people must care about something. I've seen their faces . . . they *must* care!"

"Dearest." Franklin covers my hand with his. Mine trembles. "If you're going to speak to a crowd you better learn how to say *either* with a long *e*, rather than a long *i*."

Everyone laughs uproariously because Franklin has said *rather* with an awfully broad *a*. I can't tell who they are laughing at, with, for. "I hardly think," I retort, "that I'll be speaking publicly!" and flaunt off to my stateroom. I recall my back being very straight.

"It was ossified, madam, ossified. Relax."

"What?"

"Your back was ossified. What's bothering you?"

"Oh, Franklin, it is so so . . . difficult to control my behavior."

"That's not precisely the problem, Eleanor. You are trying to control *our* behavior and you are quite out of line."

Whether the sun sets before us or behind, we go from the same harshness of railroad yard to railroad yard, broken now and then by a rough dusty tour along a country road in a

225

rented Dodge, seven or eight of us bouncing along in an open car at twenty-five big bucks a day, boss. Sometimes I have a bath in a hotel.

Shards of glass sparkle in rubble along the sidings, Russian thistle sprouts between the tracks, sunlit tiger lilies and Siberian iris spike up in muddy culverts. The curses of black men shoveling coal wove once before dawn with the terrible thin final scream of a pig in the stockyards. We go deeper into America. I have seen blood running from cement aprons before slaughterhouses along the route. I have seen a length of cobalt blue hose cut and curled like a snake on the flank of a coal pile gleaming in the rain, a jeweled beast from the center of the earth. I have seen cranes and derricks and factories with hundreds of dirty windows and brick warehouses and narrow tenements and cobblestones and cobra skins and adobe along the right-of-way under indigo skies and then back again to the narrow tenement houses, one after another, and an old sea gull circling slowly over a warehouse, looking for the river, circling over large white brick numbers raised on the walls: 1894. Starlings punctuate the 1894, three starlings to the one, seven to the eight, one to the nine and none on the four as if they too have a code. They have. At once, all attack the sea gull. He flies higher. The starlings settle into their niches again. Everywhere there is lead. Somewhere there is silver.

"You have a fine mind, Eleanor, a disciplined mind and a selfless soul. I am afraid for you that you will live a life of contradiction." Ah, Mlle. Souvestre, if you could see me now. We have a code on the train. Farmers eleven, Democrats four, League five, or is it ten? Repeal six, labor nine. Something important is ten. Brown, black, red. Red on four, move to five. Irish in Danville. Black. Factory roofs chew at the sky, vats, vents, boilers, warehouses, cranes and derricks and then we come to the river.

"That be the old Mo, ma'am," I am informed by Romeo,

who slumps further into a wing chair in the lounge area of our Pullman car and studies his Bible. He says he's a deacon and then says no more. I watch the ellipses and eddies of the river.

The Missouri flattens and moves slowly with its load of silt. Like the faces of the people who come to the rear of the observation car to hear Franklin, the river is flat, treacherous with snags, dangerous with uncharted currents. Sometimes we hire a band. Sometimes we see hawks circling under the sun. Once I saw the shadow of an eagle on the concrete and felt hackles rise on the back of my neck.

We are all dirty. My clothes are too warm. It is early October, yet the sun bakes down on the metal sides of the Pullman and the car reeks from cigar smoke, from coal fumes, from the amber jam, an insect excrement in the bottom of last night's bourbon glasses, and from Mr. Sullivan's suit. The flag draped along the rear of the observation platform is blackened and heavy with the cinders in its folds. Franklin's clothes are crumpled also. At Sedalia, the stationmaster holds the clean chemises and drawers and handkerchiefs and new black hose Mama has sent on and wires reporting poor James' recovery from his colitis during his first week at Groton.

I have nowhere to go. A few times Mr. Howe has taken me at night to the rear to see the wealth of stars in the heavenly sky ("Don't say 'heavenly sky,' Eleanor. That's redundant." "Oh.") but mostly I am in my stateroom with the shutters closed against the unending scrape and collision and rupture of the dark men shoveling coal into the cars, the cars locking and grinding, the odd stumps of people staring into our car, the buckwheat bumpkins climbing on board to meet and greet and press the flesh while I press the thorns of their wives' roses.

"Jes wanna press the flesh of the next President of the Yewnited States."

227

Someone whispers.

"Oh, *Vice*-President. Sure enough. See you in Washington."

"My." They look me up and down. "She is so tall and ugly next to him. Why did he ever marry someone who looks like her?" I move away from Franklin, shifting from one foot to the other like a cripple in a pavane until I have reached the wall and a wing chair. It is only next to Franklin that I feel ugly. I cross my arms over my breasts, over my roses, and hold myself as if I were my own child and try not to get that look on my face. Fascinated, I count cows, sumac, buttons on the horsehair upholstery.

And Franklin, conspirator par excellence, winking at them all, planning itineraries and post-office appointments, inviting them up to Washington, God help us all, making promises he would/should/could never keep and repeating their bumpkin names as if he were one of them. Slap on the back, my name is Al from Altoona and I sell anthracite. Slap on the back. Put 'er there. V. Valentine from Virginia City, votes. Come up and see me sometime. Anything I can do for you, brother, just let me know.

"How common does a man have to be, Great Commoner, in order to be in tune with the common man?"

"Have to make 'em feel comfortable, Mrs. Roosevelt," Franklin's gang would explain to me. But they were just as rough with their drink and telegraphese talk and innuendos and . . . and their yatatata. "It never stops, Franklin."

"You *know* newspapermen, darling. It's nothing personal."

"To think that men such as these inform the people."

I remember a sunbaked day with Franklin standing on the roof of a small shed, hands behind his back, leaning into the crowd, the shadows of a pale brick building sharp purple on the red clay of the right-of-way. Men wore slouch hats and shaded their eyes with one hand. Franklin was bareheaded. He did his Humble speech, preaching to them.

"The Democratic party is destined to win because, number

one, we need the League of Nations to show the war was not fought in vain."

"Hey, you a wet or a dry, mister?" They shout at Franklin. "You one of those swells who's gonna drag us into the damn League, mister?"

"And we're going to win, number two, because no one wants to adopt Mr. Hardly's plan to go back to McKinley's days. And three, we do not want to wipe out the benefits of progressive . . ."

"Hell, that's not Teddy. Where's your dad, son?"

"And, number four, because the people won't sanction the purchase of the election by a Republican campaign chest."

And some walk away or lean, hostile and smart-alec, against a Ford flivver, parked on the cement apron of the right-of-way. The band plays, dour and dirty men they are— fifer and three drummers with starvation necks and skin so luminous I can see the bones in their wrists. Franklin changes shape and now, as if he's sucked himself off the Tell It To The Marines poster, out of the pages of Carlyle, he stands with his God of War legs squarely placed, far apart, set, no delicacy, none of the genteel summer languish in wicker chairs on tranquil lawns. He has pulled a brimmed notched hat over his head, pleated its crown with a cut of his hand. Snap. And he snaps a smile from the corner of his mouth as if he's just snapped a coarse joke with someone. But who? In the crowds are dull and bland faces, bored, curious for a moment about the swells, about Franklin who is, these days, a grinning exaggeration of a football hero. Women follow him up aisles and flutter about him while Louis kindly engages me in conversation. Louis has assigned himself to me.

Louis spends his time cultivating the AP man, vying for Franklin's attention, writing poetry and talking with me. He too was left behind until this last trip. Franklin's friend who owns the mill in Massachusetts wrote him to leave Louis in Washington and "let the people see you do your own work." It was responsible advice.

"Boss," Louis would ask. "Watson's saying the Army purchased two times as many curry combs as it had horses and mules. How do we answer that, boss?"

"Uppa stump. Snug as a bug in a rug, smackeroo, smasheroo, yatatata. Forward or flounder."

While I claw through the trunk under the dirty linens looking for my own face, Franklin wrestles with that implacable sea of faces out there. I thought for so long it would be through Franklin I would find myself, play golf, say sticky wicket, even bully, laugh, save the world, love, all of it in any order. But now I am not certain it is possible to take substance from that shadow of his which looms and shrinks and slips under cracks and is without measure. It is a wretched aloneness I feel. Franklin has begun again to dream of fire. In the night I hear him shout: "Stop!" I lift up on one elbow and listen, taut. "Get water." I would hear Louis, always Louis, leave his berth, run water. Franklin mumbles something. Doors close. Lights off.

"Franklin! These people *care* about things."

"Care, Eleanor? Have you seen their faces. It's like speaking into a vacuum. The women don't care about the women's vote; the veterans don't care about the war *or* the League. The mothers don't care about their sons. They think tariff is a place in Africa. Which it well might be. Early, you have got to do something about too many speeches and too small crowds. Thirty, forty people ten times a day is . . . isn't. Can't we get any more money from headquarters?"

Early shook his head no.

So we went on. Franklin, the city swell, trying to be the big swashing hero-figure with his British accent, toying with the people and the peas at men's club suppers, trying to stir up some "sediment of sentiment," he says, winking at us all, "some residue of romance," he trills, trying to get something moving on the people's faces. "Irritirritable!" he would warn at the end of a station stop. "Let's play poker." And the men would spill from the observation platform to the front end of the car, ready with chips and bottles and cards until the next town, the next speech, the next faint clapping, the next morning searching the papers for the name of Roosevelt.

Franklin's mens' club speech is We Have Got to Reorganize the Government Along the Lines of Business. On the word *reorganize* Franklin makes peas jump on dinner plates with his fist. Off dinner plates when he hits really first-rate. We take bets as to how many peas he can displace. Fourteen is the most so far. "Waste, waste, waste." He hits the table. The peas jump. "The Republican party has betrayed every mother who sent her son to his death," he tells ladies' clubs in the Flossy speech. And for the large crowds, or the small crowds with newspapermen, he uses his favorite: the Rough, Peppy Americanism, Law and Order, No Issues speech. But his smackeroo, he calls it, his socko pseudosocratic peroration of abuse and malcontent is the Hardly Hymn of Hate speech which I cannot tolerate. I long to hear even bully once again.

By the end of the trip, Mr. McIntyre calculates, Franklin will have grinned through thirty-two states and made one thousand speeches and swallowed, Mr. Lunch adds cryptically, four million green peas and one chicken bone. Ploppit. His real talent, I heard Mr. McIntyre sigh resignedly through an open stateroom door to someone I couldn't see as I passed, "his real talent is himself." The gang was supportive outwardly, but privately, they were brutal and so I learned more from listening to what I should not have heard than to the hundreds of speeches I did hear.

One morning when I should not have, I heard Mr. Early speaking with Mr. Prenosil in the public facility at the end of the lounge. Had I stood, they would have known I'd overheard, so I thought to sit small and quiet in the wing chair and then leave when I could. The men were at the sinks, shaving, I supposed, and forgot once again forevermore to close the door of the sacrosanct room.

"Listen, I could carve a man with more backbone than him from a *banana*."

"Still, he's a lot like Teddy."

"Teddy? How?"

"You know. What they said about Teddy: ordinary intellect, extraordinary gifts."

"Never heard that."

"Don't remember who said it . . . but they said he didn't give a damn for the law. You know, could be with Frank's luck, he'll win and Cox will drop dead the day after he takes office."

"He is a lucky s.o.b., ain't he?"

"Yeah. And he hates like H. to lose. He's a real poor loser, I'll tell you that much."

"Plays every card in his hand and then some . . ."

"I'm not sure you can judge a man by the way he plays poker."

"I say you can. And I also say there's nothing more dangerous than a fool with initiative."

"Shrewd fool. That much I'll give you. You know what, though? I like him."

"Everybody does."

"Not her."

"Probably mutual."

"Don't blame him. Sourpuss lady . . ."

"Jesus, the door."

We reached the door at the same time. I saw Mr. Early's face fat with suds and his razor paused at his chin.

"Disloyal and crude," I reported to Franklin.

"Look, we're losing. He's killed himself for me. He's a damn good advance man. It's just uphill. You can't blame the man. Cox is losing hard."

"So are you."

"No, I was never trying to win."

I didn't believe that. Franklin always expected to win at anything he tried. Something about his luck was changing.

IN WHICH I RECOGNIZE A FACE IN THE CROWD

"I didn't hear you mention the League once last night, Franklin. Not once."

"You may have surmised that the League is no longer a viable issue. Also you sat on the platform as if you were at a funeral. I don't need that."

"Whatever are you talking about, dear? Of course the League's an issue. Why, Franklin, it's what we believe in!"

"Nobody around here does."

"They must believe in something, dear. People do. We do."

"We're quite different."

"Well, then, of course you'll agree that it is our duty to teach them, is it not? This is a marvelous opportunity to teach the entire country what is right. They only need to be educated."

"Amazing. Simply amazing. You have an assumption that if everyone were as clever and educated as you he would feel the same compulsions and have the same truths. You are so wrong, Eleanor. You still live in such a dream world. Anyway, I haven't forty years. I have less than three weeks. You have to hit them over the head or take away their liquor to wake them up. Or . . . or *trick* them into making me President. Yup, that'll teach 'em, won't it fellas?" His smile was crooked and did not include me.

"Never has," Prenosil added.

Everyone laughed.

"But it could," I insisted. I was near to tears that I was so misunderstood.

"Of course, Babsy, if I ever have the chance. And these old duffers here are gonna give me the chance." His grin was sportive, wise without wisdom.

"Babs." Franklin took my arm and led me gently toward the narrow corridor outside my stateroom, where we leaned against the walls and shouted truths at each other over the crashing of wheels and the hiss of steam. Lights splashed on his face, off his face, comic evil, tragic good, comic good, tragic evil; the car swayed, darkness, light, darkness, as we dipped toward the South. The train slowed. Wheels spun, a roulette wheel spun. Franklin's face was left at tragic good. "People want to believe in things, Babs. Hope . . . sympathy . . . lead them to proper destiny. Educate them . . ." The train stopped to let another pass. "And I intend to if I ever get the chance. I intend to lead the people, darling. It will be toward the very things you and I believe in."

"With honor."

"With honor."

"Not this sort of deceit."

"With intelligent politics."

I had not been misunderstood. I had been betrayed.

Mr. Lynch and Mr. Sullivan came out on the platform and heckled the crows who screeched at them from the plane trees along the tracks.

There is something about the Democrats and the Re-

publicans, this entire debate weaving across the country, that
has to do with my own life. I am not certain at all what it is. I
do see in the faces of the people something I have seen in my
children's faces when they are really ill. They call for me every
moment to stroke their foreheads and hold cold compresses
to the backs of their necks and read to them. As soon as they
are well, they are quite ready to kick me down the stairs and
any touch from me is a threat to their existence. Stay away.
Leave me alone. Don't bother me. I see that on the faces of
the people. We won the war, now leave us be. Harding is quite
correct: we'll go back to the good old days of McKinley, before
all these rich Easterners tried to redeem us, every one of them
a new Christ from Groton, transforming us, saving us. We
don't need progress. We have enough problems without
trying to change things. Progressive legislation: phooey. It is a
word my children use: "Phooey." Franklin says the issue is
the status quo versus progress. But there is something more.

Once, I believe it was before Franklin Jr. was born, my
charity boards giving me no satisfaction, I announced I
should return to a settlement house to work with the poor as
I had before my marriage. All Mama had to say was, "Well,
Eleanor, you will pick up every disease of the poor and bring
them back to your children who are already ill enough."
Germs didn't keep me from the settlement house; Mama's
unspoken Jehovan prophecy of God's Punishment trapped
me. If you do something willfully wrong, something you want
to do, you will lose a child. Amazingly, I agreed. I have since
lost a child; I have lost love, an aunt, my grandmother. I have
lost so much and behaved so perfectly. I did my duty as
Granny Hall had. I did not cut the cords of tradition as my
Aunt Pussie had. Still I had lost. I'm no longer afraid of loss.
But those people out there listening to Franklin, they are.
They want to hear nothing of progress. They are still afraid
that if they criticize the sky, it will fall in on them.

Pussie criticized the sky. She lived on the very cusp of
decency, on the edge of creativity. Dear Granny Hall, her

235

mother, my grandmother, did not. Granny Hall gave her life
to everyone and had none of her own. Rest in peace. When
Pussie died last winter suddenly, as Mama had predicted,
horribly burned to death in the converted stable with her two
children, everyone simply nodded over their sewing-bee laps
as if Pussie and her dear girls deserved such an end because—
the needles slip in and out—because she had forgotten her
beginnings and, rather than safety, chose love, freedom,
adventure. Ah. I trudged across Washington Square in a
blizzard to identify the chars that had been flesh and blood. I
shall long remember the next three days of finding Pussie's
husband and her son, arranging for the funeral, telling the
family. When the three days were over and the loved ones
sifted into the earth, Mama simply looked at me and declared:
"Pussie ought to have lived in Europe."

Granny Hall died before Pussie, only from a slower
tragedy: that of giving her entire life to her children. It would
have been too horrible if she had seen those charred bodies.
Death, I decided, crossing the square that day, lifting one
heavy foot over the crusted drifts and then the other until I
reached the remains of the stable, death is not the tragedy.
The tragedy is in what one does with one's life. I vowed never
to be Granny Hall, but I had not Pussie's courage to live her
life just as she wished, right or wrong. I wonder if she was
happy. I wonder if she was frightened. I wonder how she
decided what her duty was. I have to do my duty of course,
but less and less do I know what it is, where it lies. Does it lie
with Franklin's destiny grinning at me like some terrible
grotesque in the eaves of my life? Does it lie with the safety of
home and hearth? How odd I once again have no home.
There are all the children in school and all the things in
boxes, as though the pool has turned inside out, upside down
once again, in some strange gyre. What do I owe to Franklin
now? There are enough servants. Mama will take care of
anything that needs care with more grace, generosity and
efficiency than I. There are people to choose clothes for the

children, people to take them to school. I come when they are sick and even so, they are healthier without me. I suppose my destiny finally lies within myself. In that lump of lead that stirs now and then? Does it lie in being discovered, loved, protected by another man? Mr. Baruch sent me roses, filled my hotel room with roses. Would he have loved me? Will I sit quivering again and again hoping a General Pershing will lift me from the crowd . . . or another man, another destiny to fling my dreams onto? Shall I dream forever about a sergeant because he is safely put away? What shall I dream about? Does one dream about one's own self? If so, even my dreams shall be lonely. Could I possibly, could America, ever dare risk enough to surrender our safety to change? Only when we hit bottom. And neither America nor I have yet hit bottom enough to risk. I know the Republicans will win.

IN WHICH I AM CHALLENGED
BY FRANKLIN

I have irritated Franklin considerably in the last few days with my questions. The men are also irritated with me.

"Do you mean the law-enforcement people in the South are insisting on Prohibition? Why that's . . . you must tell them that if they insist on Prohibition, on carrying out *that* law, they should also insist on the carrying out of voting for all citizens."

"Yes, Eleanor."

"Franklin, I can't sleep for the noise. The porter has nowhere to sleep until you clear out your card game. It's a dreadful thing to keep him up until two in the morning while you . . . gamble."

"I figure the Rough, Peppy Americanism speech in Morgantown."

"How does the crowd look out there?"

"Persnickety. Talk about mothers and wives."

"But I don't understand, dear. Who are the Southern law-enforcement committees to obey and enforce one law and ignore the other? If they demand Prohibition, tell them they must therefore see that all their citizens vote."

"That'll carry the South," cracked Mr. Early.

"Wrap it right up," added Mr. Prenosil.

"You still live in such a dream world, darling. Look, fellas, how the H. can I explain the League of Nations to them? I say once and for all we drop the League as an issue."

"National has already."

"Franklin! Our own people are depending on you to carry that issue to the country!"

"Do you realize who elects . . . *what* elects a president? Those flatfaced fenmen out there. They don't want Hardly off his front porch any more than they want to get off theirs. You know what Missouri's biggest export is? They carry it in their pants. Lead. Lead. Get the lead out of your pants and vote for Roosevelt."

"Ran over one of 'em yesterday in the touring car. Three of 'em sprang right up from the very spot."

"Franklin, you don't stand for anything. How can you stand for anything if you continue to change your story each moment the wind shifts? You don't believe in anything. At all. I weep for you."

"Babs, you read too much Dickens. Just because people are poor, humble and crippled doesn't mean they're very wonderful, doesn't mean they're waiting for the Redeemer on the 10:25 from Kokomo."

"You lack in ideals. You brag. You boast. That remark about controlling the votes of Haiti . . . and that you yourself wrote the constitution for Haiti. . . . My god, Franklin!"

"And I fall flat on my face and I pick up and go out there

239

again. I had a tomato in my face last week. A tomato. Are you willing to risk yourself as I'm doing?"

"Someone has to remind you of what we stand for."

"And I thank you, Eleanor. Politics is a rough business. It isn't easy bringing ideas into a world. I need your support not your complaints. You are getting under my skin and there is quite enough irritation there already."

"But you must tell these people what America means!" I whined.

He looked away from me. "Fellas, can't we do anything about Morgantown? Maybe you can drum up more than fifty Spanish War vets who can't clap because they've got umbrellas in one hand and crutches in the other. Say, Babs, don't we own mines in Morgantown? I could get the workers."

"Sure," McIntyre answered. "That's all the folks have to see. You can't own the mines and be on the side of labor. You want national press to pick that one up? They'd love it."

"But I *am* on the side of labor."

"Not here. Not in Morgantown you're not. Here you own the mines."

"Irritirritable . . . let's play poker!"

Through a hundred miles of mountain passes and shimmering rocks and deep-cut gorges I had rehearsed my words over and over again. "You must tell them what you believe, not what they want to hear."

Franklin was very quiet. He looked at his fingernails, the circles of flesh on his knuckles, the fair hairs tufted in the circles like quivers in targets. He looked at me.

"You do believe in things, Franklin? Humanity?"

"Don't be patronizing. I really can't bear a sanctimonious woman."

"I suppose it would be easier if I were prettier."

"Come off it."

"No, really. If I were prettier, men would listen to me a little longer than they do now."

"I *am* listening to you."

"I'm not speaking of you; I'm speaking of *men!*"

"If that is a 'remark,' I would beg you to desist under the circumstances."

"Well, then, going back. What is it you believe in? You decide that, and then speak to the people, tell them what you believe and if they believe what you do, or if you can convince them to, they'll vote for you and you'll represent them."

"Really, Eleanor, you are so naïve."

"Not so. I've been watching you for fifteen years, Franklin."

"Then why don't *you* go out there on the platform and tell them what you believe and see what happens. Oh, would I like to see that! The shy lady risking herself a little. They should only know how shy you are. I wish you *were* shy!"

"Oh, Franklin, I can't speak . . ."

"You said it was easy. You said just tell them what you believe. You won't have to boast, to fight, to accuse. You can just tell them."

"I haven't . . ."

"Yes, you have. You've spoken to your Red Cross groups and your Navy League, at bond drives. You are a very efficient and capable woman. You can't have it both ways."

"I will not speak publicly."

"Then don't tell *me* what to do. I have enough people telling me what to do already."

I had never seen such challenge in his eyes. It was a breathless fiery moment for both of us and I stood at the top of the mast, dizzy, just for that moment as I looked back at him, light-headed, very light-headed, the lead forgotten, and then I backed off and climbed down. "I can't possibly . . ."

I find kidney gravy after two days, and not three, intolerable. "Franklin." I catch him by the sleeve as he passes my stateroom. "Franklin you must get Mr. Sullivan to change his clothes."

"Good Lord, Babs, I can't even get him to change his *gravy!*" He has said it loudly enough to be heard and someone laughs in another stateroom.

In a barren one-street, general-store and apothecary town, where Franklin was to have spoken, he was told with much excitement by Mr. Early that a fortnight before the Sedalia American Legion had had a bloody battle with the IWW. I had no idea what the IWW was but supposed them, from the heated significance of Franklin's reaction, to be an anarchist group threatening the peace of the community in particular and our country in general. The melting pot, he would say, which refused to melt. Fistfights around a bonfire had led to rocks and then to shotguns and, on the Sedalia picnic grounds, in a patch of greenery and mulberry trees surrounded by a large sandy plain of empty American space, six Legionnaires lay dead. Four of the other side had been killed but, it was made clear to us with a smirk by the editor of the *Sedalia Herald* whose hands shook, not during the actual fight.

Canceling his town-green speech and announcing a pilgrimage to the graves of the martyred members of the American Legion, Franklin marched stiff-armed and straightbacked like a windup Uncle Ted, along the main street to the hilltop graveyard overlooking the sandy plain. A large and excited crowd followed him to the top of a small knoll and under a singularly lonely long-limbed elm, which shed its last leaves on Franklin's shoulders, Franklin spoke with eloquence and passion to the raw graves at his feet. The Sedalians cheered at each pause and Franklin, with each cheer, grew more eloquent and more passionate as he damned the anarchists who were tearing our country asunder, who didn't own their own homes or speak our language, who didn't love their country, who should be educated with a two-by-four, then jailed and, if that didn't work, booted right out of our country, those hyphenated Americans.

"Rid this land of the alien anarchist. The American Legion

242

will carry on this cause to put into public life that new blood. " The crowd was again prepared for murder.

It wasn't until I saw a pale face on the edge of the crowd, a woman pulling at her lower lip in fear, that I recognized the alien anarchist. It was Rosie with the broken tooth, whose friends had been hung, she said, hanged I had corrected her, and she had said "It feels the same." She stood pulling at her lip, listening to Franklin, watching me, heavily shawled, her complicated hair twisted, I recalled, with rocks above her raisin face.

It must have been someone she knew, perhaps loved, who had been hanged in Sedalia. I watched the thick Breughel faces creased with red anger and hatred shouting in response to Franklin's oratory, which, to Franklin's delight, the *Sedalia Herald,* a Republican paper, reported the next day as having been inspired. I watched Franklin plant small American flags beside each tumbled bit of turf, as Rosie moved closer and closer around the periphery of the crowd toward me. I watched her sideways, not wishing to call attention to her. When she was at last behind me under the elm and Franklin's speech had ended in apocalyptic hosannas from the hilltop, I managed to stand close to her, smiling at many others, and then slipped a small diamond ring from my finger which I passed to her as I squeezed her hand. I had no money with me and I dared not give her away.

As she slipped back into the crowd and off the hilltop in a direction away from Sedalia, I knew I would forever despise the men of the American Legion who carry war in their hearts the way one harbors typhoid. I didn't know what else I could do. Rosie, at least, with my grandmother's ring, whatever would happen to her, she knew she was right. "It's hard," she had told me at the square dance. "It's so hard not to become crazy especially if you know you're right."

We were told later that the Wobblies had been hanged from the limbs of the very elm Franklin chose to speak beneath. I could not help but shudder. There had been—

indeed, I could see them clearly—small clumps of crow feathers on a sticky base of tar along the spine of the elm. Very sticky. It gets very sticky, the girls had told me.

Each time our train stopped, I looked for Rosie's face, but she was not there although there were other faces like hers, silent and sullen on the edge of the crowd.

IN WHICH I GIVE A BACK RUB

ouis sits on the edge of the wing chair in the lounge area and recites the names of the *Westboro*'s eight sister trains, trying to match the names with the turn and fall of the *Westboro*'s wheels. He says that Mr. Cox's party is on the *Painesville* and I refuse to believe anyone would name a train the *Painesville*.

"Louis, does sanctimonious mean 'unattractive'?"

"No. From saint. 'Saintly. Too saintly.' "

"Is it possible to be too saintly?"

"Well, Eleanor, it's a little like being too unique."

"I see." One either is or is not a saint. There are no steps between.

I have irritated Franklin considerably in the last three days by saying the following: "A lady's place is not in the public eye." "Of course I know what everyone is speaking about but I do not care to make a statement for the press." "Yes, I am

245

going to church today but I shall tell the newspapers that you and I are going, if that sort of lie will make you happy." "There is no point in a campaign trip. The people who do come out are from our own party; the others are trouble-makers from the other party." "The reason my face is frozen and I cannot smile is that I spend too much time looking rapt and wondrous at your speeches. I can't sleep."

Franklin's major response to all of this was not a new one. He wanted me to speak on the platform, just once. "You aren't shy, Babs. Not at all. You just don't want to put yourself in a position where you have to take criticism. You protect yourself with your shyness. It's a defense against being found out . . . being wrong. You won't risk. Well, I risk."

A few nights ago, a very clear night of susurrating crickets and river tide, which is not the way I ordinarily speak but it was a night like that, I heard Mr. Prenosil lecturing someone just outside my stateroom window on the platform. They stood between the endless aisles and alleys of wooden packing crates. It was a young woman, rather a dashing curly-bobbed young woman with her stockings rolled down to her knees, kewpie-doll lips painted in pigeon blood I am certain, and a small curly dog clasped, if it is possible, kittenishly in the crook of her arm.

"They aren't the Whitneys." I heard his voice rising on Whitney and since I knew most of the Whitneys, I didn't close my shutter but lay still and listened. "They aren't what one could call patrician, you know. They'd be laughingstocks in a real European salon. Petit bourgeois."

"Veddy peddy."

She laughed and he pinched her. Or he pinched her and she laughed.

"Oh, they're rich, but not enormously."

"Not slathers?"

"Country-squire stuff. You know, there are two types who have no airs. The lower class and the upper class. These people are middle-class. They buy things in dozens, sets, collections. They are very materialistic. You know who they are most afraid of? Jews. Because Jews are moving in on them fast. They are afraid to lose status if they don't buy their underwear and tennis balls in England. Real uppers don't worry so much about what's wrong and what's right. They do what they want. She bothers him all the time about sending the proper notes to this aunt and that aunt and going to church." I suddenly realized with a hot and terrible rush of blood that Mr. Prenosil was talking about us. "Now you name me one big English family, I mean upper-class, who pulls that kind of trick, who cares. If you belong. I mean if you really belong. Now there are some Americans who can go back and forth. They don't have to buy their tennis balls in London to get invited to the Continental salons of the real cultured people. And they're so wild about history . . . that's the first clue. They're hungry for it. I'd say the Holmeses, some of the Adamses, the really crusty old families. But the Hyde Park Roosevelts are a bit rough. What have they done?"

"Made a President."

"A. That ain't culture, sweetie, if you've ever traveled on a campaign train. B. That's another part of the family."

"C," she told him, "I think you're pretty smooth." And powdered her nose and her knees. I could see the moon reflected in the compact for a moment until he bent low and whispered something to her which I suppose was D.

"Have to file a story," he called in to Mr. Lynch who simply noted it in his account book. "See you up the line." Mr. Prenosil boarded the train in the morning, tipped his hat to me and grinned at the men.

I spoke to Franklin. "I should not have listened, of course, but that is his attitude toward us."

"It's a new world, Babs. Everyone's rolling up their shirt sleeves. He's right. It's time we gave up all this love of the English. *We're* civilization now, not them. I heard a story about a doughboy going into Germany. He found Beethoven's house, traded off a candy bar to play the piano and banged out 'The Stars and Stripes Forever.' I think that's significant."

"I'm horrified."

"I never plan to live like a feudal landlord in Hyde Park and drive around with a team of Norwegian ponies for adventure. Not I."

"Nor I."

"Then what are we to do?"

"I'm not sure," I say. There is a chink in the thick black wall with winged things fluttering all around me. Rocks move underground. "Do you think it must be one or the other, Franklin?"

"Don't press me."

"Both?"

"A life of compromise?"

"Or contradiction, Franklin."

"Hasn't it already come to that . . . it isn't easy for a man . . . to be thwarted . . . as I am."

"Enough. I can't bear it."

"Forgive me, Babs."

"Mein Gawd," Louis groaned another day as we took our places in the lounge. "Jukes. The country is full of Jukes. When I find out who the horsethief was who first said all men are equal I'm going to give him a week's vacation in Sedalia and then string him up."

"I'm beginning to think Franklin wishes to be equal."

Louis doesn't answer.

"Louis, I really feel America believes in nothing at all except itself and I think Franklin is reinventing himself along those lines."

Louis looks at me, sharply, then out the window. "Cows are stupid, aren't they?" Then, many cows later, he says very slowly, "Eleanor, once there was a saint who was going to build a church. Long time ago. In those days a priest would offer himself up as a sacrifice and they'd bury him alive under the first stone. Well, they buried a priest and started piling rocks for the wall but something wasn't just so and three times the wall collapsed until they decided to dig up the priest because he clearly wasn't pure enough. So they dig him up after three days and as soon as he sees the saint, he says, 'Hell is beautiful.' And the saint says, Eleanor, the saint says, 'Quickly, brethren, cover him up before he blurts out anything else.' "

So I say nothing else.

I am in the center, going south, going deep. That is the sound of the shoveling every morning, the shovels are scraping against the deepest nerves, the lead center, ripping it open. And I have not come up yet. We go deeper and deeper into America, south, and we stew, as Mr. Carlyle says, and soak, as Louis tells me in whispers while he watches the gang lead Franklin. "We soak in the devil's pickle. Why do you think they picked Franklin? Because he had a chance?" Louis whispers as we sit watching cows and weeds and rocks, flat and dry and hot undifferentiated America. "Why do you think they picked Franklin? Because he was expendable and Al Smith was not. And pretty enough to pull a few of the ladies' votes. Just treading water because everyone knows Harding has it so why should Tammany waste their cash. Look, Eleanor, it won't hurt him. He's made a name for himself. And he can blame the loss on Cox. Poor Cox. Their train is worse than ours. Nobody speaks. At least here we speak to each other. Somewhat." Poor Louis, Franklin has very little to do with him now. I watch the horizon for another pool, another Richebourg.

"*Conneaut, Farnham, Fontenat.*" Louis recites train names.

"Louis, however do you remember those things?"

"They just stay with me. Nothing very useful."

"You and Franklin."

"*Waldameer, Wayneport, Westboro. Waldameer, Wayneport . . .* that works," and he repeats it. I see his mouth moving while he thinks behind it. "They don't even rhyme.

Trainmen have no imagination. Imagine naming anything *Painesville.*"

Roll down your stocking and powder your knee. People from Hollywood play tennis on the wings of a biplane. In Hyde Park Mama still goes out in her basket phaeton with its white fringed top and its two piebald Norwegian ponies, and Uncle Warren one day this last July was thrown from his cart at the railroad station by those very ponies while overhead two stars played tennis on the wings of a biplane skimming the Hudson but no one can see the wires which hold them to the wings as the plane dips and falls and Uncle Warren Delano dies and James is feeling better and shall return to Groton, Mama has wired, which will make him ill again, I complain to Franklin. So are we all going mad, dancing like crickets before the fire? Where are the wires, the struts, the supports? There has been so much death around me. We've no home to go to. New York is rented to the Lamonts. We've given up Washington. I will return to live with Mama and all the children. Which would be worse? That or being the wife of the Vice-President? I'm lucky I suppose that I needn't play both roles at the same time because I could not bear that contradiction. I shall never have the phoenix freedom of Pussie or the tight web of devotion encircling Granny Hall. I wonder if I am strong enough for a life of contradiction. Perhaps. If I were to be in the public eye in Washington I would have to live such a life, and I do not yet have the strength.

"Louis, you have extraordinary eyes."

"Something had to make up for this face."

"We ought to be in pictures . . ." and we both laugh.

"It is such a degradation, Louis. I weep for him. I hate what politics is doing to him."

"Look, about the jokes. You know men with their sexual innuendos . . . we're just more interested in that sort of thing than you ladies are. No one means to offend."

250

"I see."

How is it, I would ask him but even dear Louis for all the poetry in that tortured soul would not know how it is that I am not offended so much as I am threatened, frightened, trapped by it. For you, Louis, it may be an innuendo. For me it is a child, it is hemorrhoids, blood, tears, sickness, sorrow, hatred, panic, Groton. I am terrorized as if each remark makes me that much more vulnerable to the bestial in these men I am with. And yet I too long. I too feel the train rocking beneath me, beneath my legs. I see even Mr. Prenosil under the gaslight, a lounge-lizard in his too-tight clothes. I see Franklin. I wipe cinders from the bedsheets of my tiny stateroom and pull the shutters tight to keep out the sound of coal cascading and cars lunging and crashing against each other, rupturing the night. The men joke over their card game. I hear them clearly.

"Oh, he's right side up, that Mayor Babcock from Kalamazoo."

"Right side up."

"So's his missus."

"Wish she were."

Laughter. Hush. Laughter.

"Raise two . . ."

"Hell, you can't raise one."

"Hush, lady aboard." Louis' voice.

"I say you make friends with Tammany. Hell, Murphy could have had the whole state out here if he wanted. You need Tammany. Your press is lousy. You had to fight for everything. Cox has half an outfit. You got pegged as losers and you got no budget."

"And I'll be in serious debt from this, perhaps in the tens of thousands."

"Okay, we gotta play it different from here on. You and me, boss. None of these stooges."

"Okay, Louis. You and me. None of these stooges."

"Okay, Early, as soon as I can comfortably honorably get rid of Howe I promise you I'll do my best."

"That's right, Prenosil, I know how you feel about Lynch. Can't make a team when you feel that way. You depend on me. I'll do my very best."

"Eleanor, I absolutely agree. I know you are upset that I call him Hardly. It's almost a habit by now. You've got to admit it is amusing. Warren Hardly."

"I'm constipated, Franklin. I cannot tolerate any more black coffee. I . . . I want my licorice compound. I want . . . I'm sorry. I hope they don't hear me."

"Go ahead, sweetheart. It does you good to cry."

"I'm worried about James. I miss the children. He's too young to have colitis. What's wrong with us that a child should have colitis at age twelve?"

"Brave little fellow. He looks older. Darling, maybe you should go home."

"Home? I have no home."

"There's no reason for you to hang in here with these duffers in this cattle car. We're all beginning to smell pretty ripe. You can go on ahead to Hyde Park."

"You don't want me here any longer?"

"Silly goose. Of course I want you. I need you here. You don't know how clean I feel when I look up to see your dear person sitting there against the sunset, to know you're on the train, to share your perceptions. Really, Babs. I want you to share with me. It's just another few weeks. I want you to learn from this. We've a long life ahead of us and I want you to understand the issues as well as the ropes."

"And you, Franklin? How is it with you?"

We were standing between his stateroom and mine squeezed together in that foot and a half of space which seemed smaller every moment.

"I? Why I feel fine."

"Do you?"

"I'd love a back rub. It's been a long time since I've had a

252

back rub. Would the lady consider in the interests of the Democratic party?"

"As long as it goes no further than our agreement."

"Oh, Babs, don't you ever . . . ever regret it?"

"Only in the sense that each night you go to bed with your career and I have no career to go to bed with."

IN WHICH I MAKE A SPEECH

And then there was a rainy night when we lurched into a station stop, moths floating in the yellow wet light of the mercury lamps, the light spilling silver onto the platform, gentle shapes in the crowd, umbrellas and crutches, little flags, the party loyals, a few paid onlookers. No one would have come out on such a night if they hadn't had to.

Franklin opened a shutter of his compartment's drawing room and halooed out into the blackness. "Hello out there. Hello out there. Anybody out there? Anybody here care if I'm Vice-President of the Yewnited States? Get the lead outa your pants and vote for Roosevelt. Anybody care who Roosevelt is?"

Early pulled him back and closed the shutter.

"Absolutely correct, Steve. I'm drunk and I shouldn't go

out there and talk to them. Right. Well, do me a favor and tell them I'm drunk. Tell them I'm playing poker. I can hear them already. Why should I go out in that weather for twenty lousy votes we have already? Eleanor's right. I hear them heckling already. Why should I lift my precious self out of here into that weather? I am depressed. Damn depressed and not a little drunk and I'm not about to wax eloquently for the men of the fen . . . not me."

"We can't leave them out there, boss." Early was alarmed. "It'll be in every newspaper. They've come out in the rain!"

"Tell 'em to go back in the rain."

"I'll go. I'll go." I ran for my coat and galoshes.

"What, Babs?" Franklin called after me. "That's a stupid display of bravado, Babs. It isn't worth it."

I stopped and looked into his room. He was sprawled in his bunk with a whiskey bottle, obviously empty, alongside him. "Don't be silly, Franklin. Louis, Louis!" I called. "Come here at once!" I shuddered to see Franklin so. "I'll simply go out there and tell them what I believe in and what America means to me. If Louis will go with me?" I turned to Louis who watched Franklin very carefully.

Louis looked back and forth from me to Franklin and then into the gorilla faces assembling in the corridor. "Sure, I'll go. If she can go, I sure as H. can go."

"Me too." Mr. McIntyre sighed reluctantly and went to the locker for his coat.

Franklin lifted himself from the berth and stumbled toward and past me. "Let's play poker!" He looked back at me. "Romeo! Must be Kentucky. Must be time for some good ole Kentucky bourbon. Right, Reverend? Right reverend? And we'll have a little groggy grog while my missus has a little talky-talk with the good ole folks of . . . of Tariff."

The river ran to the right of the platform. I could only hear it churning. Under the rain, which pounded on the tin roofs of the warehouses and the wood of the platforms and the docks and the crates and the awning above my head, shimmering in the sheets of rain I could see shafts of light catching a button, eyeglass frames, a belt buckle, the handle of an umbrella, a moth. There were no faces, no eyes. They were the party people, paid, I knew, from the local coffers, the faithfuls who would have printing jobs or janitor jobs or building contracts if the Democrats were to win, except the Democrats were to lose as everyone had known before we boarded the train in Washington.

I towered above Louis, behind Louis who held his arms above his head to stop the cheering except there was no sound at all coming from the crowd.

"Jesus," I heard Mr. McIntyre expel softly. "We could hire cows. They're cheaper."

"Ladies and gentlemen, fellow Democrats, loyal friends who came down in the rain to meet the campaign train. We have a very special treat for you tonight. Mr. Roosevelt, your candidate and mine, the next Vice-President of the Yewnited States, has spoken so many times today to such vast crowds, his throat is closed up and the doctors have advised him to rest but he said . . . uh, in a whisper . . . I can't leave those people out there, so he sent his dearly loved wife . . ." Louis pulled me forward by the hand into the light. I felt awkward. "She's been on the train with us from the beginning and she is here to tell you . . ."

Louis pauses, his hand tightened on mine, he vibrated to something in the air, a dangerous current, a dreadful sort of stillness, a vacuum out of which came suddenly a hesitant hiss, then a less hesitant one, then a chorus of Bronx cheers. I feel perspiration mixing with the rain on the back of my neck.

"Hey, we want Teddy."

"Yeah, where's Teddy?"

"Teddy?" I ask Louis.

"Teddy Jr.?" Louis calls into the dark fist of voices.

"No, sir, Teddy Roosevelt. Go wake him up and get him

out here." I saw one man under a shaft of light throw up an arm as if he were tossing a ball. "Aaah, for Christ's sake," he yells at me and then stalks angrily away into the blackness.

"Folks, Teddy Roosevelt has been dead more than a year now. This is his niece and the wife of Franklin Roosevelt, your next Vice-President!"

"We want Teddy," the crowd bellows in one voice. "Tell Teddy to come out. Hey, Teddy, come on out."

"Your husband want war, lady?" a woman in country clothes carrying a straw basket over one arm, yells to me. "He gonna take us to war?"

I lean over the railing, over the American flag angular now with its load of soot, and look into the woman's face in the dark. "My husband doesn't like war. He is opposed to war."

"And is your man gonna get government messing up our lives more than already?"

Long low rolls of thunder move in from over the mountains, like dogs growling. "Of course there are some ways government can help your lives."

"Bull."

"If you educate yourself, you can take part in your government. You can make your vote have great meaning."

"Hell, my man's been voting for years and we're still starvin'."

"Tell her. That a gal, you tell her. Look at her, all them fancies."

"There are issues," I try to shout over the man's voice. "There are issues that affect you, madam. Child labor, maternity protection." I try to remember the list from the Working Women's Congress. "Unions, fair pay for women."

"My man ain't lettin' me work. He'd rather have the kids starvin' than me work. Sure as hell won't let me vote anyway."

"Then why are you here?" I scream over the growing thunder and the calls of the crowd. She waves two dollar bills in my face. I feel Louis' hand on my shoulder. My voice was moth-fragile.

"C'mon, get your old man out here. Let's hear some about real politics. Come on. We didn't come down here to listen to women's talk. Go talk to the women. We came down to talk politics, lady. You hear?"

"Yeah, go talk to the women on your own time."

There was more back talk from the crowd and then within the crowd, advising each other to be reasonable and listen, people trying to save the moment by explaining to the others that this wasn't Teddy and then I could see forms moving away from the puddles of the lights and a car started up and roared off with the tires screeching along the stone bed of the siding and then more cars and I fled back to my stateroom where Franklin was lying in my berth with his arms up behind his head and he said to me, perfectly sober and golden-tongued, "Well, now, madam, my love, do you understand why I can't tell them about the League of Nations? It's not that easy, after all, is it?"

"Please leave my room."

"I was hoping for another back rub."

"Leave. Please."

"Let me dry you off, Babs."

"I am wet and chilled to the bone. Please leave or I shall."

"Ladies and gentlemen," Franklin stood and pinned me to the wall with his strong hands, his body pressed against mine. "I'd like you to meet my missus. My missus is a very interesting lady, all right. If her son murdered someone and she were the judge, she'd sentence him to death. Oh, that she would. And then she'd go out and die of a broken heart."

"What do you want, Franklin?"

"Forgive me. Forget."

"That part of my life is over."

The train rocked us against each other. I had a sense of final moments. I wanted to lay my head on his shoulder. I wanted him to smooth my hair under his hands.

"It never began, did it?"

"I suppose not, Franklin."

"Good night, Babs. Sleep well."

For three days, the porter brought me hot orange juice and my husband's regards while I kept my face to the wall of the stateroom and seethed the rest of the way across America.

IN WHICH MAMA AND I
HAVE A FURIOUS BLOWOUT
OVER CHINTZ

"Black rabble from Foggy Bottom cooking your food, shorthand lessons in a public school, women in the lowest form of politics, trips to Albany to fight with legislators. What is next, Eleanor? Threadbare clothes? What kind of example are you setting for your children? Step by step down the social ladder? I am old-fashioned but I know one thing will never change and that is the duty of a mother to set an example. You act like a . . . a . . . you act in any way you wish and you won't give your own daughter an inch of freedom for herself."

Regardless of the issues, regardless of the times, Mama feels if I had been more of a wife, Franklin would now be Vice-President of the United States. Instead, he works for an insurance firm and does very little except go to the New York office every day and come home very late every night. Mama wants us all to return to Hyde Park forever. It is my fault

Franklin lost last month's election and it is my fault the New York house looks as tawdry as it does and it is my fault that our servants, hers Continental, mine Foggy Bottom, are at each other's throats and that I no longer entertain. The Lamonts just moved from 47, my side of our twin houses, and all of us, the happy family, are together in New York for Christmas, with open passages between us, from one house to the other, on each floor, in each room. Mama decided, driven as she was, that our lives must be put into order, which meant that the rooms be redecorated now that the Lamonts have left. With chintz.

She entered the drawing room, cast a withering eye at my few things, the tear bottle, Rejeanne's *New Republic* magazines, a three-sectioned picture frame with Kodaks of Rejeanne and Caroline in their New York apartment, legislative reports in foot-high stacks, and announced that what the room needed was chintz slipcovers. "It looks cold. Men like warm rooms."

"Is it our occupation to be devout and keep rooms and rolls warm for men who like warm rooms and warm rolls?" It was her house.

Elliott was miserable and sickly upstairs. Plum pudding and Christmas gifts filled the rooms. Franklin was not even home in the evenings. I had torn deep rifts in the bottom of my heels, dried and cracked from the winter heat, and Mama was absolutely determined that nothing would ruin Christmas. And so, the next few days were filled with seamstresses measuring and stitching, wallpaper hangers, paste, ribbons, medicine. And chintz. Someday I would wrap her son in chintz for her with flounces and pounces and armrests and stuff him in a corner. Daily, hourly, Mama complained about the servants getting in the way of the seamstresses until I finally snapped, "Could we not call them help, at least, rather than servants? They are human beings."

The remark stopped her in her tracks. "And I suppose you'll have them eating below the salt at table soon? You must learn to be stronger with them. They make a fool out of you. One can't be an anarchist outside and expect to maintain authority at home. With servants or children."

"They aren't my children. They are yours and Franklin's children. I'm just the machine."

With that Mama folded up the triple frame photograph of Rejeanne and Caroline, crunching the glass.

On the street below a Jew is selling Bibles and almanacs from a wooden box and a man with a patch over his eye and a can of hot potatoes and a bushel of apples is eyeing the Jew. Yesterday on another street I saw Army veterans cheer for America, toss their hats in the air, catch them and raid the cigarmakers' union office dragging old Russian intellectuals to the gutters. The Jew has a Perfecto cigar in his mouth. The Jew is peddling perfection with the cigar twisting in his mouth. There are double-decker buses on Fifth Avenue with open tops and there are horse-drawn cars. The Jew twists his cigar in a series of three circles between his pitch. I watch. Everything is out of proportion. Franklin's uncle brought Elliott a rooster in a cage and somehow someone managed in the melee between Mama and myself to snatch a neighbor's small orange kitten and shove it into the cage with the rooster. By the time I arrived upstairs, I found Elliott in his sickbed vomiting in horror. I am sure Elliott did not do it.

My daughter doesn't speak to me at all and I wonder, poor lamb, what horrid beast rides in her breast to drag her into womanhood. What is this shadow Franklin and I spread across the world? Is this my history? Are these my stations? This ormolu, this gingerbread, this plum pudding, the cage of bloody fur and feathers? Shall I then be redeemed? Shall I redeem my silver self through them, my offspring? Are they the opus of my life and the harvest of my days? Nature's time is long and the fashion of her concoction is uniform. Shall I be them? Franklin says that James' relationship to trees is perfectly natural at his age. I shudder. Shall I then decimate the forests to rid my sons of lechery? Do men like warm rooms so they can breed? Rejeanne says that men are worms. "What do you want for Christmas, Babs?" I have been asked for the last month and I refuse to answer. I want great good to emerge from great evil. I want silver to be freed from lead.

Last summer, no, the summer before that, during the war, a group of official wives was taken on tour to the weapons factory at Watervliet to watch the production of a twenty-millimeter gun. At the last step of production one man swaddled in chamois cloth squirmed through the bore of the gun to clean it. He slid out of the muzzle, newborn, an infant, and the visiting ladies cheered and clapped for him as he stood before them, hands clasped in victory above his blackened head, grinning stupidly through a sooty face. The urine of an unpolluted boy becomes gunpowder. There is no innocence. Nonsense. Men are born to slay. They are worms. They wrap us in silk and stay in warm rooms and breed.

At dinner on the day the rooster died, Mama and Franklin and my Anna and James were discussing the merits of noble sacrifice as opposed to gracious uselessness. Mama always enjoys what she calls philosophical conversations. "Franklin, which is more exemplary?"

"If someone were to offer me a choice, which they have not, I would say I preferred noble sacrifice in war to noble sacrifice in love."

"Yes?" Mama encourages him from one end of the table. He sits at the other end. I anyplace.

"I would defend love but I would choose noble sacrifice in war because in war one doesn't have to get involved with any one single person in particular."

"I see."

We sit, a circle of elect spirits given to noble sacrifice, eating oyster crabs in cream sauce. Franklin belches over the oyster crabs. "History repeats itself," he apologizes. The children, who have not heard that chestnut as often as I, roar with laughter and try to belch. Franklin snaps shut his tortoiseshell cigarette case, snaps and opens and snaps and opens and I remember the broken picture frame and burst into tears and run from the room.

I take huge draughts of fresh air from an open window in the sitting room and I wonder how long I will last.

"It's very cold in here." Mama arrives, carrying a white owl in a domed glass case. "Must we keep the windows open." It isn't a question.

I say nothing. She leaves. Franklin arrives. He has the owl.

"Babs, are you upset?"

"Upset? Upset. Yes. I feel as if I'm dead."

"Would you like to play dominoes?"

"Don't be funny."

"I'm not. Get your mind off things."

"I have to do Christmas wrapping."

"When you tell me what you want, darling, I'll be very relieved . . . there's not much time left for shopping."

I say nothing.

"What do you want, Eleanor?"

"I need to be alone right now. I want you to stop belching at the table. I can bear it if you must, but I can't bear it if the children try to."

Franklin finally left.

It was a lonely thing to have all those children, a lonely thing that performance on my flooding bloody battlefield of a bed with hushed voices outside and my children, already born, fighting in the rooms above me.

"How is she doing?"

"Finely."

"A bit longer?"

"A bit longer. Soon."

Ypres? Loos? I am doing well. I am a good woman and a constant wife. Whatever I have you may have. I am ripping myself into shreds. I eat sour grapes and my children's eyes are gray and their pearly teeth set on edge. Wolves? I ask. To devour me? I brought two Franklins into the world. Someone

264

took the first from me, then the second became Mama's and then someone took my own Franklin from me, who was bashful in those days and shuffled like a schoolboy. Here, then, is another child as I split open like a chicken breast. I have every woman's pain. They know mine; I know theirs and I love them. I have done this six, seven times in fear and wonderment, in terror and hope. Like an ancient, in crooked clothes with crooked finger, Auntie Bye would sit at my bedside and hold my hand. Outside, my husband thought I had command of the secrets of the universe. Bright blue eye under the duckboard. The secrets were in command of me and hardly secret. One of my boys told me he wanted to marry Mademoiselle, our slender Swiss governess, and she did allow him to rub at her ankle while she read his lessons to him and he told her he would run away with her and Granny would give him all the money they needed to live happily ever after. He would climb trees, she told me, while she, seated below, read Lewis Carroll to the others in the garden and mess his pants against the shaggy bark of the tree and one day, it is not certain just why, he took a knife from the kitchen and threw it at her, grazing her arm, she insisted, tearing her starched shirtwaist. She unfolded the shirtwaist and shook it before me and wept as if the rent in its sleeve were proof. Mademoiselle insisted he was not being himself when he threw the knife, but I think he was, more than ever.

Clearly my boy was tormented and I had Mademoiselle leave, paying her without touching her hand because I was then quite certain that it was she, bored and imprisoned, who has tantalized the boy tall enough to whisper in her ear. I fired her at once and determined they would all go off to the monastery of Groton where boys become men and learn to deal with the secrets.

But how shall we protect ourselves from the secrets? What shall I tell my daughter who won't speak to me? Keep their rooms warm? They won't harm you if their rooms are warm.

"There!" Mama appeared as fresh as the morning. "Do you see how warm the chintz makes the room? It really is wonderful. And now the portraits on the easels . . . and I've brought over this bonbon dish. The three-tiered type is so idiotically difficult to find now and Franklin wants this owl. There we are." A maid placed the glass-domed owl on a spindly-legged table. Mama directed a woman to puff the pillows on the furniture, a workman to install six glass globe lamps, three seamstresses to smooth and tuck and fit the slip-covers over the furniture. We watched the hubbub from the double glass doors, caryatids.

"You seem dissatisfied, Eleanor. Don't you like the room? Franklin will love it, I know. He loves rooms like this."

"Someday I would like a room of my own. Without chintz."

"I didn't mean to . . . Oh, dear, Eleanor . . . you know I only meant to . . ." Mama noticed the rooster cage I had not yet cleaned out. She moved quickly from it.

"You always mean to." I went to the window for air.

"Eleanor, I am sorry about breaking your friends' picture frame."

"It doesn't matter. Nothing matters."

"I'm having the glass replaced."

"I said it didn't matter. Nothing matters. Can't you hear me, Mama?"

"Of course I do. Christmas is always a bad time of year for women. We get through it. We do what's best."

"Mama, I don't want anything for Christmas."

"So?"

"I don't want anything."

"You are very unhappy, aren't you? Oh, Eleanor, what do you think would make you happy? Nothing pleases you. You have five beautiful children, you have Franklin, you have your health . . . you have brought all this into the world."

"I am not beautiful yet and I have not been brought into the world yet. I haven't made myself yet and I don't want to die unmade." I told the Jew still hawking Christ on the sidewalk below, "I hate my life."

"Bite your tongue!"

"Bite my tongue? Franklin won't have me biting my tongue. He doesn't like my biting my tongue or gnawing on my wings."

"Now you listen, young woman. You are being very cheeky and I won't have it."

"Cheeky?" I laughed at cheeky and tongue and all of it because I was thirty-six and old and when I stopped laughing, I very quietly asked, "For what am I supporting Franklin? Why am I keeping his room warm? For his thrills? Where are my thrills? You know what my reward has been. I have no reward from the children and I have no reward from him. Did you see the rooster cage? I mean did you look into that rooster cage? The only people who appreciate me are . . . are . . . my friends. The only reward I'll ever get is from myself and I have to find it."

"Hooligan creatures, your friends, perverts, he-she's. What you have said is simply the most disgusting, destructive selfish statement I have ever heard in my life. Shut that window! Do you want everyone in the neighborhood to hear your madness? If they took away your children, God forbid, or your husband, God forbid, where would you be?"

"Why must we spend our lives worshiping Franklin and that pack of wild children? Why? He's not God, he's only Franklin. Why must I worship him?"

"Shame. To use the Lord's name in this self-indulgence. Shame!"

"I am so tired, Mama."

"Where would you be, Eleanor? Answer me!"

"I am so tired . . ."

"Where would you be. . . ?"

"Out there. Out there." I gestured to the street. "Helping."

"Hmmmph."

"Should I then, as you, Mama, live for every breath Franklin takes and not take any of my own? Shall I live through him as you do?"

"And why not? You couldn't find better."

"Well, I want to live through me." The Jew looked up at us. I shut the window. "I am God's creature as well as Franklin is God's creature and I want to live through me. Me me me me me *me!*"

Mama hustled the installer and the seamstresses out and the maid and the owl and the rooster cage. "My daughter is not herself. You'll have to leave now."

"I *am* myself!" I shouted after them. "Don't you understand? That is the *problem.*"

That evening I apologized to Mama. It was not her fault. Nor was it Franklin's. I couldn't blame either of them or the children for being true to what they themselves were. It was I, like the man on the sidewalk, who was caught between two worlds, stretching and bursting and tearing as I straddled each wall and the walls moved apart and my legs moved apart in rage and fire, bursting, waiting for perfection to drop out bit by bit, bone by bone.

EXCURSION SIX
Campobello, Summer 1921

IN WHICH THE NAVY SCANDAL
IS LAID TO FRANKLIN

When Van Lear Black's yacht, the *Sabalo*, rounded the island and entered the cove, a school of mackerels shimmered silver and white just beyond the beach, too near the weir. Curious gulls swooped and fought with a full-force wind driving them back across the bay and the trees shifted ominously in the sandy dryness. And when the *Sabalo* hove anchor in Passamaquoddy Bay at high noon, there on the deck for my benefit a three-piece gypsy orchestra in white satin blouses and black flared trousers fiddled something greasy and staccato, a racy party of red, white and blue males and females lined up at full attention along the rail and a gray-faced Franklin, defeated, wounded, exhausted, with a red silk gypsy scarf around his head and a golf club in hand, was jauntily leading the orchestra.

I hardly knew how to show gratitude. The singular sound

of my clapping as I stood on the sagging dock must have been a great disappointment to everyone on the imperious vessel. I was not a very good audience that day.

It was August and the Campobello water level was lower than it had ever been. The dune grass leading to the water was tall, dry, brown, razor sharp, stiff bristles on the island's back. Trees rubbed against each other scratching at the air and the air was a beast crouched and waiting, but I couldn't know yet from the claw raking the dry trees and the dune grasses, the beast. In the lupin and sea pines behind our house, thousands of cicadas chirred without end. And my wee soldiers of Cadmus, born to consume each other, had indeed taken to biting.

For the two days the *Sabalo* did anchor at Campobello, Franklin was Franklin to the tenth power, odd and brittle against the desolate backdrop of our old dock and the stone-hewn foundations and the sea-rotted shingles of the rough house, worse and awkward among the chintz and the children, ridiculous, I think, with the wild music floating at night across the bay from the boat to our rooms, to my bed and to Franklin's bed, where we lay separately and listened together first to the gypsy music and singing and laughter and splashing, then much much later to the heavy dark dangerous music I had never heard before. Franklin said it was darky music. "Darktown Strutters Ball," he called in mysteriously from his room. I thought if I were to go into his room I'd find him, longing, with his nose pressed against the window. Strung with lights and lanterns, the *Sabalo* glittered beyond our dock till dawn.

"Certainly sounds out of place here, doesn't it, Babs?" Franklin asked me in the morning.

"Very." In return I blasted the "Carnival of Venice" at the *Sabalo* all through the next day but I think ineffectually, for the dancing went on and the yacht reverberated with that dark blood-beat through the second night. Mr. Black told Franklin that his party would picnic and lay over four to five days but they refused my invitation to tea, and then refused my invitation to a cold picnic. I don't think it was the note I sent aboard with Captain Calder, our "crew," requesting that no fires be lit on the beaches and liquor-drinking be kept to the *Sabalo*. The boys had found a small cairn of hot stones and three empty liquor bottles on the beach so the note was entirely justified. I think, perhaps, for the shrieking girls in tiny bathing suits and bobbed hair who had been splashing and dancing all night, Franklin's determined daytime pageant of entertainment in the wilderness was far too strenuous and maybe even a bit of a bore. Perhaps the island was too rough, the children too awful, the chintz too chintz, I in my bathing dress too, too funny. Whatever, before the third nightfall the *Sabalo* slipped serenely off and I saw Franklin at dusk, like the children, sitting on the porch steps staring blankly out to sea. Poor man. I couldn't hold his slick friends by my teas and picnics any more than he could by his calisthenics. I sulked that evening also because I knew he was bored with me, burdened with all of us, the dull wife, the dull job selling Mr. Black's insurance, the demanding noisy children, the Howes who were visiting. Poor, poor man. But then, as Franklin alone could, for he was never a bitter man, by the next day he and the chicks and the Howe children were off to swim and foot-race the cliffs, leaving behind them a hurried promise that they would swing by in our small sail, the *Vireo*, and pick up Ma.

"All right, Ma?"

Ma should be on the dock with blankets for all in case they were wet from swimming and a breeze came up. Ma agreed.

Poor Franklin. We had so little to give him and he needed so much. He raced toward the water, the lean body flashing against the dark rocks, lovely, smooth graceful body, and the children, lovely and smooth, still colt-angular, raced after him dashing along the sands, kicking up bits of it. They were all so beautiful.

"Wait, Pa! Wait!" And he ran faster and faster toward the

water, over the brown grasses slashing at his ankles, over the rocks, over and up into the foam of the wave. And gone. How I wanted to be that wave. How I wanted to hold him, to keep him, to roll in the tides with him, to be with him always. Dear Lord—I prayed a terrible prayer, I promised a terrible promise—Dear Lord, tell me what to do. I will do anything. Just show me how to keep him with me. And how he yearned to go off on that yacht as it steamed toward the world leaving him behind to foot-race with his children up and down the cliffs under a swift sky of empty clouds. I gathered the blankets and waited that day, sitting for long hours on the dock, reading and pulling apart the pods of milkweeds, letting the silk drift through my fingers into the bay. Behind me over the fields, the seeds of the pods drifted. Where miners break up rocks by fire, great cavernous explosions of vinegar and steam under the earth, white wool floats over silver mines and the rocks make grinding noises far down below the fields.

For the last six months the beast ripping at Franklin's patchwork of destiny was a Senate investigation. It was Republican in nature, malicious and pointless, fed, we suspected, by Ted Jr. now sitting in Franklin's chair at Navy. Franklin was being accused of appointing, allowing, ignoring, covertly, overtly, a sodomy squad of older men to entrap younger men with deviate desires at the Newport Naval Base.

Louis suggested we let it blow over.

It didn't. The headlines grew worse; the details were "unprintable."

Franklin said: "I don't know what it's about, Babs. I have to look into the records. I haven't even been in the Department for a year. There are fifty-seven varieties of charges against me so far but nobody yet can make a soup." The newspapers said: "Young men in the Naval service had been compelled under orders of officers attached to the Office of Naval Intelligence to commit vile and nameless crimes on the persons of others in the Naval service or have suggested these acts be practiced on themselves. Mr. Roosevelt told Mr. Fairbrother that he gave Lt. Hudson the order by word of mouth and cited the men involved for interest and zeal in their work." The *Providence Journal* declared in print that "F. D. Roosevelt was lacking in manliness and frankness." Those were terrible months.

I told Franklin as I had told him time and time again: "When one is involved in personality politics rather than issue politics, in who is right rather than what is right, this is the sort of thing one can expect. I'm sorry for you." The Senate refused him a hearing and Franklin spent weeks writing taffy-twists of paragraphs defending himself, accusing others. He didn't know the methods of the vice net. He had only asked that the base be cleaned up. He had appointed the squad. He hadn't appointed the squad. They were all decent men. He couldn't understand what had happened to their personnel records. He wrote statements for the press proclaiming his ignorance, innocence, horror, syntax, but the statements were printed in long columns side by side with the news of the court trial in Providence. In which testimonies of local clergy condemned the unprintable, mothers swore their boys would never do the unimaginable, if not for the vice squad leading them down the path to the unmentionable. Solicitors, solicitous, solicited.

"Don't worry," Franklin wrote. "I'll be up to Campo in July as soon as I get my hearing. I'm going to singe the beards off those old ladies in the Senate."

Louis said Franklin better get his defense ready and stop writing to the newspapers. At last, in July, Franklin was summoned from the Fidelity offices to Washington for his hearing. He walked the corridors beyond the hearing room, waiting for his moment, preparing and mouthing his words and concentrating on rejoinders and widening his saucer eyes in that fixed twinkle and arching his eyebrows and lifting his voice in silvery eloquence, the voice of a god in a world of lies, the voice of lies in a world of God. Lies, whims, wishes and dreams. In Washington leaden cubes of rain reached from dark clouds to the rims of the earth. There was a kind of madness among the thunderstorms. Franklin was frightened. He was prepared to defend himself as a moral man. As a man. But they wouldn't let him in. They wouldn't hear him. He could insert nothing in the record. He could insert nothing. He stalked the Senate halls in an impotent rage, collaring, buttonholing, but no one would help.

If the accusations had been about his part in the Navy oil fields deal or the odd investment in German marks and misery or any of the dozen schemes he and Louis and others materialized from nighttime sprites into corporate vellum giants, he could have weathered the criticism. But Washington was criticizing his manhood. When Franklin had been at Harvard, even at Groton, he hadn't been invited to the clubs he had expected. In Washington, he devoted himself to being a man among men—a he-man, the *Navy Spar* wrote about him, an athlete, and now he was tainted. I am afraid by early August when the *Sabalo* arrived, life for Franklin was as bad as it could be. He had lost Lucy Mercer, my devotion, the election, the Senate hearing. And his name was muddied in large letters in every newspaper on the East Coast. Although it seemed archaic and he spoke only of his honor being lost, I am afraid it was his manhood that was threatened, something for which, having had my own femininity shattered, I could feel true empathy but in no way could restore. Poor Franklin. I sent him a milk pod, pushed it out to sea with my toe and watched it move sullenly from the dock.

IN WHICH WE PUT OUT A
FOREST FIRE

ong before I heard the bell, I heard Franklin and the children singing and laughing across the water. I hurried down to the dock with blankets and biscuits and Thermoses of tea.

Elliott was snuggled into Franklin's shoulder and rubbing his cheek against Franklin's. The other children were lined up neatly along both sides of the *Vireo*. Franklin, happier than I'd seen him in months, his favorite Dunhill at his mouth, his old slouch sailing hat tipped over his forehead, held the tiller and gave very official orders. Anna took directions at the sail. After I was settled and John climbed into my lap, Franklin called: "Ready about."

"Ready about," the children replied and in a body shifted to the high side, dipping their heads for the swing of the boom, perfectly obedient and ecstatic as the sail caught a faint breeze and we were off into the bay. The mackerels still shimmered, trembling in the still waters, waiting for something at the edge of the sea.

"How happy the chicks look, Franklin."

"Why not? Perfect day."

"Mummy, do you know what Papa told us? That cicadas are born from cuckoo spit."

"Cuckoo spit? Why, I've never even *seen* a cuckoo on the island."

"Cuckoos don't spit, do they, Mummy?"

"Moses Smith told me his grandfather cured cows with cuckoo spit," Anna offered.

And Franklin shouted across flapping sails, "Must have been a lot of cuckoo cows."

"Cuckoo cows! Cuckoo cows! Oh, Papa!" Which sent the children into wild laughter until Anna called James cuckoo and of course everyone then was off spitting at each other with Franklin laughing at the whole scene.

"If you listen," I shouted over them, "you'll hear the cicadas. Right now!"

They listened for a moment but we could hear nothing and then the laughter rose again as we tacked the *Vireo* around the gray rocks. "Stop spitting," Franklin commanded very simply. "Or I'll dunk the lot of you. Ready about, now. Ak dum and viggery!"

If only it could last forever. We could be the Fairchilds. It would be so much easier. We could live happily ever after in Hyde Park and Franklin could be with us all the time, busy with his farming, and his tree plantings and writing books about John Paul Jones and I think even I could be happy. As long as he stayed with us and the faces of my children kept shining like the little lanterns they were that day in the sailboat.

Suddenly, what had seemed moments before to be dark clouds became puffs of dark smoke rising from the shore at the far end of the cove. "Hey, look!"

"A fire!"

"Wow, a fire! Wow!"

"Oh, no, Franklin. No we don't. You call the townspeople, do you hear me?"

Oblivious, Franklin tacked and headed for the burning beach.

"You call Captain Calder. No heroics, Franklin. The children."

"We can handle it."

For the next hour we handled it, each of us, for how could I not? We snatched at blankets, dipped them into the seawater and then ran up the beach, to the edge of the woods. The flames were now shoulder high. Although it was only a thicket of bushes on fire, the danger was that the thicket twisted itself into a labyrinth of old vines and extended like electric wires back into the wall of spruce and toward the town. Franklin and I and the older boys beat down the bushes with wet blankets while Anna and the younger boys kept the blankets wet. For almost an hour, from either end of the semicircle of bushes, we beat down the flames. My arms ached and my eyes smarted and I knew when the pitchy smoke festooning the beach cleared, we would find another cairn of bottles and stones from Mr. Black's glamorous crew. At last, only a few bushes smoked. I stood back to wipe the soot from my eyes and straighten my back. Franklin finished off the last of the flames.

"Well, you see that. Didn't need the island folk at all, did we?"

"We were lucky."

"I daresay they'll think the more of us for it . . . no namby-pamby city folk are we, are we?"

"And if we had failed and their woods burned . . ."

Our argument began at the edge of the beach, continued as we rinsed the blankets which spewed soot like octopus ink in the shallows, took our places in the *Vireo* and pushed off for home. "Really, boy with finger in the dike. We would have been responsible for the entire town, Franklin! Why must you be a hero?"

"Risk and courage, Eleanor, risk and courage," he repeated as if he were teaching me those lessons. The two younger children covered their ears when the words grew rough . . . the older ones were bored for they had heard the bickering for years and knew it had nothing to do with them nor did anything ever come of it except eventual frozen silences. I didn't have the strength to argue with Franklin.

"Are you finished, Eleanor?"

"Yes."

"Don't worry about things so. Well." Franklin addressed the children as soon as it was safe to speak. "Five little smudge pots. Mama's gonna be very aggravated with us, isn't she? Soon as we get back it's bath time."

"Ooooh!" They played this way with him.

"In the bay you all will go."

"Hooray! In the bay!"

"And Anna, you will dash up on those long, lovely legs and get a bar of soap for each of us as soon as we get near the house and when your ma sees you at supper table, she won't know who you are."

"You'll know who I am, won't you, Ma?" Johnny seemed startled and everyone laughed. Even I.

"Of course. That's not what Pa meant."

After we tied up and the soap arrived, I walked up to the house. Behind me, Franklin shouted: "Last one in is a monkey's uncle."

When the splashing and lathering were over and the children off changing for supper, Franklin, still in his jersey bathing suit, insisted on reading the mail from Washington and New York. He kept tugging at one shoulder strap, absentmindedly aware in the descending night chill that he should take off the suit. The children tramped into the dining room and could barely keep their faces out of their soup bowls. After soup and bread and butter and eggs, they were grateful for bed and sprawled like dead men thrown up from the sea. I remember I was much annoyed because we were all to go off camping the next day with the Howes and everyone would be impossibly grumpy. I also remember that Franklin didn't eat that night. He shivered and burned in his bed and I gave him hot lemonade and brandy finally but still he shivered and he burned and he burned and he burned and Mr. Howe sent his family and mine off on the camping trip the next morning so that there was only himself and myself and he helped me cool Franklin's head and neck with compresses. Franklin's forehead was like a hot stone. I remember that nights had come and gone, candles, sunsets, dawns, food, and days later, we knew something was terribly wrong because Franklin did not/could not move. That was the beast clawing at the air: infantile.

"A grown man? I think it's influenza."

IN WHICH I AM FREED

I remember the soldiers going over No-Man's-Land, reciting as they took the German bullets. Fourteen times fourteen, to be or not to be. The lead moves slowly, deepening in his limbs. Do rub his muscles. Do feed him solids. Don't. Do. Whom fire doth spare, sea doth drown. Whom sea spares, pestilent air doth send to clay, whom war 'scapes, sickness takes away. And the mackerels float fermenting silver-bellied on their backs in green pools at the water's edge.

"His mind, Louis?"

"Let's not make decisions. Let's not ask questions, Eleanor. We have too much work to do. Worry about your own mind."

"If only he'd taken off the wet bathing suit, Louis."

"It's more than that. One thing I understand, Eleanor, is being sick. Let's get to work."

And so, as if being organized would help, Louis and I made up a schedule for the water after the local doctor came and warned us of dehydration, a danger I had forgotten, I was so stricken. And since I was to sleep in Franklin's room during the night, it became my duty to make certain he had water every hour and every hour I dragged myself more and more slowly from the cot to the washstand to the bed to his lips. Some nights I dreamed I had already awoken, gone to the washstand, to the bed, to his lips, and back to my cot and I would somehow cut through the dream and force myself up. Nothing existed except that fever. Once I slept through the night until I heard Franklin call for water. His head was a fiery stone and his lips were bleeding. I who had lived on dreams vowed I would never dream again as long as I lived. My dreams had nearly killed him.

I prayed. "I will look up to the hills, from whence comes my help." From whence comes my help became a question. I did not pray. But it happened so suddenly, I said to no one, a sudden storm. A cobalt sky, lightning filling the bowl of mountains. There is always that sense of yet another suddenness, waiting in the wings and sweeping in just before the curtains go down. There, my dear. You may rest now. It is over. See, the sky is blue, dear girl, and a gentle rain to cleanse your hands and see, the gulls again skim the bay and even the suicidal bellies of the mackerel turned up dead six-deep on the shore in some horror of nature beyond ken, even the mackerels will be restored and turn again on their bellies, verily, and go back to the sea, and your husband will stand and walk and run and come alive just as soon as the mackerels turn over. Just as soon as the lights dim and intermission is over.

Uncle Frederic wrote long philosophical letters about faith and character and following the doctors' orders and a good diet and the vitallic method of breathing in bed. Uncle Frederic would get Franklin the book about the vitallic method. Livy heard Franklin was ill and, never suspecting I would open my husband's mail, tried to cheer him by suggesting they write a book together about bachelor nights in Washington. "Pip of a book, F.D. Rip-snorting, mirth-provoking, blood-tingling, rib-tickling laughs, loves and surprises," Livy wrote. "What a book we'll write, F.D. I'm tearing my hair out to get up to you. Anything I can do to get you back on your feet? Of course we both agree at the outset that it's to be fiction, correct, old Rosie? See you in the city. Soon, Livy."

There was no time then to think what it meant. There was no time and what time there was, was an eternity. The heat spell dwindled to damp rain; the skies were lead, deepening, moving; the fireplaces smoked in the wind. Louis handled the business mail. I, in a firm reassuring hand, the personal. "We thought Franklin had influenza, but he did not," I reported carefully, "and he seems to be improving." "He is doing finely," I wrote, which meant today he moved his fingers. When I fell asleep before the fire, Louis would wake me to take my turn at rubbing muscles, spooning liquids, cooling Franklin. I was the sponge they gave to the thirsting Christ. For all I poured into him, Franklin still burned and turned to ashes. Although we could not admit it to each other, Louis and I were both keenly aware that the fever was only a manifestation of the disease. *That* we didn't know how to fight. My husband had been eaten away by fever, by fire, and when the fire finally receded, he was ashes. He tried to read my face. I smiled and turned away.

When one is locked in a tragedy one doesn't know it to be a tragedy until letters must be sent, until the meaning has to be suggested, until the events must be siphoned and simplified into familiar words and short sentences for others to understand and estimate, but not too precisely. And when I read the words I'd written, eulogistic, euphemistic, and looked at the cryptic wires I would send from Welshpool to the unreal world, I began slowly to realize there was a very probable chance that Franklin would never recover.

When the infantile specialist came from Boston and told ıs we had been damaging the muscles more by rubbing them, Louis and I were struck down. But he complimented us and said we were doing finely. He couldn't say as much for Franklin. "It's a matter of time," he said. "Time will tell," he said, as I walked with him to the dock where Captain Calder was waiting to take him back to the mainland. "It's a matter of degree, too, of course," he said as I bent to pick up the small skull of a herring gull filled with sand, and I stopped for a moment to pour out the sand. "You've lost your time," I told the skull.

The doctor said I must hire a professional nurse and get some rest myself. There was nothing wrong with me. Reality for me was simply very different than it was for anyone else and I didn't have time just now to act properly, to satisfy everyone's illusions about poor Eleanor.

"You must begin to make plans as to where he will be, Mrs. Roosevelt."

"Be?"

"Yes. There's no telling how long he'll be crippled. It varies with victims of infantile."

"Crippled, doctor?"

"You knew that of course. Yes. I think the country would be best in the long run, don't you?"

A victim. Franklin a victim? "That's Franklin's decision. When he's ready to make it, of course."

"Of course. Please let me know and I'll do whatever I can to help you move him."

Honorable wound, son, honorable wound. Livy's letter lay unanswered. I had never said to anyone nor even thought to say to anyone "Go to Hell," but now that I have been there, am perhaps still there, I whispered in the candlelight over Livy's letter: "Go to Hell," and then threw it in the fire.

On my husband's rip-snorting, mirth-provoking blood-tingling rib-tickling mysteries, I used a catheter; on his eyes, ice packs. I wiped him clean and diapered him, all of his black

285

bilious soured functions. I scraped and fed and washed and threw his wastes into the sea. There was only Louis and me and the letters and our zombie cheerfulness before Franklin. He cried.

Mama arrived from Europe with her trunks and her deep and terrible sorrow. "When did it happen?" she insisted. "I want the precise date. You know I had a black spot on my finger and it began to dilate in Shropshire. That must have been it. It dilates near the end. Oh, but you're a wonderful, wonderful girl, Eleanor. You've saved my boy's life."

"And Louis also."

"When can we take him home? He'll have all his books and his stamps and he'll be so comfortable at Hyde Park."

Louis and I had merely the energy to glance at each other. "Oh, Franklin, dear child, there are blessings in disguise. We must not quibble with the Lord." Mama had caught, in her own desperation, our false cheer.

"Mama," I told her one night, for she stayed long enough to pack the children and take them to Hyde Park, "Mama, I have always prayed that Franklin would stay with me, that I would have him for my own and he would give up the world and live with me. And now I've had my prayers answered. Have you?"

"Eleanor, dear, please . . ."

"Ah, I daresay you have had yours answered also. You see the Lord answered my prayer but He also demanded a bit of something from us. So much that I wish I'd never made the prayer in the first place. We must not quibble. He had His price, did He not? Franklin won't wander. God knows, there won't be another love affair."

"Poor child."

"We both have what we want, haven't we? So now we must think of what Franklin wants, mustn't we?"

"My dear, Franklin wants to walk again. I know my son. And he can learn at Hyde Park. I'll make every facility available to him. There are machines and pools and treatments . . ."

"No. Franklin wants to live. He can only live where there is life and change and movement. He doesn't want to vegetate in Hyde Park. He is going to New York."

"It will kill him. You're the one who wants to go to New York—for your politics and your perversities."

"How dare you! Who are you to say where my husband goes? Who are you to say?"

"Surely," she backed down, "we're both acting like Lilliputs cutting up the body. We shall see what's best for Franklin. We shall see . . . it's very complicated, of course."

"You can't accuse me on the one hand of cutting up his body and on the other of saving his life."

"Of course I can. Can't I? Anyway, whether I can or not, I have."

"Mama, if it is true that I have, then you have also."

"You are dismissed, Eleanor."

"I don't think so. I believe it is you who are dismissed."

That night, during a long silent hour when Franklin seemed to be at rest, Louis insisted I sleep and dutifully I lay out in the swinging sofa on the porch but my mind, like the springs beneath me, leaped and bounced against its own narrow limits, and so I walked down to the rocks, at the water's edge carrying a lantern, the windows of the house soft, yellow behind me, and I sit here now, on the gray rocks at the water's edge, the lantern behind me casting my long shadow out before me on the flank of rock, spume and spindrift on my face. I have in the deep pocket of my white apron a broken catheter. My apron is very white in the moonlight and the broken parts of the catheter tinkled as I walked to the rocks and they are there still as I sit here and wonder what will become of Franklin. Herring gulls cry single clean gypsy cries in the darkness. Behind me the field of lupin and sea pines is vague in the moonlight and to my right are the rows of charred trees and burned bushes with the moon spilling in three rivers through them onto the bay waves and the bay waves lap and roll with the silver of the moon from the burned forest.

Why Franklin? None of the children, none of the Howes, none of the help, none of the people on the *Sabalo,* not I, not Louis, none of us. Yet one has only to read the meaning of the bronze statue in Mama's entrance hall at Hyde Park . . . with its unfinished legs frozen in that block of bronze. I am so empty for an answer. Is there a pattern to anything except what we have in our shrunken traditions forced upon the world, ignoring what didn't fit? Like the green pool? Like infantile? They don't belong. What is this loom of things? It is so easy to be superstitious now, so hard to have faith. Only the very fortunate can have the sort of faith I once had. "Ah, the torso, it is so beautiful," the sculptor had said. "We only suggest the legs. Yes?"

Yes.

Lost wax, molded, cast fired. Listen to the words and extend them to the body. Listen. Fire and water and earth and air and I take the nighttime path, the nighttime strike, the vein that strikes deep and dark. Franklin is frozen in bronze. The first time the doctor came from Lubbeck on the mainland to demonstrate the catheter insertion, I sobbed and fled the room. Louis followed. "We've done so well. We'll do it, Eleanor. We can. We really can," and he pulled my too-tall head down to his face and kissed, once, each of my cheeks, and I returned and watched. Three times the delicate curved glass shattered and slipped from my terrified grasp over the mysteries of my husband and three times Louis stood by until my hands stopped shaking and I accomplished the dark task. If Franklin could have, he would have covered his eyes in shame and I mine, but his arms were paralyzed still and mine locked to my task. I learned.

Franklin's body was soured and swollen like a cow gone

loose in a field of rotten apples. And like the cow, had to be released, vented. At home, Moses Smith simply punctured the cow's side to let the filthy stinking gases explode from the balloon of her stomach. Franklin's poisons were worse for the indignity. In his most grinding of agonies, he would scream "I'm sorry, Babs. I'm sorry. I don't want to be a burden to you. Oh, Babs!" When he was clean, I would act crisp until I escaped the room and fell into Louis' lap and he would rub the ache in my shoulders and promise me, behind his own pink-lidded liquid eyes, promise me things would improve. He didn't believe it any more than I, but it was all we had and each day we made that promise and each day Franklin's body deteriorated more.

The functions. . . . The functions, I whispered into the silver spindrift over the bay. God release me from the functions. Am I to be trapped now so completely? Leave it to his mother to scrape the black and bilious things from the sheets, to rub the sores, to hear the screams. "Don't ever tell anyone I cried, darling. Please." In Flanders, Franklin told me once, long ago, the eyes of the chaffinch are burned out so the bird sings more beautifully. There are contests. One young man burned out the eyes of a chaffinch which lived in a tree near his house. Then the young man went to war. When he came home to the ruined farmhouse, blinded, he heard in the tree the beautiful song of his own chaffinch and they spent the rest of their lives singing to each other, bird and man, more beautifully as the suffering increased.

Are we both then to be the victims?

Not I. No longer. Not I drawn into the paralysis. I have been motionless too long. I have not sinned. I have not punched and burned the eyes of birds and left my wife and loved another. It is not what I deserve. Had God designed all this, assigned His own devils to putrefy the air, to putrefy the man? If not God, who? Has Franklin putrefied himself, petrified himself, sinned so to deserve this? "Edward being

now de-kinged, the assemblie rode back joyfully to Canter-
bury." O, Lady Fortune, what more atrocious stinks have you
for us in your dilly bag? What then is my reward for being
pure and doing my duty? Lead endures. Endures and endures
and endures. It is the longest way.

I am thirty-six years old. Relieve me from the functions.
Man is no mystery to me, nor is love, nor is sex. It is
animal . . . the puncturing of the cow, of the woman, the
draining of the man, the filling of the entrails. It is dignity
that is a mystery. It is happiness that is a mystery. It is
freedom. I have seen too much to sing blind songs.

I walk back, one hand supporting the lantern, the other in
my pocket stilling the tinkle of the catheter. Franklin's
forehead is again a cold stone, his eyes dull as an owl's in
sunlight, his stomach and fingers subsiding slowly. Yesterday
he gripped a pencil, held my hand. There is some hope.

Louis sits in an armchair under a bracketed oil-wick lamp.
His feet don't touch the floor and he drinks whiskey and I
throw my head on his lap once again and am grateful for the
warmth of his thighs and the rise and fall of his wise ugly
little body. We are both at last needed, aren't we, Louis? I
wrote in my diary that a woman can only be happy by being
useful to others and then I crossed that out with the nub of
my pen and the mess of my tears on the ink and then I wrote
it in again on a new page. Dear Lord, what is my duty? Have I
not done it? The ocean strand stinks now of dead mackerel;
the silken blackening kelp is a loom of entrails on the beach.
He will be grateful now; he will need me. The lead has passed
from me to him. Yes, Mr. Adams. I understand now. I was the
lead in the silver cup from which Franklin drank the wine of
life. Yes. I poisoned the Emperor with my lead. He is my
paralysis, over there, a trophy on the wall. My heart is moved,
Franklin. I bleed for you. As wretched as I am, though, I feel
the lead gone. Every night for two weeks, in delirium, in his
nightshirt, Franklin grappled face to face, mouth to mouth,

heart to heart with the beast. But last night he murmured as I sponged his face and washed between his fingers, "Plant the apricot trees on the eastern wall. Very important."

I forgive you, Franklin.

Flesh of my flesh, blood of my blood. I forgive you. The draining of his fluids, the feeding of the gruel, the changing of the sheets, the washing of the parts, the turning of the body.

"He's as heavy as lead," Louis complained, straining.

"Yes. Lead. You lift him. I'll pull out the sheets." Lead.

Louis sits by his side and reads to him. It is like the old days in Albany. Louis holds him suspended as I slip the bedpan beneath him. "Oooh, God," he cries. My touch is excruciating. "Oh, God." Louis reads from Carlyle as I give the slumbering hero a sponge bath. What the muscles have lost the nerves have gained. Louis reads and Franklin tries to listen, grimacing, crying. His tongue runs over parched lips. I rub glycerine on them lightly, with my fingers lightly. It is a kiss. And then with a glass straw he sips pineapple juice and his eyes are bowls of sorrow as he looks at me, and Louis reads. Louis reads to Franklin inviting him to dream, inviting him to insert himself someplace in the pages of history, between the sentences, between the heartbeats, in the lists of kings. "Listen, hero, we shall fill you with other things. Listen, man great enough, man wise enough. A man wise enough, a man good enough with the wisdom to determine what the Time really wants."

"Plant the apricot trees by the eastern wall."

"Hey, boss, you hear about the guy who thought he was a shellfish?"

"No, Louis, tell me."

"Can't, boss, he clammed right up soon as I asked him."

The catheter and the tear bottle and boxes of gray mushrooms in bright blue papers and yellow sickle pears in green crackly papers and braces of coots from my aunts and geese from Mr. Baruch and books and letters and wine. Captain

Calder brought the gifts to the house and I noted the sender and Captain Calder took the gifts to the island people. I wrote letters and Louis read to Franklin. " 'The first duty for a man is still that of subduing Fear. We must get rid of Fear. We cannot act at all till then. Till we have got Fear under our feet.' " I leaned, as I once had leaned against the door frame, and listened. " 'A man shall and must be valiant. He must march forward and quit himself like a man, trusting imperturbably in the appointment and choice of the upper powers and on the whole not fear at all. Now and always the completeness of his victory, over Fear, will determine how much of a man he is.' "

Franklin lost his manhood to prove he was a man.

"Victory over fear, Louis?"

"That's right, boss. Carlyle never led you wrong yet. You can't fear Fear!"

"Babs, are you there?"

"Yes, darling. Right here."

"Babs, I hate to ask you this . . ."

"Yes, Franklin?" Write to Lucy? Let him die?

"You've been singing under your breath since this began. Change the song."

"Singing?"

" 'Carnival of Venice.' "

I asked Louis. Yes, I had, constantly, like breathing. I would rush to the window, suck in great gulps of fresh air and come back and sing "Carnival of Venice."

"And you have a terrible voice." Franklin laughed.

"Oh, darling, it's so good to hear you laugh."

"It will be so good to hear you sing something else. Two weeks of 'Carnival of Venice.' Reminds me of my honeymoon."

"I will. Oh, I will. Oh, Franklin. Oh, darling, I love you so. You *are* better. You *are* better. Oh, Franklin."

"You must stay with me, Babs."

"If you'll let us take you to New York soon, to a hospital."

"Whatever you think is right, you do. You and the doctor. Not Mama."

"Yes, Franklin."

"It's you and I, Eleanor."

"Hey, hey, don't forget *me!*"

"And you, Louis, my two dearest most beloved friends."

I have done my duty. I forgive. I don't forget.

It takes a forest fire and after the fire a triple stream of silver runs down the mountainside from the charred stumps. The moon shines on the waves. The waves dance and are a thousand silver mirrors, a cold strange brightness, something imprisoned released. The gloomy valley and the sterile mountains and the charred forest, that I may draw forth my silver.

"There are letters from Livy, Franklin. A number of them."

"Damn Livy, don't want to hear."

"And some from Miss LeHand who addresses you as Your Excellency." I see part of a smile. "Shall I write her? You'll be needing a secretary." If Missy makes you smile, you shall have Missy.

"What for? I have no more work to do."

"Of course you have. If you just begin to answer the letters you've received, you'll need a secretary. There are even requests for speeches . . . in time, Franklin." I cannot make you smile.

"I don't want sympathy."

"Aunt Maude has sent drawn coots. We have four dozen coots."

"Coots won't wash, I'm afraid. Oh, Babs, I'm such a burden. The sheets hurt my toes. Can you loosen them?"

"They are loose, Franklin."

"Everything hurts so terribly or doesn't hurt at all."

"I know, darling, but you're doing finely, just finely. Shall I write Miss LeHand to meet us in New York?"

"Not yet."

"He didn't say no, did he?" Louis whispered to me outside the room. "That's something. Also, he doesn't want you reading Livy's letters."

"Louis, Babs, where are you? Don't leave me alone, you two!"

"Hear about the man who thought he was a shellfish, boss?"

"Nope. He clammed right up."

Childhood is over. Back we would go to the Dresden chandeliers, the English sideboards, the worn leather on Mama's dining room chairs, the pincushions on the marble-topped bureaus, the crocheted hangar covers, the soft-collar shirts and the Palm Beach suits and nothing, not even the sugar maples nor the snowball bushes, not even my footfall on the pine needles, not even the children shouting "Navel cord and belly button, Mr. Howe eats only mutton," nothing would be the same ever again. It is like flying. The higher you go, the smaller things become, smaller and smaller.

The island men carry the stretcher down to the dock and with the utmost care Franklin is placed in the bow of the boat. Poor Franklin, he is so frightened. Poor man. Poor, poor man.

ACKNOWLEDGMENTS

In the course of gathering materials for this book, I have been helped by many people. I wish to thank the archivists at the F. D. Roosevelt Library at Hyde Park, who led me for three tedious years through the materials with patience and generosity. In particular, I am grateful to Dr. William Emerson, Director; Frances Seeber, Archivist; Joseph Marshall, Librarian; and Ray Teichman, Audio-Visual Archivist.

There is, of course, no question of the usefulness of Joseph Lash's superb scholarship in *Eleanor and Franklin.* I am also in debt to the friends of Mrs. Roosevelt who offered me insights into the substance of the woman I never knew. In particular, Esther Lape, who helped me to understand the character of Mrs. Roosevelt, and Mayris Cheney (Mrs. Harry Pokras), who showed me Eleanor Roosevelt as a loving woman with deep family ties to an adopted family. Marion Dickerman gave me invaluable insight into Mrs. Roosevelt's loneliness and vulnerability. I am grateful, too, to Harlan Cook and Otto Berge. Many who knew State Trooper Earl Miller as well as the family maids, cooks, and other servants were very forthcoming. In particular, Bucky Golden, Supervisor of Hyde Park and son of the Roosevelt's chauffeur in Washington during World War I.

For background material, I am in debt to: Caroline Gould, biographer of Dorothy Payne Whitney Strait, whose labor organizing and homesteading activities heavily influenced Mrs. Roosevelt; Alice Cook, Professor Emeritus of Cornell University and close friend of Frances Perkins, who was particularly informative about the position and attitudes of women in the early days of Mrs. Roosevelt's life; C. R. Smith of American Airlines, a close friend of Mrs. Roosevelt; Katie Hansen, who shared her memories of the rules and mores of the upper classes; Faith Knapp, descendant of Henry Adams, who shared her impressions of Clover Adams and the Washington house; Peter Tilp, Pullman-car historian, who sent me pictures and diagrams of the *Westboro;* Sarah and Howland Auchincloss, who offered insights into the lifestyles of the old upstate families; Janet Cook, who, as a newspaperwoman in Albany, reported on Mrs. Roosevelt as the Governor's wife; and Anna Roosevelt Halstead, Eleanor's daughter, who told me more, I think, than I wanted to know.

I am indebted to the careful records of the League of Women Voters, to Curtis Roosevelt who interviewed Alice Roosevelt on my behalf, and who made possible access to the FBI files on Eleanor Roosevelt, as well as private papers relating to the family. To Van Seagraves, executor of the Anna Roosevelt Halstead materials in the Oral History Section at Columbia University; to the Hamlin Letters at the Albany State Historical Society; to the Library of Congress; to Frank Friedel for opening his private files on Mrs. Roosevelt.

I feel a special indebtedness to the poetic vision of Paul Fussell's *The Great War and Modern Memory.*

I owe personal debts to my mother-in-law for her research

assistance, to the women at the Cazenovia College Women's Writer's Center for their help and support, and to Layne Hamilton for her writer's insights and her typing.

It is to Jean Stapleton that I owe my deepest gratitude. Through her act of imagination in bringing to life the words of Mrs. Roosevelt that I had written, she gave me the confidence to write this book in Eleanor Roosevelt's voice. For the film, *Soul of Iron*, in which Jean performs my script, I am indebted to Robert Benjamin of the Eleanor Roosevelt Institute, who contributed to the cost of the initial performance, and to Norman Lear at Tandem Productions, who produced the final film. To Esther Peterson, an old, old friend of Mrs. Roosevelt and still energetically active today as Economic Adviser to President Carter, I shall be forever grateful; when she whispered to me that the film made her cry, she gave me the last push to finish the book.

I owe much to my agent, Julie Coopersmith, who lived with the book, and to my editor, Marian Wood, who saw it at the beginning, better than I.

Finally, I want to acknowledge Kay Wheelin, my housekeeper, who carried the entire family through what I can now look back on as my Roosevelt years—years that were painful and difficult but, in the end, years that I hope produced what Mrs. Roosevelt herself would feel was an honest attempt at her truth.